Friends and Neighbors
Or, Two Ways of Living in the World

by
T. S. Arthur

Friends and Neighbors
Or, Two Ways of Living in the World
by T. S. Arthur

Copyright © 2024

All Rights reserved.

No part of this publication may be reproduced, stored in a retrieval system, or transmitted in any form or by any means, electronic, mechanical, photocopying or Otherwise, without the written permission of the publisher.
The author/editor asserts the moral right to be identified as the author/editor of this work.

ISBN: 978-93-62206-65-7

Published by

DOUBLE 9 BOOKS

2/13-B, Ansari Road
Daryaganj, New Delhi – 110002
info@double9books.com
www.double9books.com
Tel. 011-40042856

This book is under public domain

ABOUT THE AUTHOR

Timothy Shay Arthur, or T. S. Arthur was born on June 6, 1809, and died on March 6, 1885. S. Arthur was a well-known American author in the 1800s. Many people know him for the 1854 book Ten Nights in a Bar-Room and What I Saw There, which was a temperance story. It helped make Americans dislike alcohol. When he wrote his stories with care and compassion, he shared beliefs and ideas that were common in American "respectable middle class" life. A story of his called "An Angel in Disguise" shows how much he believed in the healing and changing power of love. He also wrote dozens of stories for Godey's Lady's Book, which was the most famous American monthly magazine before the Civil War. For many years, he published and edited his own magazine, Arthur's Home Magazine, which was modeled after Godey's. Arthur did a lot to explain and spread the values, beliefs, and habits that made up proper middle-class life in America. He is almost lost today. While a child, Arthur lived in Fort Montgomery, New York. He was born in Newburgh, New York. By 1820, Arthur's miller father had moved to Baltimore, Maryland, and Arthur went to school there for a short time.

CONTENTS

PREFACE 7
GOOD IN ALL 8
HUMAN PROGRESS 11
MY WASHERWOMAN 15
FORGIVE AND FORGET 19
OWE NO MAN ANYTHING 20
RETURNING GOOD FOR EVIL 29
PUTTING YOUR HAND IN YOUR NEIGHBOUR'S POCKET 32
KIND WORDS 42
NEIGHBOURS' QUARRELS 45
GOOD WE MIGHT DO 47
THE TOWN LOT 48
THE SUNBEAM AND THE RAINDROP 56
A PLEA FOR SOFT WORDS 58
MR. QUERY'S INVESTIGATION 63
ROOM IN THE WORLD 69
WORDS 70
THE THANKLESS OFFICE 74
LOVE 79
"EVERY LITTLE HELPS" 80
LITTLE THINGS 81
CARELESS WORDS 82
HOW TO BE HAPPY 88

CHARITY.—ITS OBJECTS	90
THE VISION OF BOATS	94
REGULATION OF THE TEMPER	97
MANLY GENTLENESS	100
SILENT INFLUENCE	106
ANTIDOTE FOR MELANCHOLY	111
THE SORROWS OF A WEALTHY CITIZEN	115
"WE'VE ALL OUR ANGEL SIDE"	122
BLIND JAMES	125
DEPENDENCE	137
TWO RIDES WITH THE DOCTOR	147
KEEP IN STEP	154
JOHNNY COLE	157
THE THIEF AND HIS BENEFACTOR	163
JOHN AND MARGARET GREYLSTON	166
THE WORLD WOULD BE THE BETTER FOR IT	183
TWO SIDES TO A STORY	185
LITTLE KINDNESSES	192
LEAVING OFF CONTENTION BEFORE IT BE MEDDLED WITH	194
"ALL THE DAY IDLE"	197
THE BUSHEL OF CORN	198
THE ACCOUNT	208
CONTENTMENT BETTER THAN WEALTH	210
RAINBOWS EVERYWHERE	215

PREFACE

WE were about preparing a few words of introduction to this volume, the materials for which have been culled from the highways and byways of literature, where our eyes fell upon these fitting sentiments, the authorship of which we are unable to give. They express clearly and beautifully what was in our own mind:—

"If we would only bring ourselves to look at the subjects that surround as in their true flight, we should see beauty where now appears deformity, and listen to harmony where we hear nothing but discord. To be sure there is a great deal of vexation and anxiety in the world; we cannot sail upon a summer sea for ever; yet if we preserve a calm eye and a steady hand, we can so trim our sails and manage our helm, as to avoid the quicksands, and weather the storms that threaten shipwreck. We are members of one great family; we are travelling the same road, and shall arrive at the same goal. We breathe the same air, are subject to the same bounty, and we shall, each lie down upon the bosom of our common mother. It is not becoming, then, that brother should hate brother; it is not proper that friend should deceive friend; it is not right that neighbour should deceive neighbour. We pity that man who can harbour enmity against his fellow; he loses half the enjoyment of life; he embitters his own existence. Let us tear from our eyes the coloured medium that invests every object with the green hue of jealousy and suspicion; turn, a deal ear to scandal; breathe the spirit of charity from our hearts; let the rich gushings of human kindness swell up as a fountain, so that the golden age will become no fiction and islands of the blessed bloom in more than Hyperian beauty."

It is thus that friends and neighbours should live. This is the right way. To aid in the creation of such true harmony among men, has the book now in your hand, reader, been compiled. May the truths that glisten on its pages be clearly reflected in your mind; and the errors it points out be shunned as the foes of yourself and humanity.

GOOD IN ALL

THERE IS GOOD IN ALL. Yes! we all believe it: not a man in the depth of his vanity but will yield assent. But do you not all, in practice, daily, hourly deny it? A beggar passes you in the street: dirty, ragged, importunate. "Ah! he has a *bad* look," and your pocket is safe. He starves—and he steals. "I thought he was *bad*." You educate him in the State Prison. He does not improve even in this excellent school. "He is," says the gaoler, "thoroughly *bad*." He continues his course of crime. All that is bad in him having by this time been made apparent to himself, his friends, and the world, he has only to confirm the decision, and at length we hear when he has reached his last step. "Ah! no wonder—there was never any *Good* in him. Hang him!"

Now much, if not all this, may be checked by a word.

If you believe in Good, *always appeal to it*. Be sure whatever there is of Good—is of God. There is never an utter want of resemblance to the common Father. "God made man in His own image." "What! yon reeling, blaspheming creature; yon heartless cynic; yon crafty trader; yon false statesman?" Yes! All. In every nature there is a germ of eternal happiness, of undying Good. In the drunkard's heart there is a memory of something better—slight, dim: but flickering still; why should you not by the warmth of your charity, give growth to the Good that is in him? The cynic, the miser, is not all self. There is a note in that sullen instrument to make all harmony yet; but it wants a patient and gentle master to touch the strings.

You point to the words "There is *none* good." The truths do not oppose each other. "There is none good—*save one*." And He breathes in all. In our earthliness, our fleshly will, our moral grasp, we are helpless, mean, vile. But there is a lamp ever burning in the heart: a guide to the source of Light, or an instrument of torture. We can make it either. If it burn in an atmosphere of purity, it will warm, guide, cheer us. If in the midst of selfishness, or under the pressure of pride, its flame will be unsteady, and we shall soon have good reason to trim our light, and find new oil for it.

There is Good in All—the impress of the Deity. He who believes not in the image of God in man, is an infidel to himself and his race. There is no difficulty about discovering it. You have only to appeal to it. Seek in every one the *best* features: mark, encourage, educate *them*. There is no man to whom some circumstance will not be an argument.

And how glorious in practice, this faith! How easy, henceforth, all the labours of our law-makers, and how delightful, how practical the theories of our philanthropists! To educate the *Good*—the good in *All*: to raise every man in his own opinion, and yet to stifle all arrogance, by showing that all possess this Good. *In* themselves, but not *of* themselves. Had we but faith in this truth, how soon should we all be digging through the darkness, for this Gold of Love—this universal Good. A Howard, and a Fry, cleansed and humanized our prisons, to find this Good; and in the chambers of all our hearts it is to be found, by labouring eyes and loving hands.

Why all our harsh enactments? Is it from experience of the strength of vice in ourselves that we cage, chain, torture, and hang men? Are none of us indebted to friendly hands, careful advisers; to the generous, trusting guidance, solace, of some gentler being, who has loved us, despite the evil that is in *us*—for our little Good, and has nurtured that Good with smiles and tears and prayers? O, we know not how like we are to those whom we despise! We know not how many memories of kith and kin the murderer carries to the gallows—how much honesty of heart the felon drags with him to the hulks.

There is Good in All. Dodd, the forger, was a better man than most of us: Eugene Aram, the homicide, would turn his foot from a worm. Do not mistake us. Society demands, requires that these madmen should be rendered harmless. There is no nature dead to all Good. Lady Macbeth would have slain the old king, Had he not resembled her father as he slept.

It is a frequent thought, but a careless and worthless one, because never acted on, that the same energies, the same will to great vices, had given force to great virtues. Do we provide the opportunity? Do we *believe* in Good? If we are ourselves deceived in any one, is not all, thenceforth, deceit? if treated with contempt, is not the whole world clouded with scorn? if visited with meanness, are not all selfish? And if from one of our frailer fellow-creatures we receive the blow, we cease to believe in women. Not the breast at which we have drank life—not the sisterly hands that have guided ours—not the one voice that has so often soothed us in our darker hours, will save the sex: All are massed in one common sentence: all bad. There may be Delilahs: there are many Ruths. We should not lightly give them up. Napoleon lost France when he lost Josephine. The one light in Rembrandt's gloomy life was his sister.

And all are to be approached at some point. The proudest bends to some feeling—Coriolanus conquered Rome: but the husband conquered the hero. The money-maker has influences beyond his gold—Reynolds made an exhibition of his carriage, but he was generous to Northcote, and had time to think of the poor Plympton schoolmistress. The cold are not all ice. Elizabeth slew Essex—the queen triumphed; the woman *died*.

There is Good in All. Let us show our faith in it. When the lazy whine of the mendicant jars on your ears, think of his unaided, unschooled childhood; think that his lean cheeks never knew the baby-roundness of content that ours have worn; that his eye knew no youth of fire—no manhood of expectancy. Pity, help, teach him. When you see the trader, without any pride of vocation, seeking how he can best cheat you, and degrade himself, glance into the room behind his shop and see there his pale wife and his thin children, and think how cheerfully he meets that circle in the only hour he has out of the twenty-four. Pity his narrowness of mind; his want of reliance upon the God of Good; but remember there have been Greshams, and Heriots, and Whittingtons; and remember, too, that in our happy land there are thousands of almshouses, built by the men of trade alone. And when you are discontented with the great, and murmur, repiningly, of Marvel in his garret, or Milton in his hiding-place, turn in justice to the Good among the great. Read how John of Lancaster loved Chaucer and sheltered Wicliff. There have been Burkes as well as Walpoles. Russell remembered Banim's widow, and Peel forgot not Haydn.

Once more: believe that in every class there is Good; in every man, Good. That in the highest and most tempted, as well as in the lowest, there is often a higher nobility than of rank. Pericles and Alexander had great, but different virtues, and although the refinement of the one may have resulted in effeminacy, and the hardihood of the other in brutality, we ought to pause ere we condemn where we should all have fallen.

Look only for the Good. It will make you welcome everywhere, and everywhere it will make you an instrument to good. The lantern of Diogenes is a poor guide when compared with the Light God hath set in the heavens; a Light which shines into the solitary cottage and the squalid alley, where the children of many vices are hourly exchanging deeds of kindness; a Light shining into the rooms of dingy warehousemen and thrifty clerks, whose hard labour and hoarded coins are for wife and child and friend; shining into prison and workhouse, where sin and sorrow glimmer with sad eyes through rusty bars into distant homes and mourning hearths; shining through heavy curtains, and round sumptuous tables, where the heart throbs audibly through velvet mantle and silken vest, and where eye meets eye with affection and sympathy; shining everywhere upon God's creatures, and with its broad beams lighting up a virtue wherever it falls, and telling the proud, the wronged, the merciless, or the despairing, that there is "Good in All."

HUMAN PROGRESS

WE are told to look through nature
Upward unto Nature's God;
We are told there is a scripture
Written on the meanest sod;
That the simplest flower created
Is a key to hidden things;
But, immortal over nature,
Mind, the lord of nature, springs!

Through*Humanity* look upward,—
Alter ye the olden plan,—
Look through man to the Creator,
Maker, Father, God of Man!
Shall imperishable spirit
Yield to perishable clay?
No! sublime o'er Alpine mountains
Soars the Mind its heavenward way!

Deeper than the vast Atlantic
Rolls the tide of human thought;
Farther speeds that mental ocean
Than the world of waves o'er sought!
Mind, sublime in its own essence
Its sublimity can lend
To the rocks, and mounts, and torrents,
And, at will, their features bend!

Some within the humblest *floweret*
"Thoughts too deep for tears" can see;
Oh, the humblest man existing
Is a sadder theme to me!
Thus I take the mightier labour
Of the great Almighty hand;
And, through man to the Creator,
Upward look, and weeping stand.

Thus I take the mightier labour,
—Crowning glory of *His* will;
And believe that in the meanest
Lives a spark of Godhead still:
Something that, by Truth expanded,
Might be fostered into worth;
Something struggling through the darkness,
Owning an immortal birth!

From the Genesis of being
Unto this imperfect day,
Hath Humanity held onward,
Praying God to aid its way!
And Man's progress had been swifter,
Had he never turned aside,
To the worship of a symbol,
Not the spirit signified!

And Man's progress had been higher,
Had he owned his brother man,
Left his narrow, selfish circle,
For a world-embracing plan!
There are some for ever craving,

Ever discontent with place,
In the eternal would find briefness,
In the infinite want space.

If through man unto his Maker
We the source of truth would find,
It must be through man enlightened,
Educated, raised, refined:
That which the Divine hath fashioned
Ignorance hath oft effaced;
Never may we see God's image
In man darkened—man debased!

Something yield to Recreation,
Something to Improvement give;
There's a Spiritual kingdom
Where the Spirit hopes to live!
There's a mental world of grandeur,
Which the mind inspires to know;
Founts of everlasting beauty
That, for those who seek them, flow!

Shores where Genius breathes immortal—
Where the very winds convey
Glorious thoughts of Education,
Holding universal sway!
Glorious hopes of Human Freedom,
Freedom of the noblest kind;
That which springs from Cultivation,
Cheers and elevates the mind!
Let us hope for Better Prospects,
Strong to struggle for the night,

We appeal to Truth, and ever
Truth's omnipotent in might;
Hasten, then, the People's Progress,
Ere their last faint hope be gone;
Teach the Nations that their interest
And the People's good, ARE ONE.

MY WASHERWOMAN

SOME people have a singular reluctance to part with money. If waited on for a bill, they say, almost involuntarily, "Call to-morrow," even though their pockets are far from being empty.

I once fell into this bad habit myself; but a little incident, which I will relate, cured me. Not many years after I had attained my majority, a poor widow, named Blake, did my washing and ironing. She was the mother of two or three little children, whose sole dependence for food and raiment was on the labour of her hands.

Punctually, every Thursday morning, Mrs. Blake appeared with my clothes, "white as the driven snow;" but not always, as punctually, did I pay the pittance she had earned by hard labour.

"Mrs. Blake is down stairs," said a servant, tapping at my room-door one morning, while I was in the act of dressing myself.

"Oh, very well," I replied. "Tell her to leave my clothes. I will get them when I come down."

The thought of paying the seventy-five cents, her due, crossed my mind. But I said to myself,—"It's but a small matter, and will do as well when she comes again."

There was in this a certain reluctance to part with money. My funds were low, and I might need what change I had during the day. And so it proved. As I went to the office in which I was engaged, some small article of ornament caught my eye in a shop window.

"Beautiful!" said I, as I stood looking at it. Admiration quickly changed into the desire for possession; and so I stepped in to ask the price. It was just two dollars.

"Cheap enough," thought I. And this very cheapness was a further temptation.

So I turned out the contents of my pockets, counted them over, and found the amount to be two dollars and a quarter.

"I guess I'll take it," said I, laying the money on the shopkeeper's counter.

"I'd better have paid Mrs. Blake." This thought crossed my mind, an hour afterwards, by which time the little ornament had lost its power of pleasing. "So much would at least have been saved."

I was leaving the table, after tea, on the evening that followed, when the waiter said to me,

"Mrs. Blake is at the door, and wishes to see you."

I felt a little worried at hearing this; for I had no change in my pockets, and the poor washerwoman had, of course, come for her money.

"She's in a great hurry," I muttered to myself, as I descended to the door.

"You'll have to wait until you bring home my clothes next week, Mrs. Blake. I haven't any change, this evening."

The expression of the poor woman's face, as she turned slowly away, without speaking, rather softened my feelings.

"I'm sorry," said I, "but it can't be helped now. I wish you had said, this morning, that you wanted money. I could have paid you then."

She paused, and turned partly towards me, as I said this. Then she moved off, with something so sad in her manner, that I was touched sensibly.

"I ought to have paid her this morning, when I had the change about me. And I wish I had done so. Why didn't she ask for her money, if she wanted it so badly?"

I felt, of course, rather ill at ease. A little while afterwards I met the lady with whom I was boarding.

"Do you know anything about this Mrs. Blake, who washes for me?" I inquired.

"Not much; except that she is very poor, and has three children to feed and clothe. And what is worst of all, she is in bad health. I think she told me, this morning, that one of her little ones was very sick."

I was smitten with a feeling of self-condemnation, and soon after left the room. It was too late to remedy the evil, for I had only a sixpence in my pocket; and, moreover, did not know where to find Mrs. Blake.

Having purposed to make a call upon some young ladies that evening, I now went up into my room to dress. Upon my bed lay the spotless linen brought home by Mrs. Blake in the morning. The sight of it rebuked me; and

I had to conquer, with some force, an instinctive reluctance, before I could compel myself to put on a clean shirt, and snow-white vest, too recently from the hand of my unpaid washerwoman.

One of the young ladies upon whom I called was more to me than a mere pleasant acquaintance. My heart had, in fact, been warming towards her for some time; and I was particularly anxious to find favour in her eyes. On this evening she was lovelier and more attractive than ever, and new bonds of affection entwined themselves around my heart.

Judge, then, of the effect produced upon me by the entrance of her mother—at the very moment when my heart was all a-glow with love, who said, as she came in—

"Oh, dear! This is a strange world!"

"What new feature have you discovered now, mother?" asked one of her daughters, smiling.

"No new one, child; but an old one that looks more repulsive than ever," was replied. "Poor Mrs. Blake came to see me just now, in great trouble."

"What about, mother?" All the young ladies at once manifested unusual interest.

Tell-tale blushes came instantly to my countenance, upon which the eyes of the mother turned themselves, as I felt, with a severe scrutiny.

"The old story, in cases like hers," was answered. "Can't get her money when earned, although for daily bread she is dependent on her daily labour. With no food in the house, or money to buy medicine for her sick child, she was compelled to seek me to-night, and to humble her spirit, which is an independent one, so low as to ask bread for her little ones, and the loan of a pittance with which to get what the doctor has ordered her feeble sufferer at home."

"Oh, what a shame!" fell from the lips of Ellen, the one in whom my heart felt more than a passing interest; and she looked at me earnestly as she spoke.

"She fully expected," said the mother, "to get a trifle that was due her from a young man who boards with Mrs. Corwin; and she went to see him this evening. But he put her off with some excuse. How strange that any one should be so thoughtless as to withhold from the poor their hard-earned pittance! It is but a small sum at best, that the toiling seamstress or washerwoman can gain by her wearying labour. That, at least, should be promptly paid. To withhold it an hour is to do, in many cases, a great wrong."

For some minutes after this was said, there ensued a dead silence. I felt that the thoughts of all were turned upon me as the one who had withheld from poor Mrs. Blake the trifling sum due her for washing. What my feelings were, it is impossible for me to describe; and difficult for any one, never himself placed in so unpleasant a position, to imagine.

My relief was great when the conversation flowed on again, and in another channel; for I then perceived that suspicion did not rest upon me. You may be sure that Mrs. Blake had her money before ten o'clock on the next day, and that I never again fell into the error of neglecting, for a single week, my poor washerwoman.

FORGIVE AND FORGET

THERE'S a secret in living, if folks only knew;
An Alchymy precious, and golden, and true,
More precious than "gold dust," though pure and refined,
For its mint is the heart, and its storehouse the mind;
Do you guess what I mean—for as true as I live
That dear little secret's—forget and forgive!

When hearts that have loved have grown cold and estranged,
And looks that beamed fondness are clouded and changed,
And words hotly spoken and grieved for with tears
Have broken the trust and the friendship of years—
Oh! think 'mid thy pride and thy secret regret,
The balm for the wound is—forgive and forget!

Yes! look in thy spirit, for love may return
And kindle the embers that still feebly burn;
And let this true whisper breathe high in thy heart,
'Tis better to love than thus suffer apart—

Let the Past teach the Future more wisely than yet,
For the friendship that's true can forgive and forget.

And now, an adieu! if you list to my lay
May each in your thoughts bear my motto away,
'Tis a crude, simple ryhme, but its truth may impart
A joy to the gentle and loving of heart;
And an end I would claim far more practical yet
In behalf of the Rhymer—*forgive and forget!*

OWE NO MAN ANYTHING

THUS says an Apostle; and if those who are able to "owe no man anything" would fully observe this divine obligation, many, very many, whom their want of punctuality now compels to live in violation of this precept, would then faithfully and promptly render to every one their just dues.

"What is the matter with you, George?" said Mrs. Allison to her husband, as he paced the floor of their little sitting-room, with an anxious, troubled expression of countenance.

"Oh! nothing of much consequence: only a little worry of business," replied Mr. Allison.

"But I know better than that, George. I know it is of consequence; you are not apt to have such a long face for nothing. Come, tell me what it is that troubles you. Have I not a right to share your griefs as well as your joys?"

"Indeed, Ellen, it is nothing but business, I assure you; and as I am not blessed with the most even temper in the world, it does not take much you know to upset me: but you heard me speak of that job I was building for Hillman?"

"Yes. I think you said it was to be five hundred dollars, did you not?"

"I did; and it was to have been cash as soon as done. Well, he took it out two weeks ago; one week sooner than I promised it. I sent the bill with it, expecting, of course, he would send me a check for the amount; but I was disappointed. Having heard nothing from him since, I thought I would call on him this morning, when, to my surprise, I was told he had gone travelling with his wife and daughter, and would not be back for six weeks or two months. I can't tell you how I felt when I was told this."

"He is safe enough for it I suppose, isn't he, George?"

"Oh, yes; he is supposed to be worth about three hundred thousand. But what good is that to me? I was looking over my books this afternoon, and, including this five hundred, there is just fifteen hundred dollars due me now, that I ought to have, but can't get it. To a man doing a large business it would not be much; but to one with my limited means, it is a good deal. And this is all in the hands of five individuals, any one of whom could pay immediately, and feel not the least inconvenience from it."

"Are you much pressed for money just now, George?"

"I have a note in bank of three hundred, which falls due to-morrow, and one of two hundred and fifty on Saturday. Twenty-five dollars at least will be required to pay off my hands; and besides this, our quarter's rent is due on Monday, and my shop rent next Wednesday. Then there are other little bills I wanted to settle, our own wants to be supplied, &c."

"Why don't you call on those persons you spoke of; perhaps they would pay you?"

"I have sent their bills in, but if I call on them so soon I might perhaps affront them, and cause them to take their work away; and that I don't want to do. However, I think I shall have to do it, let the consequence be what it may."

"Perhaps you could borrow what you need, George, for a few days."

"I suppose I could; but see the inconvenience and trouble it puts me to. I was so certain of getting Hillman's money to meet these two notes, that I failed to make any other provision."

"That would not have been enough of itself."

"No, but I have a hundred on hand; the two together would have paid them, and left enough for my workmen too."

As early as practicable the next morning Mr. Allison started forth to raise the amount necessary to carry him safely through the week. He thought it better to try to collect some of the amounts owing to him than to borrow. He first called on a wealthy merchant, whose annual income was something near five thousand.

"Good morning, Mr. Allison," said he, as that individual entered his counting-room. "I suppose you want some money."

"I should like a little, Mr. Chapin, if you please."

"Well, I intended coming down to see you, but I have been so busy that I have not been able. That carriage of mine which you did up a few weeks ago does not suit me altogether."

"What is the matter with it?"

"I don't like the style of trimming, for one thing; it has a common look to me."

"It is precisely what Mrs. Chapin ordered. You told me to suit her."

"Yes, but did she not tell you to trim it like General Spangler's?"

"I am very much mistaken, Mr. Chapin, if it is not precisely like his."

"Oh! no; his has a much richer look than mine."

"The style of trimming is just the same, Mr. Chapin; but you certainly did not suppose that a carriage trimmed with worsted lace, would look as well as one trimmed with silk lace?"

"No, of course not; but there are some other little things about it that don't suit me. I will send my man down with it to-day, and he will show you what they are. I would like to have it to-morrow afternoon, to take my family out in. Call up on Monday, and we will have a settlement."

Mr. Allison next called at the office of a young lawyer, who had lately come into possession of an estate valued at one hundred thousand dollars. Mr. Allison's bill was three hundred dollars, which his young friend assured him he would settle immediately, only that there was a slight error in the way it was made out, and not having the bill with him, he could not now correct it.

He would call on Mr. Allison with it, sometime during the next week, and settle it.

A Custom-House gentleman was next sought, but his time had been so much taken up with his official duties, that he had not yet been able to examine the bill. He had no doubt but it was all correct; still, as he was not accustomed to doing business in a loose way, he must claim Mr. Allison's indulgence a few days longer.

Almost disheartened, Mr. Allison entered the store of the last individual who was indebted to him for any considerable amount, not daring to hope that he would be any more successful with him than with the others he had called on. But he was successful; the bill, which amounted to near one hundred and fifty dollars, was promptly paid, Mr. Allison's pocket, in consequence, that much heavier, and his heart that much lighter. Fifty dollars was yet lacking of the sum requisite for that day. After calling on two or three individuals, this amount was obtained, with the promise of being returned by the middle of the next week.

"I shall have hard work to get through to-day, I know," said he to himself, as he sat at his desk on the following morning.

"Two hundred and fifty dollars to be raised by borrowing. I don't know where I can get it."

To many this would be a small sum, but Mr. Allison was peculiarly situated. He was an honest, upright mechanic, but he was poor. It was with difficulty he had raised the fifty dollars on the day previous. Although he had never once failed in returning money at the time promised, still, for some reason or other, everybody appeared unwilling to lend him. It was nearly two O'clock and he was still a hundred dollars short.

"Well," said he to himself, "I have done all I could, and if Hall won't renew the note for the balance, it will have to be protested. I'll go and ask him, though I have not much hope that he will do it."

As he was about leaving his shop for that purpose, a gentleman entered who wished to buy a second-hand carriage. Mr. Allison had but one, and that almost new, for which he asked a hundred and forty dollars.

"It is higher than I wished to go," remarked the gentleman. "I ought to get a new one for that price."

"So you can, but not like this. I can sell you a new one for a hundred and twenty-five dollars. But what did you expect to pay for one?"

"I was offered one at Holton's for seventy-five; but I did not like it. I will give you a hundred for yours."

"It is too little, indeed, sir: that carriage cost three hundred dollars when it was new. It was in use a very short time. I allowed a hundred and forty dollars for it myself."

"Well, sir, I would not wish you to sell at a disadvantage, but if you like to, accept of my offer I'll take it. I'm prepared to pay the cash down."

Mr. Allison did not reply for some minutes. He was undecided as to what was best.

"Forty dollars," said he to himself, "is a pretty heavy discount. I am almost tempted to refuse his offer and trust to Hall's renewing the note. But suppose he won't—then I'm done for. I think, upon the whole, I had better accept it. I'll put it at one hundred and twenty-five, my good friend," said he, addressing the customer.

"No, sir; one hundred is all I shall give."

"Well, I suppose you must have it, then; but indeed you have got a bargain."

"It is too bad," muttered Allison to himself, as he left the bank after having paid his note. "There is just forty dollars thrown away. And why? Simply because those who are blessed with the means of discharging their debts promptly, neglect to do so."

"How did you make out to-day, George?" asked his wife, as they sat at the tea-table that same evening.

"I met my note, and that was all."

"Did you give your men anything?"

"Not a cent. I had but one dollar left after paying that. I was sorry for them, but I could not help them. I am afraid Robinson's family will suffer, for there has been sickness in his house almost constantly for the last twelvemonth. His wife, he told me the other day, had not been out; of her bed for six weeks. Poor fellow! He looked quite dejected when I told him I had nothing for him."

At this moment; the door-bell rang and a minute or two afterwards, a young girl entered the room in which Mr. and Mrs. Allison were sitting. Before introducing her to our readers, we will conduct them to the interior of an obscure dwelling, situated near the outskirts of the city. The room is small, and scantily furnished, and answers at once for parlour, dining-room, and kitchen. Its occupants, Mrs. Perry and her daughter, have been, since the earliest dawn of day, intently occupied with their needles, barely allowing themselves time to partake of their frugal meal.

"Half-past three o'clock!" ejaculated the daughter, her eyes glancing, as she spoke, at the clock on the mantelpiece. "I am afraid we shall not get this work done in time for me to take it home before dark, mother."

"We must try hard, Laura, for you know we have not a cent in the house, and I told Mrs. Carr to come over to-night, and I would pay her what I owe her for washing. Poor thing! I would not like to disappoint her, for I know she needs it."

Nothing more was said for near twenty minutes, when Laura again broke the silence.

"Oh, dear!" she exclaimed, "what a pain I have in my side!" And for a moment she rested from her work, and straightened herself in her chair, to afford a slight relief from the uneasiness she experienced. "I wonder, mother, if I shall always be obliged to sit so steady?"

"I hope not, my child; but bad as our situation is, there are hundreds worse off than we. Take Annie Carr, for instance—how would you like to exchange places with her?"

"Poor Annie! I was thinking of her awhile go, mother. How hard it must be for one so young to be so afflicted as she is!"

"And yet, Laura, she never complains; although for five years she has never left her bed, and has often suffered, I know, for want of proper nourishment."

"I don't think she will suffer much longer, mother. I stopped in to see her the other day, and I was astonished at the change which had taken place in a short time. Her conversation, too, seems so heavenly, her faith in the Lord so strong, that I could not avoid coming to the conclusion that a few days more, at the most, would terminate her wearisome life."

"It will be a happy release for her, indeed, my daughter. Still, it will be a sore trial for her mother."

It was near six when Mrs. Perry and her daughter finished the work upon which they were engaged.

"Now Laura, dear," said the mother, "get back as soon as you can, for I don't like you to be out after night, and more than that, if Mrs. Carr comes, she won't want to wait."

About twenty minutes after the young girl had gone, Mrs. Carr called. "Pray, be seated, my dear friend," said Mrs. Perry, "my daughter has just gone to Mrs. Allison's with some work, and as soon as she returns I can pay you."

"I think I had better call over again, Mrs. Perry," answered the poor woman; "Mary begged me not to stay long."

"Is Annie any worse, then?"

"Oh, yes, a great deal; the doctor thinks she will hardly last till morning."

"Well, Mrs. Carr, death can be only gain to her."

"Very true; still, the idea of losing her seems dreadful to me."

"How does Mary get on at Mrs. Owring's?"

"Not very well; she has been at work for her just one month to-day; and although she gave her to understand that her wages would be at least a dollar and a quarter a week, yet to-night, when she settled with her, she wouldn't give her but three dollars, and at the same time told her that if she didn't choose to work for that she could go."

"What do you suppose was the reason for her acting so?"

"I don't know, indeed, unless it is because she does not get there quite as early as the rest of her hands; for you see I am obliged to keep her a little while in the morning to help me to move Annie while I make her bed. Even that little sum, small it was, would have been some help to us, but it had all to go for rent. My landlord would take no denial. But I must go; you think I can depend on receiving your money to-night?"

"I do. Mrs. Allison is always prompt in paying for her work as soon as it is done. I will not trouble you to come again for it, Mrs. Carr. Laura shall bring it over to you."

Let us now turn to the young girl we left at Mr. Allison's, whom our readers, no doubt, recognise as Laura Perry.

"Good evening, Laura," said Mrs. Allison, as she entered the room; "not brought my work home already! I did not look for it till next week. You and your mother, I am afraid, confine yourselves too closely to your needles for your own good. But you have not had your tea? sit up, and take some."

"No, thank you, Mrs. Allison; mother will be uneasy if I stay long."

"Well, Laura, I am sorry, but I cannot settle with you to-night. Tell your mother Mr. Allison was disappointed in collecting to-day, or she certainly should have had it. Did she say how much it was?"

"Two dollars, ma'am."

"Very well: I will try and let her have it next week."

The expression of Laura's countenance told too plainly the disappointment she felt. "I am afraid Mrs. Perry is in want of that money," remarked the husband after she had gone.

"Not the least doubt of it," replied his wife. "She would not have sent home work at this hour if she had not been. Poor things! who can tell the amount of suffering and wretchedness that is caused by the rich neglecting to pay promptly."

"You come without money, Laura," said her mother, as she entered the house.

"How do you know that, mother?" she replied, forcing a smile.

"I read it in your countenance. Is it not so?"

"It is: Mr. Allison was disappointed in collecting—what will we do, mother?"

"The best we can, my child. We will have to do without our beef for dinner to-morrow; but then we have plenty of bread; so we shall not starve."

"And I shall have to do without my new shoes. My old ones are too shabby to go to church in; so I shall have to stay at home."

"I am sorry for your disappointment, my child, but I care more for Mrs. Carr than I do for ourselves. She has been here, and is in a great deal of trouble. The doctor don't think Annie will live till morning, and Mrs. Owrings hag refused to give Mary more than three dollars for her month's work, every cent of which old Grimes took for rent. I told her she might depend on getting what I owed her, and that I would send you over with it when you returned. You had better go at once and tell her, Laura; perhaps she may be able to get some elsewhere."

"How much is it, mother?"

"Half a dollar."

"It seems hard that she can't get that small sum."

With a heavy heart Laura entered Mrs. Carr's humble abode.

"Oh how glad I am that you have come, my dear!" exclaimed the poor woman. "Annie has been craving some ice cream all day; it's the only thing she seems to fancy. I told her she should have it as soon as you came."

Mrs. Carr's eyes filled with tears as Laura told of her ill success. "I care not for myself," she said "but for that poor suffering child."

"Never mind me, mother," replied Annie. "It was selfish in me to want it, when I know how hard you and Mary are obliged to work for every cent you get. But I feel that I shall not bother you much longer; I have a strange feeling here now." And she placed her hand upon her left side.

"Stop!" cried Laura; "I'll try and get some ice cream for you Annie." And off she ran to her mother's dwelling. "Mother," said she, as she entered the house, "do you recollect that half dollar father gave me the last time he went to sea?"

"Yes, dear."

"Well, I think I had better take it and pay Mrs. Carr. Annie is very bad, and her mother says she has been wanting some ice cream all day."

"It is yours, Laura, do as you like about it."

"It goes hard with me to part with it, mother, for I had determined to keep it in remembrance of my father. It is just twelve years to-day since he went away. But poor Annie—yes, mother, I will take it."

So saying, Laura went to unlock the box which contained her treasure, but unfortunately her key was not where she had supposed it was. After a half hour's search she succeeded in finding it. Tears coursed down her cheeks like rain as she removed from the corner of the little box, where it had lain for so many years, this precious relic of a dear father, who in all probability, was buried beneath the ocean. Dashing them hastily away, she started again for Mrs. Carr's. The ice cream was procured on the way, and, just as the clock struck eight, she arrived at the door. One hour has elapsed since she left. But why does she linger on the threshold? Why but because the sounds of weeping and mourning have reached her ears, and she fears that all is over with her poor friend, Her fears are indeed true, for the pure spirit of the young sufferer has taken its flight to that blest land where hunger and thirst are known no more. Poor Annie! thy last earthly wish, a simple glass of ice-cream, was denied thee—and why? We need not pause to answer: ye who have an abundance of this world's goods, think, when ye are about to turn from your doors the poor seamstress or washerwoman, or even those less destitute than they, without a just recompense for their labour, whether the sufferings and privations of some poor creatures will not be increased thereby.

RETURNING GOOD FOR EVIL

OBADIAH LAWSON and Watt Dood were neighbours; that is, they lived within a half mile of each other, and no person lived between their respective farms, which would have joined, had not a little strip of prairie land extended itself sufficiently to keep them separated. Dood was the oldest settler, and from his youth up had entertained a singular hatred against Quakers; therefore, when he was informed that Lawson, a regular disciple of that class of people had purchased the next farm to his, he declared he would make him glad to move away again. Accordingly, a system of petty annoyances was commenced by him, and every time one of Lawson's hogs chanced to stray upon Dood's place, he was beset by men and dogs, and most savagely abused. Things progressed thus for nearly a year, and the Quaker, a man of decidedly peace principles, appeared in no way to resent the injuries received at the hands of his spiteful neighbour. But matters were drawing to a crisis; for Dood, more enraged than ever at the quiet of Obadiah, made oath that he would do something before long to wake up the spunk of Lawson. Chance favoured his design. The Quaker had a high-blooded filly, which he had been very careful in raising, and which was just four years old. Lawson took great pride in this animal, and had refused a large sum of money for her.

One evening, a little after sunset, as Watt Dood was passing around his cornfield, he discovered the filly feeding in the little strip of prairie land that separated the two farms, and he conceived the hellish design of throwing off two or three rails of his fence, that the horse might get into his corn during the night. He did so, and the next morning, bright and early, he shouldered his rifle and left the house. Not long after his absence, a hired man, whom he had recently employed, heard the echo of his gun, and in a few minutes Dood, considerably excited and out of breath, came hurrying to the house, where he stated that he had shot at and wounded a buck; that the deer attacked him, and he hardly escaped with his life.

This story was credited by all but the newly employed hand, who had taken a dislike to Watt, and, from his manner, suspected that something was wrong. He therefore slipped quietly away from the house, and going through the field in the direction of the shot, he suddenly came upon Lawson's filly, stretched upon the earth, with a bullet hole through the head, from which the warm blood was still oozing.

The animal was warm, and could not have been killed an hour. He hastened back to the dwelling of Dood, who met him in the yard, and demanded, somewhat roughly, where he had been.

"I've been to see if your bullet made sure work of Mr. Lawson's filly," was the instant retort.

Watt paled for a moment, but collecting himself, he fiercely shouted,

"Do you dare to say I killed her?"

"How do you know she is dead?" replied the man.

Dood bit his lip, hesitated a moment, and then turning, walked into the house.

A couple of days passed by, and the morning of the third one had broken, as the hired man met friend Lawson, riding in search of his filly.

A few words of explanation ensued, when, with a heavy heart, the Quaker turned his horse and rode home, where he informed the people of the fate of his filly. No threat of recrimination escaped him; he did not even go to law to recover damages; but calmly awaited his plan and hour of revenge. It came at last.

Watt Dood had a Durham heifer, for which he had paid a heavy price, and upon which he counted to make great gains.

One morning, just as Obadiah was sitting down, his eldest son came in with the information that neighbour Dood's heifer had broken down the fence, entered the yard, and after eating most of the cabbages, had trampled the well-made beds and the vegetables they contained, out of all shape—a mischief impossible to repair.

"And what did thee do with her, Jacob?" quietly asked Obadiah.

"I put her in the farm-yard."

"Did thee beat her?"

"I never struck her a blow."

"Right, Jacob, right; sit down to thy breakfast, and when done eating I will attend to the heifer."

Shortly after he had finished his repast, Lawson mounted a horse, and rode over to Dood's, who was sitting under the porch in front of his house, and who, as he beheld the Quaker dismount, supposed he was coming to demand pay for his filly, and secretly swore he would have to law for it if he did.

"Good morning, neighbour Dood; how is thy family?" exclaimed Obadiah, as he mounted the steps and seated himself in a chair.

"All well, I believe," was the crusty reply.

"I have a small affair to settle with you this morning, and I came rather early."

"So I suppose," growled Watt.

"This morning, my son found thy Durham heifer in my garden, where she has destroyed a good deal."

"And what did he do with her?" demanded Dood, his brow darkening.

"What would thee have done with her, had she been my heifer in thy garden?" asked Obadiah.

"I'd a shot her!" retorted Watt, madly, "as I suppose you have done; but we are only even now. Heifer for filly is only 'tit for tat.'"

"Neighbour Dood, thou knowest me not, if thou thinkest I would harm a hair of thy heifer's back. She is in my farm-yard, and not even a blow has been struck her, where thee can get her at any time. I know thee shot my filly; but the evil one prompted thee to do it, and I lay no evil in my heart against my neighbours. I came to tell thee where thy heifer is, and now I'll go home."

Obadiah rose from his chair, and was about to descend the steps, when he was stopped by Watt, who hastily asked,

"What was your filly worth?"

"A hundred dollars is what I asked for her," replied Obediah.

"Wait a moment!" and Dood rushed into the house, from whence he soon returned, holding some gold in his hand. "Here's the price of your filly; and hereafter let there be a pleasantness between us."

"Willingly, heartily," answered Lawson, grasping the proffered hand of the other; "let there be peace between us."

Obadiah mounted his horse, and rode home with a lighter heart, and from that day to this Dood has been as good a neighbour as one could wish to have; being completely reformed by the RETURNING GOOD FOR EVIL.

PUTTING YOUR HAND IN YOUR NEIGHBOUR'S POCKET

"DO you recollect Thomas, who lived with us as waiter about two years ago, Mary?" asked Mr. Clarke, as he seated himself in his comfortable arm-chair, and slipped his feet into the nicely-warmed, embroidered slippers, which stood ready for his use.

"Certainly," was the reply of Mrs. Clarke. "He was a bright, active fellow, but rather insolent."

"He has proved to be a regular pickpocket," continued her husband, "and is now on his way to Blackwell's Island."

"A very suitable place for him. I hope he will be benefited by a few months' residence there," returned the lady.

"Poor fellow!" exclaimed Mr. Joshua Clarke, an uncle of the young couple, who was quietly reading a newspaper in another part of the room. "There are many of high standing in the world, who deserve to go to Blackwell's Island quite as much as he does."

"You are always making such queer speeches, Uncle Joshua," said his niece. "I suppose you do not mean that there are pickpockets among respectable people?"

"Indeed, there are, my dear niece. Your knowledge of the world must be very limited, if you are not aware of this. Putting your hand in your neighbour's pocket, is one of the most fashionable accomplishments of the day."

Mrs. Clarke was too well acquainted with her uncle's peculiarities to think of arguing with him. She therefore merely smiled, and said to her husband:—

"Well, Henry, I am glad that neither you nor myself are acquainted with this fashionable accomplishment."

"Not acquainted with it!" exclaimed the old gentleman. "I thought you knew yourselves better. Why, you and Henry are both regular pickpockets!"

"I wonder that you demean yourself by associating with us!" was the playful reply.

"Oh, you are no worse than the rest of the world; and, besides, I hope to do you some good, when you grow older and wiser. At present, Henry's whole soul is absorbed in the desire to obtain wealth."

"In a fair and honourable way, uncle," interrupted Mr. Clarke, "and for honourable purposes."

"Certainly," replied Uncle Joshua, "in the common acceptation of the words *fair* and *honourable*. But, do you never, in your mercantile speculations, endeavour to convey erroneous impressions to the minds of those with whom you are dealing? Do you not sometimes suppress information which would prevent your obtaining a good bargain? Do you never allow your customers to purchase goods under false ideas of their value and demand in the market? If you saw a man, less skilled in business than yourself, about to take a step injurious to him, but advantageous to you, would you warn him of his danger—thus obeying the command to love your neighbour as yourself?"

"Why, uncle, these questions are absurd. Of course, when engaged in business, I endeavour to do what is for my own advantage—leaving others to look out for themselves."

"Exactly so. You are perfectly willing to put your hand in your neighbour's pocket and take all you can get, provided he is not wise enough to know that your hand is there."

"Oh, for shame, Uncle Joshua! I shall not allow you to talk to Henry in this manner," exclaimed Mrs. Clarke perceiving that her husband looked somewhat irritated. "Come, prove your charge against me. In what way do I pick my neighbour's pockets?"

"You took six shillings from the washerwoman this morning," coolly replied Uncle Joshua.

"*Took* six shillings from the washerwoman! Paid her six shillings, you mean, uncle. She called for the money due for a day's work, and I gave it to her."

"Yes, but not till you had kept her waiting nearly two hours. I heard her say, as she left the house, 'I have lost a day's work by this delay, for I cannot go to Mrs. Reed's at this hour; so I shall be six shillings poorer at the end of the week.'"

"Why did she wait, then? She could have called again. I was not ready to attend to her at so early an hour."

"Probably she needed the money to-day. You little know the value of six shillings to the mother of a poor family, Mary; but, you should remember that her time is valuable, and that it is as sinful to deprive her of the use of it, as if you took money from her purse."

"Well, uncle, I will acknowledge that I did wrong to keep the poor woman waiting, and I will endeavour to be more considerate in future. So draw your chair to the table, and take a cup of tea and some of your favourite cakes."

"Thank you, Mary; but I am engaged to take tea with your old friend, Mrs. Morrison. Poor thing! she has not made out very well lately. Her school has quite run down, owing to sickness among her scholars; and her own family have been ill all winter; so that her expenses have been great."

"I am sorry to hear this," replied Mrs. Clarke. "I had hoped that her school was succeeding. Give my love to her, uncle, and tell her I will call upon her in a day or two."

Uncle Joshua promised to remember the message, and bidding Mr. and Mrs. Clarke good evening, he was soon seated in Mrs. Morrison's neat little parlour, which, though it bore no comparison with the spacious and beautifully furnished apartments he had just left, had an air of comfort and convenience which could not fail to please.

Delighted to see her old friend, whom she also, from early habit, addressed by the title of Uncle Joshua, although he was no relation, Mrs. Morrison's countenance, for awhile beamed with that cheerful, animated expression which it used to wear in her more youthful days; but an expression of care and anxiety soon over shadowed it, and, in the midst of her kind attentions to her visiter, and her affectionate endearment to two sweet children, who were playing around the room, she would often remain thoughtful and abstracted for several minutes.

Uncle Joshua was an attentive observer, and he saw that something weighed heavily upon her mind. When tea was over, and the little ones had gone to rest, he said, kindly,

"Come, Fanny, draw your chair close to my side, and tell me all your troubles, as freely as you used to do when a merry-hearted school-girl. How often have listened to the sad tale of the pet pigeon, that had flown away, or the favourite plant killed by the untimely frost. Come, I am ready, now as then, to assist you with my advice, and my purse, too, if necessary."

Tears started to Mrs. Morrison's eyes, as she replied.

"You were always a kind friend to me, Uncle Joshua, and I will gladly confide my troubles to you. You know that after my husband's death I took this house, which, though small, may seem far above my limited income, in the hope of obtaining a school sufficiently large to enable me to meet the rent, and also to support myself and children. The small sum left them by their father I determined to invest for their future use. I unwisely intrusted it to one who betrayed the trust, and appropriated the money to some wild speculation of his own. He says that he did this in the hope of increasing my little property. It may be so, but my consent should have been asked. He failed and there is little hope of our ever recovering more, than a small part of what he owes us. But, to return to my school. I found little difficulty in obtaining scholars, and, for a short time, believed myself to be doing well, but I soon found that a large number of scholars did not insure a large income from the school. My terms were moderate, but still I found great difficulty in obtaining what was due to me at the end of the term.

"A few paid promptly, and without expecting me to make unreasonable deductions for unpleasant weather, slight illness, &c., &c. Others paid after long delay, which often put me to the greatest inconvenience; and some, after appointing day after day for me to call, and promising each time that the bill should be settled without fail, moved away, I knew not whither, or met me at length with a cool assurance that it was not possible for them to pay me at present—if it was ever in their power they would let me know."

"Downright robbery!" exclaimed Uncle Joshua. "A set of pickpockets! I wish they were all shipped for Blackwell's Island."

"There are many reasons assigned for not paying," continued Mrs. Morrison. "Sometimes the children had not learned as much as the parents expected. Some found it expedient to take their children away long before the expiration of the term, and then gazed at me in astonishment when I declared my right to demand pay for the whole time for which they engaged. One lady, in particular, to whose daughter I was giving music lessons, withdrew the pupil under pretext of slight indisposition, and sent me the amount due for a half term. I called upon her, and stated that I considered the engagement binding for twenty-four lessons, but would willingly wait until the young lady was quite recovered. The mother appeared to assent with willingness to this arrangement, and took the proffered money without comment. An hour or two after I received a laconic epistle stating that the lady had already engaged another teacher, whom she thought preferable— that she had offered me the amount due for half of the term, and I had declined receiving it—therefore she should not offer it again. I wrote a polite, but very plain, reply to this note, and enclosed my bill for the whole term, but have never heard from her since."

"Do you mean to say that she actually received the money which you returned to her without reluctance, and gave you no notice of her intention to employ another teacher?" demanded the old gentleman.

"Certainly; and, besides this, I afterwards ascertained that the young lady was actually receiving a lesson from another teacher, when I called at the house—therefore the plea of indisposition was entirely false. The most perfect satisfaction had always been expressed as to the progress of the pupil, and no cause was assigned for the change."

"I hope you have met with few cases as bad as this," remarked Uncle Joshua. "The world must be in a worse state than even I had supposed, if such imposition is common."

"This may be an extreme case," replied Mrs. Morrison, "but I could relate many others which are little better. However, you will soon weary of my experience in this way, Uncle Joshua, and I will therefore mention but one other instance. One bitter cold day in January, I called at the house of a lady who had owed me a small amount for nearly a year, and after repeated delay had reluctantly fixed this day as the time when she would pay me at least a part of what was due. I was told by the servant who opened the door that the lady was not at home.

"What time will she be in?" I inquired.

"Not for some hours," was the reply.

Leaving word that I would call again towards evening, I retraced my steps, feeling much disappointed at my ill success, as I had felt quite sure of obtaining the money. About five o'clock I again presented myself at the door, and was again informed that the lady was not at home.

"I will walk in, and wait for her return," I replied.

The servant appeared somewhat startled at this, but after a little delay ushered me into the parlour. Two little boys, of four and six years of age, were playing about the room. I joined in their sports, and soon became quite familiar with them. Half an hour had passed away, when I inquired of the oldest boy what time he expected his mother?

"Not till late," he answered, hesitatingly.

"Did she take the baby with her this cold day?" I asked.

"Yes, ma'am," promptly replied the girl, who, under pretence of attending to the children, frequently came into the room.

The youngest child gazed earnestly in my face, and said, smilingly,

"Mother has not gone away, she is up stairs. She ran away with baby when she saw you coming, and told us to say she had gone out. I am afraid brother will take cold, for there is no fire up stairs."

"It is no such thing," exclaimed the girl and the eldest boy. "She is not up stairs, ma'am, or she would see you."

But even as they spoke the loud cries of an infant were heard, and a voice at the head of the stairs calling Jenny.

The girl obeyed, and presently returned with the child in her arms, its face, neck, and hands purple with cold.

"Poor little thing, it has got its death in that cold room," she said. "Mistress cannot see you, ma'am, she is sick and gone to bed."

"This last story was probably equally false with the other, but I felt that it was useless to remain, and with feelings of deep regret for the poor children who were so early taught an entire disregard for truth, and of sorrow for the exposure to cold to which I had innocently subjected the infant, I left the house. A few days after, I heard that the little one had died with croup. Jenny, whom I accidentally met in the street, assured me that he took the cold which caused his death from the exposure on the afternoon of my call, as he became ill the following day. I improved the opportunity to endeavour to impress upon the mind of the poor girl the sin of which she had been guilty, in telling a falsehood even in obedience to the commands of her mistress; and I hope that what I said may be useful to her.

"The want of honesty and promptness in the parents of my pupils often caused me great inconvenience, and I frequently found it difficult to meet my rent when it became due. Still I have struggled through my difficulties without contracting any debts until this winter, but the sickness which has prevailed in my school has so materially lessened my income, and my family expenses have, for the same reason, been so much greater, that I fear it will be quite impossible for me to continue in my present situation."

"Do not be discouraged," said Uncle Joshua; "I will advance whatever sum you are in immediate need of, and you may repay me when it is convenient to yourself. I will also take the bills which are due to you from various persons, and endeavour to collect them. Your present term is, I suppose, nearly ended. Commence another with this regulation:—That the price of tuition, or at least one-half of it, shall be paid before the entrance of the scholar. Some will complain of this rule, but many will not hesitate to comply with it, and you will find the result beneficial. And now I would leave you, Fanny, for I have another call to make this evening. My young friend, William Churchill, is, I hear, quite ill, and I feel desirous to see him. I will call upon you in a day or two, and then we will have another talk about your affairs, and see what can be done for you. So good night, Fanny; go to sleep and dream of your old friend."

Closing the door after Uncle Joshua, Mrs. Morrison returned to her room with a heart filled with thankfulness that so kind a friend had been sent to her in the hour of need; while the old gentleman walked with rapid steps through several streets until he stood at the door of a small, but pleasantly situated house in the suburbs of the city. His ring at the bell was answered by a pretty, pleasant-looking young woman, whom he addressed as Mrs. Churchill, and kindly inquired for her husband.

"William is very feeble to-day, but he will be rejoiced to see you, sir. His disease is partly owing to anxiety of mind, I think, and when his spirits are raised by a friendly visit, he feels better."

Uncle Joshua followed Mrs. Churchill to the small room which now served the double purpose of parlour and bedroom. They were met at the door by the invalid, who had recognised the voice of his old friend, and had made an effort to rise and greet him. His sunken countenance, the hectic flush which glowed upon his cheek, and the distressing cough, gave fearful evidence that unless the disease was soon arrested in its progress, consumption would mark him for its victim.

The friendly visitor was inwardly shocked at his appearance, but wisely made no allusion to it, and soon engaged him in cheerful conversation. Gradually he led him to speak openly of his own situation,—of his health, and of the pecuniary difficulties with which he was struggling. His story was a common one. A young family were growing up around him, and an aged mother and invalid sister also depended upon him for support. The small salary which he obtained as clerk in one of the most extensive mercantile establishments in the city, was quite insufficient to meet his necessary expenses. He had, therefore, after being constantly employed from early morning until a late hour in the evening, devoted two or three hours of the night to various occupations which added a trifle to his limited income. Sometimes he procured copying of various kinds; at others, accounts, which he could take to his own house, were intrusted to him. This incessant application had gradually ruined his health, and now for several weeks he had been unable to leave the house.

"Have you had advice from an experienced physician, William?" inquired Uncle Joshua. The young man blushed, as he replied, that he was unwilling to send for a physician, knowing that he had no means to repay his services.

"I will send my own doctor to see you," returned his friend. "He can help you if any one can, and as for his fee I will attend to it, and if you regain your health I shall be amply repaid.—No, do not thank me," he continued, as Mr. Churchill endeavoured to express his gratitude. "Your father has done me many a favour, and it would be strange if I could not extend a hand to help his son when in trouble. And now tell me, William, is not your salary very small, considering the responsible situation which you have so long held in the firm of Stevenson & Co.?"

"It is," was the reply; "but I see no prospect of obtaining more. I believe I have always given perfect satisfaction to my employer, although it is difficult to ascertain the estimation in which he holds me, for he is a man who never praises. He has never found fault with me, and therefore I suppose him satisfied, and indeed I have some proof of this in his willingness to wait two or three months in the hope that I may recover from my present illness before making a permanent engagement with a new clerk. Notwithstanding this, he has never raised my salary, and when I ventured to say to him about a year ago, that as his business had nearly doubled since I had been with him, I felt that it would be but just that I should derive some benefit from the change, he coolly replied that my present salary was all that he had ever paid a clerk, and he considered it a sufficient equivalent for my services. He knows very well that it is difficult to obtain a good situation, there are so many who stand ready to fill any vacancy, and therefore he feels quite safe in refusing to give me, more."

"And yet," replied Uncle Joshua, "he is fully aware that the advantage resulting from your long experience and thorough acquaintance with his business, increases his income several hundred dollars every year, and this money he quietly puts into his own pocket, without considering or caring that a fair proportion of it should in common honesty go into yours. What a queer world we live in! The poor thief who robs you of your watch or pocket-book, is punished without delay; but these wealthy defrauders maintain their respectability and pass for honest men, even while withholding what they know to be the just due of another.

"But cheer up, William, I have a fine plan for you, if you can but regain your health. I am looking for a suitable person to take charge of a large sheep farm, which I propose establishing on the land which I own in Virginia. You acquired some knowledge of farming in your early days. How would you like to undertake this business? The climate is delightful, the employment easy and pleasant; and it shall be my care that your salary is amply sufficient for the support of your family."

Mr. Churchill could hardly command his voice sufficiently to express his thanks, and his wife burst into tears, as she exclaimed,

"If my poor husband had confided his troubles to you before, he would not have been reduced to this feeble state."

"He will recover," said the old gentleman. "I feel sure, that in one month, he will look like a different man. Rest yourself, now, William, and to-morrow I will see you again."

And, followed by the blessings and thanks of the young couple, Uncle Joshua departed.

"Past ten o'clock," he said to himself, as he paused near a lamp-post and looked at his watch. "I must go to my own room."

As he said this he was startled by a deep sigh from some one near, and on looking round, saw a lad, of fourteen or fifteen years of age, leaning against the post, and looking earnestly at him.

Uncle Joshua recognised the son of a poor widow, whom he had occasionally befriended, and said, kindly,

"Well, John, are you on your way home from the store? This is rather a late hour for a boy like you."

"Yes, sir, it is late. I cannot bear to return home to my poor mother, for I have bad news for her to-night. Mr. Mackenzie does not wish to employ me any more. My year is up to-day."

"Why, John, how is this? Not long ago your employer told me that he was perfectly satisfied with you; indeed, he said that he never before had so trusty and useful a boy."

"He has always appeared satisfied with me, sir, and I have endeavoured to serve him faithfully. But he told me to-day that he had engaged another boy."

Uncle Joshua mused for a moment, and then asked,

"What was he to give you for the first year, John?"

"Nothing, sir. He told my mother that my services would be worth nothing the first year, but the second he would pay me fifty dollars, and so increase my salary as I grew older. My poor mother has worked very hard to support me this year, and I had hoped that I would be able to help her soon. But it is all over now, and I suppose I must take a boy's place again, and work another year for nothing."

"And then be turned off again. Another set of pickpockets," muttered his indignant auditor.

"Pickpockets!" exclaimed the lad. "Did any one take your watch just now, sir? I saw a man look at it as you took it out. Perhaps we can overtake him. I think he turned into the next street."

"No, no, my boy. My watch is safe enough. I am not thinking of street pickpockets, but of another class whom you will find out as you grow older. But never mind losing your place, John. My nephew is in want of a boy who has had some experience in your business, and will pay him a fair salary—more than Mr. Mackenzie agreed to give you for the second year. I will mention you to him, and you may call at his store to-morrow at eleven o'clock, and we will see if you will answer his purpose."

"Thank you, Sir, I am sure I thank you; and mother will bless you for your kindness," replied the boy, his countenance glowing with animation; and with a grateful "good night," he darted off in the direction of his own home.

"There goes a grateful heart," thought Uncle Joshua, as he gazed after the boy until he turned the corner of the street and disappeared. "He has lost his situation merely because another can be found who will do the work for nothing for a year, in the vain hope of future recompense. I wish Mary could have been with me this evening; I think she would have acknowledged that there are many respectable pickpockets who deserve to accompany poor Thomas to Blackwell's Island;" and thus soliloquizing, Uncle Joshua reached the door of his boarding-house, and sought repose in his own room.

KIND WORDS

WE have more than once, in our rapidly written reflections, urged the policy and propriety of kindness, courtesy, and good-will between man and man. It is so easy for an individual to manifest amenity of spirit, to avoid harshness, and thus to cheer and gladden the paths of all over whom he may have influence or control, that it is really surprising to find any one pursuing the very opposite course. Strange as it may appear, there are among the children of men, hundreds who seem to take delight in making others unhappy. They rejoice at an opportunity of being the messengers of evil tidings. They are jealous or malignant; and in either case they exult in inflicting a wound. The ancients, in most nations, had a peculiar dislike to croakers, prophets of evil, and the bearers of evil tidings. It is recorded that the messenger from the banks of the Tigris, who first announced the defeat of the Roman army by the Persians, and the death of the Emperor Julian, in a Roman city of Asia Minor, was instantly buried under a heap of stones thrown upon him by an indignant populace. And yet this messenger was innocent, and reluctantly discharged a painful duty. But how different the spirit and the motive of volunteers in such cases—those who exult in an opportunity of communicating bad news, and in some degree revel over the very agony which it produces. The sensitive, the generous, the honourable, would ever be spared from such painful missions. A case of more recent occurrence may be referred to as in point. We allude to the murder of Mr. Roberts, a farmer of New Jersey, who was robbed and shot in his own wagon, near Camden. It became necessary that the sad intelligence should be broken to his wife and family with as much delicacy as possible. A neighbour was selected for the task, and at first consented. But, on consideration, his heart failed him. He could not, he said, communicate the details of a tragedy so appalling and he begged to be excused. Another, formed it was thought of sterner stuff, was then fixed upon: but he too, rough and bluff as he was in his ordinary manners, possessed the heart of a generous and sympathetic human being, and also respectfully declined. A third made a like objection, and at last a female friend of the family was with much difficulty persuaded, in company with another, to undertake the mournful task. And yet, we repeat, there are in society, individuals who delight in contributing to the misery of others—who are eager to circulate a slander, to chronicle a ruin, to revive a forgotten error, to wound, sting, and annoy, whenever they may do so with impunity. How much better the gentle, the generous, the magnanimous policy! Why not do everything that may be done for the happiness of our fellow creatures, without seeking out their weak points, irritating their half-healed wounds, jarring their sensibilities, or embittering their thoughts! The magic of kind words and a kind manner can scarcely be over-estimated. Our fellow creatures are more sensitive than is generally imagined. We have known cases in which a gentle courtesy has been remembered with pleasure for years. Who indeed cannot look back into "bygone time," and discover some smile, some look or other demonstration of regard or esteem, calculated to bless and brighten every hour of after existence! "Kind words," says an eminent writer, "do not cost much. It does not take long to utter them. They never blister the tongue or lips on their passage into the world, or occasion any other kind of bodily suffering; and we have never heard of any mental trouble arising from this quarter. Though they do not cost much, yet they accomplish much. 1. They help one's own good nature and good will. One cannot be in a habit of this kind, without thereby pecking away something of the granite roughness of his own nature. Soft words will soften his own soul. Philosophers tell us that the angry words a man uses in his passion are fuel to the flame of his wrath, and make it blaze the more fiercely. Why, then, should not words of the opposite character produce opposite results, and that most blessed of all passions of the soul, kindness, be augmented by kind words? People that are for ever speaking kindly, are for ever disinclining themselves to ill-temper. 2. Kind words make other people good-natured. Cold words freeze people, and hot words scorch them, and sarcastic words irritate them, and bitter words make them bitter, and wrathful words make them wrathful. And kind words also produce their own image on men's souls; and a beautiful image it is. They soothe, and quiet, and comfort the hearer. They shame him out of his sour, morose, unkind feelings; and he has to become kind himself. There is such a rush of all other kinds of words in our days, that it seems desirable to give kind words a chance among them. There are vain words, idle words, hasty words, spiteful words, silly words, and empty words. Now kind words are better than the whole of them; and it is a pity that, among the improvements of the present age, birds of this feather might not have more of a chance than they have had to spread their wings."

It is indeed! Kind words should be brought into more general use. Those in authority should employ them more frequently, when addressing the less fortunate among mankind. Employers should use them in their intercourse with their workmen. Parents should utter them on every occasion to their children. The rich should never forget an opportunity of speaking kindly to the poor. Neighbours and friends should emulate each other in the employment of mild, gentle, frank, and kindly language. But this cannot be done unless each endeavours to control himself. Our passions and our prejudices must be kept in check. If we find that we have a neighbour on the other side of the way, who has been more fortunate in a worldly sense than we have been, and if we discover a little jealousy or envy creeping into our opinions and feelings concerning said neighbour—let us be careful, endeavour to put a rein upon our tongues, and to avoid the indulgence of malevolence or ill-will. If we, on the other hand, have been fortunate, have enough and to spare, and there happens to be in our circle some who are dependent upon us, some who look up to us with love and respect—let us be generous, courteous, and kind—and thus we shall not only discharge a duty, but prove a source of happiness to others.

NEIGHBOURS' QUARRELS

MOST people think there are cares enough in the world, and yet many are very industrious to increase them:—One of the readiest ways of doing this is to quarrel with a neighbour. A bad bargain may vex a man for a week, and a bad debt may trouble him for a month; but a quarrel with his neighbours will keep him in hot water all the year round.

Aaron Hands delights in fowls, and his cocks and hens are always scratching up the flowerbeds of his neighbour William Wilkes, whose mischievous tom-cat every now and then runs off with a chicken. The consequence is, that William Wilkins is one half the day occupied in driving away the fowls, and threatening to screw their long ugly necks off; while Aaron Hands, in his periodical outbreaks, invariably vows to skin his neighbour's cat, as sure as he can lay hold of him.

Neighbours! Neighbours! Why can you not be at peace? Not all the fowls you can rear, and the flowers you can grow, will make amends for a life of anger, hatred, malice, and uncharitableness. Come to some kind-hearted understanding one with another, and dwell in peace.

Upton, the refiner, has a smoky chimney, that sets him and all the neighbourhood by the ears. The people around abuse him without mercy, complaining that they are poisoned, and declaring that they will indict him at the sessions. Upton fiercely sets them at defiance, on the ground that his premises were built before theirs, that his chimney did not come to them, but that they came to his chimney.

Neighbours! Neighbours! practise a little more forbearance. Had half a dozen of you waited on the refiner in a kindly spirit, he would years ago have so altered his chimney, that it would not have annoyed you.

Mrs. Tibbets is thoughtless—if it were not so she would never have had her large dusty carpet beaten, when her neighbour, who had a wash, was having her wet clothes hung out to dry. Mrs. Williams is hasty and passionate, or she would never have taken it for granted that the carpet was beaten on purpose to spite her, and give her trouble. As it is, Mrs. Tibbets and Mrs. Williams hate one another with a perfect hatred.

Neighbours! Neighbours! bear with one another. We are none of us angels, and should not, therefore, expect those about us to be free from faults.

They who attempt to out-wrangle a quarrelsome neighbour, go the wrong way to work. A kind word, and still more a kind deed, will be more likely to be successful. Two children wanted to pass by a savage dog: the one took a stick in his hand and pointed it at him, but this only made the enraged creature more furious than before. The other child adopted a different plan; for by giving the dog a piece of his bread and butter, he was allowed to pass, the subdued animal wagging his tail in quietude. If you happen to have a quarrelsome neighbour, conquer him by civility and kindness; try the bread and butter system, and keep your stick out of sight. That is an excellent Christian admonition, "A soft answer turneth away wrath, but grievous words stir up anger."

Neighbours' quarrels are a mutual reproach, and yet a stick or a straw is sufficient to promote them. One man is rich, and another poor; one is a churchman, another a dissenter; one is a conservative, another a liberal; one hates another because he is of the same trade, and another is bitter with his neighbour because he is a Jew or a Roman Catholic.

Neighbours! Neighbours! live in love, and then while you make others happy, you will be happier yourselves.

"That happy man is surely blest,
Who of the worst things makes the best;
Whilst he must be of temper curst,
Who of the best things makes the worst."

"Be ye all of one mind," says the Apostle, "having compassion one of another; love as brethren, be pitiful, be courteous; not rendering evil for evil, or railing for railing, but contrariwise blessing. "To a rich man I would say, bear with and try to serve those who are below you; and to a poor one—

"Fear God, love peace, and mind your labour;
And never, never quarrel with your neighbour."

GOOD WE MIGHT DO

WE all might do good
Where we often do ill;
There is always the way,
If we have but the will;
Though it be but a word
Kindly breathed or supprest,
It may guard off some pain,
Or give peace to some breast.

We all might do good
In a thousand small ways—
In forbearing to flatter,
Yet yielding *due* praise—
In spurning ill humour,
Reproving wrong done,
And treating but kindly
Each heart we have won.

We all might do good,
Whether lowly or great,
For the deed is not gauged
By the purse or estate;
If it be but a cup
Of cold water that's given,
Like "the widow's two mites,"
It is something for Heaven.

THE TOWN LOT

ONCE upon a time it happened that the men who governed the municipal affairs of a certain growing town in the West, resolved, in grave deliberation assembled, to purchase a five-acre lot at the north end of the city—recently incorporated—and have it improved for a park or public square. Now, it also happened, that all the saleable ground lying north of the city was owned by a man named Smith—a shrewd, wide-awake individual, whose motto was "Every man for himself," with an occasional addition about a certain gentleman in black taking "the hindmost."

Smith, it may be mentioned, was secretly at the bottom of this scheme for a public square, and had himself suggested the matter to an influential member of the council; not that he was moved by what is denominated public spirit—no; the spring of action in the case was merely "private spirit," or a regard for his own good. If the council decided upon a public square, he was the man from whom the ground would have to be bought; and he was the man who could get his own price therefor.

As we have said, the park was decided upon, and a committee of two appointed whose business it was to see Smith, and arrange with him for the purchase of a suitable lot of ground. In due form the committee called upon the landholder, who was fully prepared for the interview.

"You are the owner of those lots at the north end?" said the spokesman of the committee.

"I am," replied Smith, with becoming gravity.

"Will you sell a portion of ground, say five acres, to the city?"

"For what purpose?" Smith knew very well for what purpose the land was wanted.

"We have decided to set apart about five acres of ground, and improve it as a kind of park, or public promenade."

"Have you, indeed? Well, I like that," said Smith, with animation. "It shows the right kind of public spirit."

"We have, moreover, decided that the best location will be at the north end of the town."

"Decidedly my own opinion," returned Smith.

"Will you sell us the required acres?" asked one of the councilmen.

"That will depend somewhat upon where you wish to locate the park."

The particular location was named.

"The very spot," replied Smith, promptly, "upon which I have decided to erect four rows of dwellings."

"But it is too far out for that," was naturally objected.

"O, no; not a rod. The city is rapidly growing in that direction. I have only to put up the dwellings referred to, and dozens will, be anxious to purchase lots, and build all around them. Won't the ground to the left of that you speak of answer as well?"

But the committee replied in the negative. The lot they had mentioned was the one decided upon as most suited for the purpose, and they were not prepared to think of any other location.

All this Smith understood very well. He was not only willing, but anxious for the city to purchase the lot they were negotiating for. All he wanted was to get a good round price for the same—say four or five times the real value. So he feigned indifference, and threw difficulties in the way.

A few years previous to this time, Smith had purchased a considerable tract of land at the north of the then flourishing village, at fifty dollars an acre. Its present value was about three hundred dollars an acre. After a good deal of talk on both sides, Smith finally agreed to sell the particular lot pitched upon. The next thing was to arrange as to price.

"At what do you hold this ground per acre?"

It was some time before Smith answered this question. His eyes were cast upon the floor, and earnestly did he enter into debate with himself as to the value he should place upon the lot. At first he thought of five hundred dollars per acre. But his cupidity soon caused him to advance on that sum, although, a month before, he would have caught at such an offer. Then he advanced to six, to seven, and to eight hundred. And still he felt undecided.

"I can get my own price," said he to himself. "The city has to pay, and I might just as well get a large sum as a small one."

"For what price will you sell?" The question was repeated.

"I must have a good price."

"We are willing to pay what is fair and right."

"Of course. No doubt you have fixed a limit to which you will go."

"Not exactly that," said one of the gentlemen.

"Are you prepared to make an offer?"

"We are prepared to hear your price, and to make a report thereon," was replied.

"That's a very valuable lot of ground," said Smith.

"Name your price," returned one of the committeemen, a little impatiently.

Thus brought up to the point, Smith, after thinking hurriedly for a few moments, said—

"One thousand dollars an acre."

Both the men shook their heads in a very positive way. Smith said that it was the lowest he would take; and so the conference ended.

At the next meeting of the city councils, a report on the town lot was made, and the extraordinary demand of Smith canvassed. It was unanimously decided not to make the proposed purchase.

When this decision reached the landholder, he was considerably disappointed. He wanted money badly, and would have "jumped at" two thousand dollars for the five acre lot, if satisfied that it would bring no more. But when the city came forward as a purchaser, his cupidity was subjected to a very strong temptation. He believed that he could get five thousand dollars as easily as two; and quieted his conscience by the salvo—"An article is always worth what it will bring."

A week or two went by, and Smith was about calling upon one of the members of the council, to say that, if the city really wanted the lot he would sell at their price, leaving it with the council to act justly and generously, when a friend said to him,

"I hear that the council had the subject of a public square under consideration again this morning."

"Indeed!" Smith was visibly excited, though he tried to appear calm.

"Yes; and I also hear that they have decided to pay the extravagant price you asked for a lot of ground at the north end of the city."

"A thousand dollars an acre?"

"Yes."

"Its real value, and not cent more," said Smith.

"People differ about that. How ever, you are lucky," the friend replied. "The city is able to pay."

"So I think. And I mean they shall pay."

Before the committee, to whom the matter was given in charge, had time to call upon Smith, and close with him for the lot, that gentleman had concluded in his own mind that it would be just as easy to get twelve hundred dollars an acre as a thousand. It was plain that the council were bent upon having the ground, and would pay a round sum for it. It was just the spot for a public square; and the city must become the owner. So, when he was called upon, by the gentlemen, and they said to him,

"We are authorized to pay you your price," he promptly answered, "The offer is no longer open. You declined it when it was made. My price for that property is now twelve hundred dollars an acre."

The men offered remonstrance; but it was of no avail. Smith believed that he could get six thousand dollars for the ground as easily as five thousand. The city must have the lot, and would pay almost any price.

"I hardly think it right, Mr. Smith," said one of his visitors, "for you to take such an advantage. This square is for the public good."

"Let the public pay, then," was the unhesitating answer. "The public is able enough."

"The location of this park, at the north end of the city, will greatly improve the value of your other property."

This Smith understood very well. But he replied,

"I am not so sure of that. I have some very strong doubts on the subject. It's my opinion, that the buildings I contemplated erecting will be far more to my advantage. Be that as it may, however, I am decided in selling for nothing less than six thousand dollars."

"We are only authorized to pay five thousand," replied the committee. "If you agree to take that sum, will close the bargain on the spot."

Five thousand dollars was a large sum of money, and Smith felt strongly tempted to close in with the liberal offer. But six thousand loomed up before his imagination still more temptingly.

"I can get it," said he to himself; "and the property is worth what it will bring."

So he positively declined to sell it at a thousand dollars per acre.

"At twelve hundred you will sell?" remarked one of the committee, as they were about retiring.

"Yes. I will take twelve hundred the acre. That is the lowest rate, and I am not anxious even at that price. I can do quite as well by keeping it in my own possession. But, as you seem so bent on having it, I will not stand in your way. When will the council meet again?"

"Not until next week."

"Very well. If they then accept my offer, all will be right. But, understand me; if they do not accept, the offer no longer remains open. It is a matter of no moment to me which way the thing goes."

It was a matter of moment to Smith, for all this assertion—a matter of very great moment. He had several thousand dollars to pay in the course of the next few months on land purchases, and no way to meet the payments, except by mortgages, or sales of property; and, it may naturally be concluded, that he suffered considerable uneasiness during the time which passed until the next meeting of the council.

Of course, the grasping disposition shown by Smith, became the town talk; and people said a good many hard things of him. Little, however, did he care, so that he secured six thousand dollars for a lot not worth more than two thousand.

Among other residents and property holders in the town, was a simple-minded, true-hearted, honest man, named Jones. His father had left him a large farm, a goodly portion of which, in process of time, came to be included in the limits of the new city; and he found a much more profitable employment in selling building lots than in tilling the soil. The property of Mr. Jones lay at the west side of the town.

Now, when Mr. Jones heard of the exorbitant demand made by Smith for a five acre lot, his honest heart throbbed with a feeling of indignation.

"I couldn't have believed it of him," said he. "Six thousand dollars! Preposterous! Why, I would give the city a lot of twice the size, and do it with pleasure."

"You would?" said a member of the council, who happened to hear this remark.

"Certainly I would."

"You are really in earnest?"

"Undoubtedly. Go and select a public square from any of my unappropriated land on the west side of the city, and I will pass you the title as a free gift to-morrow, and feel pleasure in doing so."

"That is public spirit," said the councilman.

"Call it what you will. I am pleased in making the offer."

Now, let it not be supposed that Mr. Jones was shrewdly calculating the advantage which would result to him from having a park at the west side of the city. No such thought had yet entered his mind. He spoke from the impulse of a generous feeling.

Time passed on, and the session day of the council came round—a day to which Smith had looked forward with no ordinary feelings of interest, that were touched at times by the coldness of doubt, and the agitation of uncertainty. Several times he had more than half repented of his refusal to accept the liberal offer of five thousand dollars, and of having fixed so positively upon six thousand as the "lowest figure."

The morning of the day passed, and Smith began to grow uneasy. He did not venture to seek for information as to the doings of the council, for that would be to expose the anxiety he felt in the result of their deliberations. Slowly the afternoon wore away, and it so happened that Smith did not meet any one of the councilmen; nor did he even know whether the council was still in session or not. As to making allusion to the subject of his anxious interest to any one, that was carefully avoided; for he knew that his exorbitant demand was the town talk—and he wished to affect the most perfect indifference on the subject.

The day closed, and not a whisper about the town lot had come to the ears of Mr. Smith. What could it mean? Had his offer to sell at six thousand been rejected? The very thought caused his heart to grow heavy in his bosom. Six, seven, eight o'clock came, and still it was all dark with Mr. Smith. He could bear the suspense no longer, and so determined to call upon his neighbour Wilson, who was a member of the council, and learn from him what had been done.

So he called on Mr. Wilson.

"Ah, friend Smith," said the latter; "how are you this evening?"

"Well, I thank you," returned Smith, feeling a certain oppression of the chest. "How are you?"

"Oh, very well."

Here there was a pause. After which Smith said, "About that ground of mine. What did you do?"

"Nothing," replied Wilson, coldly.

"Nothing, did you say?" Smith's voice was a little husky.

"No. You declined our offer; or, rather, the high price fixed by yourself upon the land."

"You refused to buy it at five thousand, when it was offered," said Smith.

"I know we did, because your demand was exorbitant."

"Oh, no, not at all," returned Smith quickly.

"In that we only differ," said Wilson. "However, the council has decided not to pay you the price you ask."

"Unanimously?"

"There was not a dissenting voice."

Smith began to feel more and more uncomfortable.

"I might take something less," he ventured to say, in a low, hesitating voice.

"It is too late now," was Mr. Wilson's prompt reply.

"Too late! How so?"

"We have procured a lot."

"Mr. Wilson!" Poor Smith started to his feet in chagrin and astonishment.

"Yes; we have taken one of Jones's lots on the west side of the city. A beautiful ten acre lot."

"You have!" Smith was actually pale.

"We have; and the title deeds are now being made out."

It was some time before Smith had sufficiently recovered from the stunning effect of this unlooked-for intelligence, to make the inquiry,

"And pray how much did Jones ask for his ten acre lot."

"He presented it to the city as a gift," replied the councilman.

"A gift! What folly!"

"No, not folly—but true worldly wisdom; though I believe Jones did not think of advantage to himself when he generously made the offer. He is worth twenty thousand dollars more to-day than he was yesterday, in the simple advanced value of his land for building lots. And I know of no man in this town whose good fortune affects me with more pleasure."

Smith stole back to his home with a mountain of disappointment on his heart. In his cupidity he had entirely overreached himself, and he saw that the consequences were to react upon all his future prosperity. The public square at the west end of the town would draw improvements in that direction, all the while increasing the wealth of Mr. Jones, while lots at the north end would remain at present prices, or, it might be, take a downward range.

And so it proved. In ten years, Jones was the richest man in the town, while half of Smith's property had been sold for taxes. The five acre lot passed from his hands, under the hammer, in the foreclosure of a mortgage, for one thousand dollars!

Thus it is that inordinate selfishness and cupidity overreach themselves; while the liberal man deviseth liberal things, and is sustained thereby.

THE SUNBEAM AND THE RAINDROP

A SUNBEAM and a raindrop met together in the sky
One afternoon in sunny June, when earth was parched and dry; Each quarrelled for the precedence ('twas so the story ran), And the golden sunbeam, warmly, the quarrel thus began:—

"What were the earth without me? I come with beauty bright,
She smiles to hail my presence, and rejoices in my light;
I deck the hill and valley with many a lovely hue,
I give the rose its blushes, and the violet its blue.

"I steal within the window, and through the cottage door,
And my presence like a blessing gilds with smiles the broad earth o'er; The brooks and streams flow dancing and sparkling in my ray,
And the merry, happy children in the golden sunshine play."

Then the tearful raindrop answered—"Give praise where praise is due, The earth indeed were lonely without a smile from you;
But without my visits, also, its beauty would decay, The flowers droop and wither, and the streamlets dry away.

"I give the flowers their freshness, and you their colours gay,
My jewels would not sparkle, without your sunny ray.
Since each upon the other so closely must depend,
Let us seek the earth together, and our common blessings blend."

The raindrops, and the sunbeams, came laughing down to earth,
And it woke once more to beauty, and to myriad tones of mirth; The river and the streamlet went dancing on their way,

And the raindrops brightly sparkled in the sunbeam's golden ray.

The drooping flowers looked brighter, there was fragrance in the air, The earth seemed new created, there was gladness everywhere; And above the dark clouds, gleaming on the clear blue arch of Heaven, The Rainbow, in its beauty, like a smile of love was given.

'Twas a sweet and simple lesson, which the story told, I thought, Not alone and single-handed our kindliest deeds are wrought; Like the sunbeam and the raindrop, work together, while we may, And the bow of Heaven's own promise shall smile upon our way.

A PLEA FOR SOFT WORDS

STRANGE and subtle are the influences which affect the spirit and touch the heart. Are there bodiless creatures around us, moulding our thoughts into darkness or brightness, as they will? Whence, otherwise, come the shadow and the sunshine, for which we can discern no mortal agency?

Oftener, As we grow older, come the shadows; less frequently the sunshine. Ere I took up my pen, I was sitting with a pleasant company of friends, listening to music, and speaking, with the rest, light words.

Suddenly, I knew not why, my heart was wrapt away in an atmosphere of sorrow. A sense of weakness and unworthiness weighed me down, and I felt the moisture gather to my eyes and my lips tremble, though they kept the smile.

All my past life rose up before me, and all my short-comings—all, my mistakes, and all my wilful wickedness, seemed pleading trumpet-tongued against me.

I saw her before me whose feet trod with mine the green holts and meadows, when the childish thought strayed not beyond the near or the possible. I saw her through the long blue distances, clothed in the white beauty of an angel; but, alas! she drew her golden hair across her face to veil from her vision the sin-darkened creature whose eyes dropped heavily to the hem of her robe!

O pure and beautiful one, taken to peace ere the weak temptation had lifted itself up beyond thy stature, and compelled thee to listen, to oppose thy weakness to its strength, and to fall—sometimes, at least, let thy face shine on me from between the clouds. Fresh from the springs of Paradise, shake from thy wings the dew against my forehead. We two were coming up together through the sweet land of poesy and dreams, where the senses believe what the heart hopes; our hands were full of green boughs, and our laps of cowslips and violets, white and purple. We were talking of that more beautiful world into which childhood was opening out, when that spectre met us, feared and dreaded alike by the strong man and the little child, and one was taken, and the other left.

One was caught away sinless to the bosom of the Good Shepherd, and one was left to weep pitiless tears, to eat the bread of toil, and to think the bitter thoughts of misery,—left "to clasp a phantom and to find it air." For often has the adversary pressed me sore, and out of my arms has slid ever that which my soul pronounced good: slid out of my arms and coiled about my feet like a serpent, dragging me back and holding me down from all that is high and great.

Pity me, dear one, if thy sweet sympathies can come out of the glory, if the lovelight of thy beautiful life can press through the cloud and the evil, and fold me again as a garment; pity and plead for me with the maiden mother whose arms in human sorrow and human love cradled our blessed Redeemer.

She hath known our mortal pain and passion—our more than mortal triumph—she hath heard the "blessed art thou among women." My unavailing prayers goldenly syllabled by her whose name sounds from the manger through all the world, may find acceptance with Him who, though our sins be as scarlet, can wash them white as wool.

Our hearts grew together as one, and along the headlands and the valleys one shadow went before us, and one shadow followed us, till the grave gaped hungry and terrible, and I was alone. Faltering in fear, but lingering in love, I knelt by the deathbed—it was the middle night, and the first moans of the autumn came down from the hills, for the frost specks glinted on her golden robes, and the wind blew chill in her bosom. Heaven was full of stars, and the half-moon scattered abroad her beauty like a silver rain. Many have been the middle nights since then, for years lie between me and that fearfulest of all watches; but a shadow, a sound, or a thought, turns the key of the dim chamber, and the scene is reproduced.

I see the long locks on the pillow, the smile on the ashen lips, the thin, cold fingers faintly pressing my own, and hear the broken voice saying, "I am going now. I am not afraid. Why weep ye? Though I were to live the full time allotted to man, I should not be more ready, nor more willing than now." But over this there comes a shudder and a groan that all the mirthfulness of the careless was impotent to drown.

Three days previous to the death-night, three days previous to the transit of the soul from the clayey tabernacle to the house not; made with hands—from dishonour to glory—let me turn theme over as so many leaves.

The first of the November mornings, but the summer had tarried late, and the wood to the south of our homestead lifted itself like a painted wall against the sky—the squirrel was leaping nimbly and chattering gayly among the fiery tops of the oaks or the dun foliage of the hickory, that shot up its shelving trunk and spread its forked branches far over the smooth, moss-spotted boles of the beeches, and the limber boughs of the elms. Lithe and blithe he was, for his harvest was come.

From the cracked beech-burs was dropping the sweet, angular fruit, and down from the hickory boughs with every gust fell a shower of nuts—shelling clean and silvery from their thick black hulls.

Now and then, across the stubble-field, with long ears erect, leaped the gray hare, but for the most part he kept close in his burrow, for rude huntsmen were on the hills with their dogs, and only when the sharp report of a rifle rung through the forest, or the hungry yelping of some trailing hound startled his harmless slumber, might you see at the mouth of his burrow the quivering lip and great timid eyes.

Along the margin of the creek, shrunken now away from the blue and gray and yellowish stones that made its cool pavement, and projected in thick layers from the shelving banks, the white columns of gigantic sycamores leaped earthward, their bases driven, as it seemed, deep into the ground—all their convolutions of roots buried out of view. Dropping into the stagnant waters below, came one by one the broad, rose-tinted leaves, breaking the shadows of the silver limbs.

Ruffling and widening to the edges of the pools went the circles, as the pale, yellow walnuts plashed into their midst; for here, too, grew the parent trees, their black bark cut and jagged and broken into rough diamond work.

That beautiful season was come when

"Rustic girls in hoods Go gleaning through the woods."

Two days after this, we said, my dear mate and I, we shall have a holiday, and from sunrise till sunset, with our laps full of ripe nuts and orchard fruits, we shall make pleasant pastime.

Rosalie, for so I may call her, was older than I, with a face of beauty and a spirit that never flagged. But to-day there was heaviness in her eyes, and a flushing in her cheek that was deeper than had been there before.

Still she spoke gayly, and smiled the old smile, for the gaunt form of sickness had never been among us children, and we knew not how his touch made the head sick and the heart faint.

The day looked forward to so anxiously dawned at last; but in the dim chamber of Rosalie the light fell sad. I must go alone.

We had always been together before, at work and in play, asleep and awake, and I lingered long ere I would be persuaded to leave her; but when she smiled and said the fresh-gathered nuts and shining apples would make her glad, I wiped her forehead, and turning quickly away that she might not see my tears, was speedily wading through winrows of dead leaves.

The sensations of that day I shall never forget; a vague and trembling fear of some coming evil, I knew not what, made me often start as the shadows drifted past me, or a bough crackled beneath my feet.

From the low, shrubby hawthorns, I gathered the small red apples, and from beneath the maples, picked by their slim golden stems the notched and gorgeous leaves. The wind fingered playfully my hair, and clouds of birds went whirring through the tree-tops; but no sight nor sound could divide my thoughts from her whose voice had so often filled with music these solitary places.

I remember when first the fear distinctly defined itself. I was seated on a mossy log, counting the treasures which I had been gathering, when the clatter of hoof-strokes on the clayey and hard-beaten road arrested my attention, and, looking up—for the wood thinned off in the direction of the highway, and left it distinctly in view—I saw Doctor H——, the physician, in attendance upon my sick companion. The visit was an unseasonable one. She, whom I loved so, might never come with me to the woods any more.

Where the hill sloped to the roadside, and the trees, as I said, were but few, was the village graveyard. No friend of mine, no one whom I had ever known or loved, was buried there—yet with a child's instinctive dread of death, I had ever passed its shaggy solitude (for shrubs and trees grew there wild and unattended) with a hurried step and averted face.

Now, for the first time in my life, I walked voluntarily thitherward, and climbing on a log by the fence-side, gazed long and earnestly within. I stood beneath a tall locust-tree, and the small, round leaves; yellow now as the long cloud-bar across the sunset, kept dropping, and dropping at my feet, till all the faded grass was covered up. There the mattock had never been struck; but in fancy I saw the small Heaves falling and drifting about a new and smooth-shaped mound—and, choking with the turbulent outcry in my heart, I glided stealthily homeward—alas! to find the boding shape I had seen through mists and, shadows awfully palpable. I did not ask about Rosalie. I was afraid; but with my rural gleanings in my lap, opened the door of her chamber. The physician had preceded me but a moment, and, standing by the bedside, was turning toward the lessening light the little wasted hand, the one on which I had noticed in the morning a small purple spot. "Mortification!" he said, abruptly, and moved away, as though his work were done.

There was a groan expressive of the sudden and terrible consciousness which had in it the agony of agonies—the giving up of all. The gift I had brought fell from my relaxed grasp, and, hiding my face in the pillow, I gave way to the passionate sorrow of an undisciplined nature.

When at last I looked up, there was a smile on her lips that no faintest moan ever displaced again.

A good man and a skilful physician was Dr. H— —, but his infirmity was a love of strong drink; and, therefore, was it that he softened not the terrible blow which must soon have fallen. I link with his memory no reproaches now, for all this is away down in the past; and that foe that sooner or later biteth like a serpent, soon did his work; but then my breaking heart judged him, hardly. Often yet, for in all that is saddest memory is faithfulest, I wake suddenly out of sleep, and live over that first and bitterest sorrow of my life; and there is no house of gladness in the world that with a whisper will not echo the moan of lips pale with the kisses of death.

Sometimes, when life is gayest about me, an unseen hand leads me apart, and opening the door of that still chambers I go in—the yellow leaves are at my feet again, and that white band between me and the light.

I see the blue flames quivering and curling close and the smouldering embers on the hearth. I hear soft footsteps and sobbing voices and see the clasped hands and placid smile of her who, alone among us all, was untroubled; and over the darkness and the pain I hear voice, saying, "She is not dead, but sleepeth." Would, dear reader, that you might remember, and I too all ways, the importance of soft and careful words. One harsh or even thoughtlessly chosen epithet, may bear with it a weight which shall weigh down some heart through all life. There are for us all nights of sorrow, in which we feel their value. Help us, our Father, to remember it!

MR. QUERY'S INVESTIGATION

"HE is a good man, suppose, and an excellent doctor," said Mrs. Salina Simmons, with a dubious shake of her head but — —"

"But what, Mrs. Simmons?"

"They say he *drinks!*"

"No, impossible!" exclaimed Mr. Josiah Query, with emphasis.

"Impossible? I hope so," said Mrs. Simmons. "And—mind you, I don't say he *drinks*, but that such is the report. And I have it upon tolerably good authority, too, Mr. Query."

"What authority?"

"Oh, I couldn't tell that: for you know I never like to make mischief. I can only say that the *report* is—he drinks."

Mr. Josiah Query scratched his head.

"Can it be that Dr. Harvey drinks?" he murmured. "I thought him pure Son of Temperance. And his my family physician, too! I must look into this matter forthwith. Mrs. Simmons, you still decline slating who is your authority for this report?"

Mrs. Simmons was firm; her companion could gain no satisfaction. She soon compelled him to promise that he would not mention her name, if he spoke of the affair elsewhere, repeating her remark that she never liked to make mischief.

Dr. Harvey was a physician residing in a small village, where he shared the profits of practice with another doctor, named Jones. Dr. Harvey was generally liked and among his friends was Mr. Josiah Query, whom Mrs. Simmons shocked with the bit of gossip respecting the doctor's habits of intemperance. Mr. Query was a good-hearted man, and he deemed it his duty to inquire into the nature of the report, and learn if it had any foundation in truth. Accordingly, he went to Mr. Green, who also employed the doctor in his family.

"Mr. Green," said he, "have you heard anything about this report of Dr. Harvey's intemperance?"

"Dr. Harvey's intemperance?" cried Mr. Green, astonished.

"Yes—a flying report."

"No, I'm sure I haven't."

"Of course, then, you don't know whether it is true or not?"

"What?"

"That he drinks."

"I never heard of it before. Dr. Harvey is my family physician, and I certainly would not employ a man addicted to the use of ardent spirits."

"Nor I," said Mr. Query "and for this reason, and for the doctor's sake, too, I want to know the truth of the matter. I don't really credit it myself; but I thought it would do no harm to inquire."

Mr. Query next applied to Squire Worthy for information.

"Dear me!" exclaimed the squire, who was a nervous man; "does Dr. Harvey drink?"

"Such is the rumour; how true it is, I can't say."

"And what if he should give one of my family a dose of arsenic instead of the tincture of rhubarb, some time, when he is intoxicated? My mind is made up now. I shall send for Dr. Jones in future."

"But, dear sir," remonstrated Mr. Query. "I don't say the report is true."

"Oh, no; you wouldn't wish to commit yourself. You like to know the safe side, and so do I. I shall employ Dr. Jones."

Mr. Query turned sorrowfully away.

"Squire Worthy must have bad suspicions of the doctor's intemperance before I came to him," thought he; "I really begin to fear that there is some foundation for the report. I'll go to Mrs. Mason; she will know."

Mr. Query found Mrs. Mason ready to listen to and believe any scandal. She gave her head a significant toss, as if she knew more about the report than she chose to confess.

Mr. Query begged of her to explain herself.

"Oh, *I* sha'n't say anything," exclaimed Mrs. Mason; "I've no ill will against Dr. Harvey, and I'd rather cut off my right hand than injure him."

"But is the report true?"

"True, Mr. Query? Do you suppose *I* ever saw Dr. Harvey drunk? Then how can you expect me to know? Oh, I don't wish to say anything against the man, and I won't."

After visiting Mrs. Mason, Mr. Query went to half a dozen others to learn the truth respecting Dr. Harvey's habits. Nobody would confess that they knew anything, about his drinking; but Mr. Smith "was not as much surprised as others might be;" Mr. Brown "was sorry if the report was true," adding, that the best of men had their faults. Miss Single had frequently remarked the doctor's florid complexion, and wondered if his colour was natural; Mr. Clark remembered that the doctor appeared unusually gay, on the occasion of his last visit to his family; Mrs. Rogers declared that, when she came to reflect, she believed she had once or twice smelt the man's breath; and Mr. Impulse had often seen him riding at an extraordinary rate for a sober Gentleman. Still Mr. Query was unable to ascertain any definite facts respecting the unfavourable report.

Meanwhile, with his usual industry, Dr. Harvey went about his business, little suspecting the scandalous gossip that was circulating to his discredit. But he soon perceived he was very coldly received by some of his old friends, and that others employed Dr. Jones. Nobody sent for him, and he might have begun to think that the health of the town was entirely re-established, had he not observed that his rival appeared driven with business, and that he rode night and day.

One evening Dr. Harvey sat in his office, wondering what could have occasioned the sudden and surprising change in his affairs, when, contrary to his expectations, he received a call to visit a sick child of one of his old friends, who had lately employed his rival. After some hesitation, and a struggle between pride and a sense of duty, he resolved to respond to the call, and at the same time learn, if possible, why he had been preferred to Dr. Jones, and why Dr. Jones had on other occasions been preferred to him.

"The truth is, Dr. Harvey," said Mr. Miles, "we thought the child dangerously ill, and as Dr. Jones could not come immediately, we concluded to send for you."

"I admire your frankness," responded Dr. Harvey, smiling; "and shall admire it still more, if you will inform me why you have lately preferred Dr. Jones to me. Formerly I had the honour of enjoying your friendship and esteem, and you have frequently told me yourself, that you would trust no other physician."

"Well," replied Mr. Miles, "I am a plain man, and never hesitate to tell people what they wish to know. I sent for Dr. Jones instead of you, I confess not that I doubted your skill—"

"What then?"

"It is a delicate subject, but I will, nevertheless, speak out. Although I had the utmost confidence in your skill and faithfulness—I—you know, I—in short, I don't like to trust a physician who drinks."

"Sir!" cried the astonished doctor.

"Yes—drinks," pursued Mr. Miles. "It is plain language, but I am a plain man. I heard of your intemperance, and thought it unsafe—that is, dangerous—to employ you."

"My intemperance!" ejaculated Dr. Harvey.

"Yes, sir! and I am sorry to know it. But the fact that you sometimes drink a trifle too much is now a well known fact, and is generally talked of in the village."

"Mr. Miles," cried the indignant doctor, "this is scandalous—it is false! Who is your authority for this report?"

"Oh, I have heard it from several mouths but I can't say exactly who is responsible for the rumour."

And Mr. Miles went on to mention several names, as connected with the rumour, and among which was that of Mr. Query.

The indignant doctor immediately set out on a pilgrimage of investigation, going from one house to another, in search of the author of the scandal.

Nobody, however, could state where it originated, but it was universally admitted that the man from whose lips it was first heard, was Mr. Query.

Accordingly Dr. Harvey hastened to Mr. Query's house, and demanded of that gentleman what he meant by circulating such scandal.

"My dear doctor," cried Mr. Query, his face beaming with conscious innocence, "*I* haven't been guilty of any mis-statement about you, I can take my oath. I heard that there was a report of your drinking, and all I did was to tell people I didn't believe it, nor know anything about it, and to inquire were it originated. Oh, I assure you, doctor, I haven't slandered you in any manner."

"You are a poor fool!" exclaimed Dr. Harvey, perplexed and angry. "If you had gone about town telling everybody that you saw me drunk, daily, you couldn't have slandered me more effectually than you have."

"Oh, I beg your pardon," cried Mr. Query, very sad; "but I thought I was doing you a service!"

"Save me from my friends!" exclaimed the doctor, bitterly. "An *enemy* could not have done me as much injury as you have done. But I now insist on knowing who first mentioned the report to you."

"Oh, I am not at liberty to say that."

"Then I shall hold you responsible for the scandal—for the base lies you have circulated. But if you are really an honest man, and my friend, you will not hesitate to tell me where this report originated."

After some reflection, Mr. Query, who stood in mortal fear of the indignant doctor, resolved to reveal the secret, and mentioned the name of his informant, Mrs. Simmons. As Dr. Harvey had not heard her spoken of before, as connected with the report of his intemperance, he knew very well that Mr. Query's "friendly investigations" had been the sole cause of his loss of practice. However, to go to the roots of this Upas tree of scandal, he resolved to pay an immediate visit to Mrs. Simmons.

This lady could deny nothing; but she declared that she had not given the rumour as a fact, and that she had never spoken of it except to Mr. Query. Anxious to throw the responsibility of the slander upon others, she eagerly confessed that, on a certain occasion upon entering a room in which were Mrs. Guild and Mrs. Harmless, she overheard one of these ladies remark that "Dr. Harvey drank more than ever," and the other reply, that "she had heard him say he could not break himself, although he knew his health suffered in consequence."

Thus set upon the right track, Dr. Harvey visited Mrs. Guild and Mrs. Harmless without delay.

"Mercy on us!" exclaimed those ladies, when questioned respecting the matter, "we perfectly remember talking about your *drinking coffee*, and making such remarks as you have heard through Mrs. Simmons. But with regard to your *drinking liquor*, we never heard the report until a week ago, and never believed it at all."

As what these ladies had said of his *coffee-drinking* propensities was perfectly true, Dr. Harvey readily acquitted them of any designs against his character for sobriety, and well satisfied with having at last discovered the origin of the rumour, returned to the friendly Mr. Query.

The humiliation of this gentleman was so deep, that Dr. Harvey avoided reproaches, and confined himself to a simple narrative of his discoveries.

"I see, it is all my fault," said Mr. Query. "And I will do anything to remedy it. I never could believe you drank—and now I'll go and tell everybody that the report *was* false."

"Oh! bless you," cried the doctor, "I wouldn't have you do so for the world. All I ask of you, is to say nothing whatever on the subject, and if you ever again hear a report of the kind, don't make it a subject of friendly investigation."

Mr. Query promised; and, after the truth was known, and, Dr. Harvey had regained the good-will of the community, together with his share of medical practice, he never had reason again to exclaim—"Save me from my friends!" And Mr. Query was in future exceedingly careful how he attempted to make friendly investigations.

ROOM IN THE WORLD

THERE is room in the world for the wealthy and great,
For princes to reign in magnificent state;
For the courtier to bend, for the noble to sue,
If the hearts of all these are but honest and true.

And there's room in the world for the lowly and meek,
For the hard horny hand, and the toil-furrow'd cheek;
For the scholar to think, for the merchant to trade,
So these are found upright and just in their grade.

But room there is none for the wicked; and nought
For the souls that with teeming corruption are fraught.
The world would be small, were its oceans all land,
To harbour and feed such a pestilent band.

Root out from among ye, by teaching the mind,
By training the heart, this chief curse of mankind!
'Tis a duty you owe to the forthcoming race—
Confess it in time, and discharge it with grace!

WORDS

"THE foolish thing!" said my Aunt Rachel, speaking warmly, "to get hurt at a mere word. It's a little hard that people can't open their lips but somebody is offended."

"Words are things!" said I, smiling.

"Very light things! A person must be tender indeed, that is hurt by a word."

"The very lightest thing may hurt, if it falls on a tender place."

"I don't like people who have these tender places," said Aunt Rachel. "I never get hurt at what is said to me. No—never! To be ever picking and mincing, and chopping off your words—to be afraid to say this or that—for fear somebody will be offended! I can't abide it."

"People who have these tender places can't help it, I suppose. This being so, ought we not to regard their weakness?" said I. "Pain, either of body or mind, is hard to bear, and we should not inflict it causelessly."

"People who are so wonderfully sensitive," replied Aunt Rachel, growing warmer, "ought to shut themselves up at home, and not come among sensible, good-tempered persons. As far as I am concerned, I can tell them, one and all, that I am not going to pick out every hard word from a sentence as carefully as I would seeds from a raisin. Let them crack them with their teeth, if they are afraid to swallow them whole."

Now, for all that Aunt Rachel went on after this strain, she was a kind, good soul, in the main, and, I could see, was sorry for having hurt the feelings of Mary Lane. But she didn't like to acknowledge that she was in the wrong; that would detract too much from the self-complacency with which she regarded herself. Knowing her character very well, I thought it best not to continue the little argument about the importance of words, and so changed the subject. But, every now and then, Aunt Rachel would return to it, each time softening a little towards Mary. At last she said,

"I'm sure it was a little thing. A very little thing. She might have known that nothing unkind was intended on my part."

"There are some subjects, aunt," I replied, "to which we cannot bear the slightest allusion. And a sudden reference to them is very apt to throw us off of our guard. What you said to Mary has, in all probability touched some weakness of character, or probed some wound that time has not been able to heal. I have always thought her a sensible, good-natured girl."

"And so have I. But I really cannot think that she has showed her good sense or good nature in the present case. It is a very bad failing this, of being over sensitive; and exceedingly annoying to one's friends."

"It is, I know; but still, all of, us have a weak point, and to her that is assailed, we are very apt to betray our feelings."

"Well, I say now, as I have always said—I don't like to have anything to do with people who have these weak points. This being hurt by a word, as if words were blows, is something that does not come within the range of my sympathies."

"And yet, aunt," said I, "all have weak points. Even you are not entirely free from them."

"Me!" Aunt Rachel bridled.

"Yes; and if even as light a thing as a word were to fall upon them, you would suffer pain."

"Pray, sir," said Aunt Rachel, with much dignity of manner; she was chafed by my words, light as they were, "inform me where these weaknesses, of which you are pleased to speak, lie."

"Oh, no; you must excuse me. That would be very much out of place. But I only stated a general fact that appertains to all of us."

Aunt Rachel looked very grave. I had laid the weight of words upon a weakness of her character, and it had given her pain. That weakness was a peculiarly good opinion of herself. I had made no allegation against her; and there was none in my mind. My words simply expressed the general truth that we all have weaknesses, and included her in their application. But she imagined that I referred to some particular defect or fault, and mail-proof as she was against words, they had wounded her.

For a day or two Aunt Rachel remained more sober than was her wont. I knew the cause, but did not attempt to remove from her mind any impression my words had made. One day, about a week after, I said to her,

"Aunt Rachel, I saw Mary Lane's mother this morning."

"Ah?" The old lady looked up at me inquiringly.

"I don't wonder your words hurt the poor girl," I added.

"Why? What did I say?" quickly asked Aunt Rachel.

"You said that she was a jilt."

"But I was only jest, and she knew it. I did not really mean anything. I'm surprised that Mary should be so foolish."

"You will not be surprised when you know all," was my answer.

"All? What all? I'm sure I wasn't in earnest. I didn't mean to hurt the poor girl's feelings." My aunt looked very much troubled.

"No one blames you, Aunt Rachel," said I. "Mary knows you didn't intend wounding her."

"But why should she take a little word go much to heart? It must have had more truth in it than I supposed."

"Did you know that Mary refused an offer of marriage from Walter Green last week?"

"Why no! It can't be possible! Refused Walter Green?"

"They've been intimate for a long time."

"I know."

"She certainly encouraged him."

"I think it more than probable."

"Is it possible, then, that she did really jilt the young man?" exclaimed Aunt Rachel.

"This has been said of her," I replied. "But so far as I can learn, she was really attached to him, and suffered great pain in rejecting his offer. Wisely she regarded marriage as the most important event of her life, and refused to make so solemn a contract with one in whose principles she had not the fullest confidence."

"But she ought not to have encouraged Walter, if she did not intend marrying him," said Aunt Rachel, with some warmth.

"She encouraged him so long as she thought well of him. A closer view revealed points of character hidden by distance. When she saw these her feelings were already deeply involved. But, like a true woman, she turned from the proffered hand, even though while in doing so her heart palpitated with pain. There is nothing false about Mary Lane. She could no more trifle with a lover than she could commit a crime. Think, then, how almost impossible it would be for her to hear herself called, under existing circumstances, even in sport, a jilt, without being hurt. Words sometimes have power to hurt more than blows. Do you not see this, now, Aunt Rachel?"

"Oh, yes, yes. I see it; and I saw it before," said the old lady. "And in future I will be more careful of my words. It is pretty late in life to learn this lesson—but we are never too late to learn. Poor Mary! It grieves me to think that I should have hurt her so much."

Yes, words often have in them a smarting force, and we cannot be too guarded how we use them. "Think twice before you speak once," is a trite but wise saying. We teach it to our children very carefully, but are too apt to forget that it has not lost its application to ourselves.

THE THANKLESS OFFICE

"AN object of real charity," said Andrew Lyon to his wife, as a poor woman withdrew from the room in which they were seated.

"If ever there was a worthy object she is one," returned Mrs. Lyon. "A widow, with health so feeble that even ordinary exertion is too much for her; yet obliged to support, with the labour of her own hands, not only herself, but three young children. I do not wonder that she is behind with her rent."

"Nor I," said Mr. Lyon, in a voice of sympathy. "How much, did she say, was due to her landlord?"

"Ten dollars."

"She will not be able to pay it."

"I fear not. How can she? I give her all my extra sewing, and have obtained work for her from several ladies; but with her best efforts she can barely obtain food and decent clothing for herself and babes."

"Does it not seem hard," remarked Mr. Lyon, "that one like Mrs. Arnold, who is so earnest in her efforts to take care of herself and family, should not receive a helping hand from some one of the many who could help her without feeling the effort? If I didn't find it so hard to make both ends meet, I would pay off her arrears of rent for her, and feel happy in so doing."

"Ah!" exclaimed the kind-hearted wife, "how much I wish that we were able to do this! But we are not."

"I'll tell you what we can do," said Mr. Lyon, in a cheerful voice; "or rather what *I* can do. It will be a very light matter for say ten persons to give a dollar apiece, in order to relieve Mrs. Arnold from her present trouble. There are plenty who would cheerfully contribute, for this good purpose; all that is wanted is some one to take upon himself the business of making the collections. That task shall be mine."

"How glad I am, James, to hear you say so!" smilingly replied Mrs. Lyon. "Oh, what a relief it will be to poor Mrs. Arnold. It will make her heart as light as a feather. That rent has troubled her sadly. Old Links, her landlord, has been worrying her about it a good deal, and, only a week ago, threatened to put her things in the street, if she didn't pay up."

"I should have thought of this before," remarked Andrew Lyon. "There are hundreds of people who are willing enough to give if they were only certain in regard to the object. Here is one worthy enough in every way. Be it my business to present her claims to benevolent consideration. Let me see. To whom shall I go? There are Jones, and Green, and Tompkins. I can get a dollar from each of them. That will be three dollars,—and one from myself, will make four. Who else is there? Oh, Malcolm! I'm sure of a dollar from him; and also from Smith, Todd, and Perry."

Confident in the success of his benevolent scheme, Mr. Lyon started forth, early on the very next day, for the purpose of obtaining, by subscription, the poor widow's rent. The first person he called on was Malcolm.

"Ah, friend Lyon!" said Malcolm, smiling blandly, "Good morning! What can I do for you, to-day?"

"Nothing for me, but something for a poor widow, who is behind with her rent," replied Andrew Lyon. "I want just one dollar from you, and as much more from some eight or nine as benevolent as yourself."

At the word poor widow the countenance of Malcolm fell, and when his visitor ceased, he replied, in a changed and husky voice, clearing his throat two or three times as he spoke.

"Are you sure she is deserving, Mr. Lyon?" The man's manner had become exceedingly grave.

"None more so," was the prompt answer. "She is in poor health, and has three children to support with the product of her needle. If any one needs assistance, it is Mrs. Arnold."

"Oh! Ah! The widow of Jacob Arnold?"

"The same," replied Andrew Lyon.

Malcolm's face did not brighten with a feeling of heart-warm benevolence. But he turned slowly away, and opening his money-drawer, *very slowly* toyed with his fingers amid its contents. At length he took therefrom a dollar bill, and said, as he presented it to Lyon,—signing involuntarily as he did so,—

"I suppose I must do my part. But we are called upon so often."

The ardour of Andrew Lyon's benevolent feelings suddenly cooled at this unexpected reception. He had entered upon his work under the glow of a pure enthusiasm; anticipating a hearty response the moment his errand was made known.

"I thank you in the widow's name," said he, as he took the dollar. When he turned from Mr. Malcolm's store, it was with a pressure on his feelings, as if he had asked the coldly-given favour for himself.

It was not without an effort that Lyon compelled himself to call upon Mr. Green, considered the "next best man" on his list. But he entered his place of business with far less confidence than he had felt when calling upon Malcolm. His story told, Green, without a word or smile, drew two half dollars from his pocket and presented them.

"Thank you," said Lyon.

"Welcome," returned Green.

Oppressed with a feeling of embarrassment, Lyon stood for a few moments. Then bowing, he said,

"Good morning."

"Good morning," was coldly and formally responded.

And thus the alms-seeker and alms-giver parted.

"Better be at his shop, attending to his work," muttered Green to himself, as his visiter retired. "Men ain't very apt to get along too well in the world who spend their time in begging for every object of charity that happens to turn up. And there are plenty of such, dear knows. He's got a dollar out of me; may it do him, or the poor widow he talked so glibly about, much good."

Cold water had been poured upon the feelings of Andrew Lyon. He had raised two dollars for the poor widow, but, at what a sacrifice for one so sensitive as himself! Instead of keeping on in his work of benevolence, he went to his shop, and entered upon the day's employment. How disappointed he felt;—and this disappointment was mingled with a certain sense of humiliation, as if he had been asking alms for himself.

"Catch me at this work again!" he said half aloud, as his thoughts dwelt upon what had so recently occurred. "But this is not right," he added, quickly. "It is a weakness in me to feel so. Poor Mrs. Arnold must be relieved; and it is my duty to see that she gets relief. I had no thought of a reception like this. People can talk of benevolence; but putting the hand in the pocket is another affair altogether. I never dreamed that such men as Malcolm and Green could be insensible to an appeal like the one I made."

"I've got two dollars towards paying Mrs. Arnold's rent," he said to himself, in a more cheerful tone, some time afterwards; "and it will go hard if I don't raise the whole amount for her. All are not like Green and Malcolm. Jones is a kind-hearted man, and will instantly respond to the call of humanity. I'll go and see him."

So, off Andrew Lyon started to see this individual.

"I've come begging, Mr. Jones," said he, on meeting him. And he spoke in a frank, pleasant manner,

"Then you've come to the wrong shop; that's all I have to say," was the blunt answer.

"Don't say that, Mr. Jones. Hear my story first."

"I do say it, and I'm in earnest," returned Jones. "I feel as poor as Job's turkey to-day."

"I only want a dollar to help a poor widow pay her rent," said Lyon.

"Oh, hang all the poor widows! If that's your game, you'll get nothing here. I've got my hands full to pay my own rent. A nice time I'd have in handing out a dollar to every poor widow in town to help pay her rent! No, no, my friend, you can't get anything here."

"Just as you feel about it," said Andrew Lyon. "There's no compulsion in the matter."

"No, I presume not," was rather coldly replied.

Lyon returned to his shop, still more disheartened than before. He had undertaken a thankless office.

Nearly two hours elapsed before his resolution to persevere in the good work he had begun came back with sufficient force to prompt to another effort. Then he dropped in upon his neighbour Tompkins, to whom he made known his errand.

"Why, yes, I suppose I must do something in a case like this," said Tompkins, with the tone and air of a man who was cornered. "But there are so many calls for charity, that we are naturally enough led to hold on pretty tightly to our purse strings. Poor woman! I feel sorry for her. How much do you want?"

"I am trying to get ten persons, including myself, to give a dollar each."

"Well, here's my dollar." And Tompkins forced a smile to his face as he handed over his contribution,—but the smile did not conceal an expression which said very plainly—

"I hope you will not trouble me again in this way."

"You may be sure I will not," muttered Lyon, as he went away. He fully understood the meaning of the expression.

Only one more application did the kind-hearted man make. It was successful; but there was something in the manner of the individual who gave his dollar, that Lyon felt as a rebuke.

"And so poor Mrs. Arnold did not get the whole of her arrears of rent paid off," says some one who has felt an interest in her favour.

Oh, yes she did. Mr. Lyon begged five dollars, and added five more from his own slender purse. But, he cannot be induced again to undertake the thankless office of seeking relief from the benevolent for a fellow creature in need. He has learned that a great many who refuse alms on the plea that the object presented is not worthy, are but little more inclined to charitable deeds, when on this point there is no question.

How many who read this can sympathize with Andrew Lyon! Few men who have hearts to feel for others but have been impelled, at some time in their lives, to seek aid for a fellow creature in need. That their office was a thankless one, they have too soon become aware. Even those who responded to their call most liberally, in too many instances gave in a way that left an unpleasant impression behind. How quickly has the first glow of generous feeling, that sought to extend itself to others, that they might share the pleasure of humanity, been chilled; and, instead of finding the task an easy one, it has proved to be hard, and, too often, humiliating! Alas that this should be! That men should shut their hearts so instinctively at the voice of charity!

We have not written this to discourage active efforts in the benevolent; but to hold up a mirror in which another class may see themselves. At best, the office of him who seeks of his fellow men aid for the suffering and indigent, is an unpleasant one. It is all sacrifice on his part, and the least that can be done is to honour his disinterested regard for others in distress, and treat him with delicacy and consideration.

LOVE

OH! if there is one law above the rest,
Written in Wisdom—if there is a word
That I would trace as with a pen of fire
Upon the unsullied temper of a child—
If there is anything that keeps the mind
Open to angel visits, and repels
The ministry of ill—'tis *Human Love!*
God has made nothing worthy of contempt;
The smallest pebble in the well of Truth
Has its peculiar meanings, and will stand
When man's best monuments wear fast away.
The law of Heaven is*Love*—and though its name
Has been usurped by passion, and profaned
To its unholy uses through all time,
Still, the external principle is pure;
And in these deep affections that we feel
Omnipotent within us, can we see
The lavish measure in which love is given.
And in the yearning tenderness of a child
For every bird that sings above its head,
And every creature feeding on the hills,
And every tree and flower, and running brook,
We see how everything was made to love,
And how they err, who, in a world like this,
Find anything to hate but human pride.

"EVERY LITTLE HELPS"

WHAT if a drop of rain should plead—
"So small a drop as I
Can ne'er refresh the thirsty mead;
I'll tarry in the sky?"

What, if the shining beam of noon
Should in its fountain stay;
Because its feeble light alone
Cannot create a day?

Does not each rain-drop help to form
The cool refreshing shower?
And every ray of light, to warm
And beautify the flower?

LITTLE THINGS

SCORN not the slightest word or deed,
Nor deem it void of power;
There's fruit in each wind-wafted seed,
Waiting its natal hour.
A whispered word may touch the heart,
And call it back to life;
A look of love bid sin depart,
And still unholy strife.

No act falls fruitless; none can tell
How vast its power may be,
Nor what results enfolded dwell
Within it silently.
Work and despair not; give thy mite,
Nor care how small it be;
God is with all that serve the right,
The holy, true, and free!

CARELESS WORDS

FIVE years ago, this fair November day,—five years? it seems but yesterday, so fresh is that scene in my memory; and, I doubt not, were the period ten times multiplied, it would be as vivid still to us—the surviving actors in that drama! The touch of time, which blunts the piercing thorn, as well as steals from the rose its lovely tints, is powerless here, unless to give darker shades to that picture engraven on our souls; and tears—ah, they only make it more imperishable!

We do not speak of her now; her name has not passed our lips in each other's presence, since we followed her—grief-stricken mourners-to the grave, to which—alas, alas! but why should not the truth be spoken? the grave to which our careless words consigned her. But on every anniversary of that day we can never forget, uninvited by me, and without any previous arrangement between themselves, those two friends have come to my house, and together we have sat, almost silently, save when Ada's sweet voice has poured forth a low, plaintive strain to the mournful chords Mary has made the harp to breathe. Four years ago, that cousin came too; and since then, though he has been thousands of miles distant from us, when, that anniversary has returned, he has written to me: he cannot look into my face when that letter is penned; he but looks into his own heart, and he cannot withhold the words of remorse and agony.

Ada and Mary have sat with me to-day, and we knew that Rowland, in thought, was here too; ah, if we could have known another had been among us,—if we could have felt that an eye was upon us, which will never more dim with tears, a heart was near us which carelessness can never wound again;—could we have known she had been here—that pure, bright angel, with the smile of forgiveness and love on that beautiful face—the dark veil of sorrow might have been lifted from our souls! but we saw only with mortal vision; our faith was feeble, and we have only drawn that sombre mantle more and more closely about us. The forgiveness we have so many times prayed for, we have not yet dared to receive, though we know it is our own.

That November day was just what this has been fair, mild, and sweet; and how much did that dear one enjoy it! The earth was dry, and as we looked from the window we saw no verdure but a small line of green on the south side of the garden enclosure, and around the trunk of the old pear-tree, and here and there a little oasis from which the strong wind of the previous day, had lifted the thick covering of dry leaves, and one or two shrubs, whose foliage feared not the cold breath of winter. The gaudy hues, too, which nature had lately worn, were all faded; there was a pale, yellow-leafed vine clambering over the verdureless lilac, and far down in the garden might be seen a shrub covered with bright scarlet berries. But the warm south wind was sweet and fragrant, as if it had strayed through bowers of roses and eglantines. Deep-leaden and snow-white clouds blended together, floated lazily through the sky, and the sun coquetted all day with the earth, though his glance was not, for once, more than half averted, while his smile was bright and loving, as it bad been months before, when her face was fair and blooming.

But how sadly has this day passed, and how unlike is this calm, sweet evening to the one which closed that November day! Nature is the same. The moonbeams look as bright and silvery through the brown, naked arms of the tall oaks, and the dark evergreen forest lifts up its head to the sky, striving, but in vain, to shut out the soft light from the little stream, whose murmurings, seem more sad and complaining than at another season of the year, perhaps because it feels how soon the icy bands of winter will stay its free course, and hush its low whisperings. The soft breeze sighs as sadly through the vines which still wreath themselves around the window; though seemingly conscious they have ceased to adorn it, they are striving to loosen their hold, and bow themselves to the earth; and the chirping of a cricket in the chimney is as sad and mournful as it was then. But the low moan of the sufferer, the but half-smothered, agonized sobs of those fair girls, the deep groan which all my proud cousin's firmness could not hush, and the words of reproach, which, though I was so guilty myself, and though I saw them so repentant, I could not withhold, are all stilled now.

Ada and Mary have just left me, and I am sitting alone in my apartment. Not a sound reaches me but the whisperings of the wind, the murmuring of the stream, and the chirping of that solitary cricket. The family know my heart is heavy to-night, and the voices are hushed, and the footsteps fall lightly. Lily, dear Lily, art thou near me?

Five years and some months ago—it was in early June—there came to our home from far away in the sunny South, a fair young creature, a relative of ours, though we had never seen her before. She had been motherless rather less than a year, but her father had already found another partner, and feeling that she would not so soon see the place of the dearly-loved parent filled by a stranger, she had obtained his permission to spend a few months with those who could sympathize with her in her griefs.

Lily White! She was rightly named; I have never seen such a fair, delicate face and figure, nor watched the revealings of a nature so pure and gentle as was hers. She would have been too fair and delicate to be beautiful, but for the brilliancy of those deep blue eyes, the dark shade of that glossy hair, and the litheness of that fragile form; but when months had passed away, and, though the brow was still marble white, and the lip colourless, the cheek wore that deep rose tint, how surpassingly beautiful she was! We did not dream what had planted that rose-tint there—we thought her to be throwing off the grief which alone, we believed, had paled her cheek; and we did not observe that her form was becoming more delicate, and that her step was losing its lightness and elasticity. We loved the sweet Lily dearly at first sight, and she had been with us but a short time before we began to wonder how our home had ever seemed perfect to us previous to her coming. And our affection was returned by the dear girl. We knew how much she loved us, when, as the warm season had passed, and her father sent for her to return home, we saw the expression of deep sorrow in every feature, and the silent entreaty that we would persuade him to allow her to remain with us still.

She did not thank me when a letter reached me from her father, in reply to one which, unknown to her, I had sent him, saying, if I thought Lily's health would not be injured by a winter's residence in our cold climate, he would comply with my urgent request, and allow her to remain with us until the following spring—the dear girl could not speak. She came to me almost totteringly, and wound her arms about my neck, resting her head on mine, and tears from those sweet eyes fell fast over my face; and all the remainder of that afternoon she lay on her couch. Oh, why did I not think wherefore she was so much overcome?

Ada L——and Mary R——, two friends whom I had loved from childhood, I had selected as companions for our dear Lily on her arrival among us, and the young ladies, from their first introduction to her, had vied with me in my endeavours to dispel the gloom from that fair face, and to make her happy; and they shared, almost equally with her relatives, dear Lily's affections.

Ada—she is changed now—was a gay, brilliant, daring girl; Mary, witty and playful, though frank and warm-hearted; but it made me love them more than ever. The gaiety and audacity of the one was forgotten in the presence of the thoughtful, timid Lily: and the other checked the merry jest which trembled on her lips, and sobered that roguish eye beside the earnest, sensitive girl; so that, though we were together almost daily, dear Lily did not understand the character of the young ladies.

The warm season had passed away, and October brought an addition to our household—Cousin Rowland—as handsome, kind-hearted, and good-natured a fellow as ever lived, but a little cowardly, if the dread of the raillery of a beautiful woman may be called cowardice.

Cousin Rowland and dear Lily were mutually pleased with each other, it was very evident to me, though Ada and Mary failed to see it; for, in the presence of the young ladies, Rowland did not show her those little delicate attentions which, alone with me, who was very unobservant, he took no pains to conceal; and Lily did not hide from me her blushing face—her eyes only thanked me for the expression which met her gaze.

That November day—I dread to approach it! Lily and I were sitting beside each other, looking down the street, and watching the return of the carriage which Rowland had gone out with to bring Ada and Mary to our house; or, rather, Lily was looking for its coming—my eyes were resting on her face. It had never looked so beautiful to me before. Her brow was so purely white, her cheek was so deeply red, and that dark eye was so lustrous; but her face was very thin, and her breathing, I observed, was faint and difficult. A pang shot through my heart.

"Lily, are you well?" I exclaimed, suddenly.

She fixed her eyes on mine. I was too much excited by my sudden fear to read their expression, but when our friends came in, the dear girl seemed so cheerful and happy—I remembered, afterwards, I had never seen her so gay as on that afternoon—that my suspicions gradually left me.

The hours were passing pleasantly away, when a letter was brought in for Lily. It was from her father, and the young lady retired to peruse it. The eye of Rowland followed her as she passed out of the room, and I observed a shadow flit across his brow. I afterwards learned that at the moment a thought was passing through his mind similar to that which had so terrified me an hour before. Our visiters remarked it, too, but little suspected its cause; and Mary's eye met, with a most roguish look, Ada's rather inquiring gaze.

"When does Lily intend to return home, S——?" she inquired, as she bent, very demurely, over her embroidery. "I thought she was making preparations to go before Rowland came here!" and she raised her eyes so cunningly to my face, that I could not forbear answering,

"I hear nothing of her return, now. Perhaps she will remain with us during the winter."

"Indeed!" exclaimed Ada, and her voice expressed much surprise. "I wonder if I could make such a prolonged visit interesting to a friend!"

"Why, Lily considers herself conferring a great favour by remaining here," replied Mary.

"On whom?" asked Rowland, quickly.

"On all of use of course;" and to Mary's great delight she perceived that her meaning words had the effect she desired on the young man.

"I hope she will not neglect the duty she owes her family, for the sake of showing us this great kindness," said Rowland, with affected carelessness, though he walked across the apartment with a very impatient step.

"Lily has not again been guilty of the error she so frequently commits, has she, S— —?" asked Ada, in a lower but still far too distinct tone; "that of supposing herself loved and admired where she is only pitied and endured?" and the merry creature fairly exulted in the annoyance which his deepened colour told her she was causing the young man.

A slight sound from the apartment adjoining the parlour attracted my attention. Had Lily stopped there to read her letter instead of going to her chamber? and had she, consequently, overheard our foolish remarks? The door was slightly ajar, and I pushed it open. There was a slight rustling, but I thought it only the waving of the window curtain.

A half-hour passed away, and Lily had not returned to us. I began to be alarmed, and my companions partook of my fears. Had she overheard us? and, if so, what must that sensitive heart be suffering?

I went out to call her; but half way up the flight of stairs I saw the letter from her father lying on the carpet, unopened, though it had been torn from its envelope. I know not how I found my way up stairs, but I stood by Lily's bed.

Merciful Heaven! what a sight was presented to my gaze. The white covering was stained with blood, and from those cold, pale lips the red drops were fast falling. Her eyes turned slowly till they rested on mine. What a look was that! I see it now; so full of grief; so full of reproach; and then they closed. I thought her dead, and my frantic shrieks called my companions to her bedside. They aroused her, too, from that swoon, but they did not awaken her to consciousness. She never more turned a look of recognition on us, or seemed to be aware that we were near her. Through all that night, so long and so full of agony to us, she was murmuring, incoherently, to herself,

"They did not know I was dying," she would say; "that I have been dying ever since I have been here! They have not dreamed of my sufferings through these long months; I could not tell them, for I believed they loved me, and I would not grieve them. But no one loves me—not one in the wide world cares for me! My mother, you will not have forgotten your child when you meet me in the spirit-land! Their loved tones made me deaf to the voice which was calling to me from the grave, and the sunshine of *his* smile broke through the dark cloud which death was drawing around me. Oh, I would have lived, but death, I thought, would lose half its bitterness, could I breathe my last in their arms! But, now, I must die alone! Oh, how shall I reach my home—how shall I ever reach my home?"

Dear Lily! The passage was short; when morning dawned, she was *there*.

HOW TO BE HAPPY

A BOON of inestimable worth is a calm, thankful heart—a treasure that few, very few, possess. We once met an old man, whose face was a mixture of smiles and sunshine. Wherever he went, he succeeded in making everybody about him as pleasant as himself.

Said we, one day,—for he was one of that delightful class whom everybody feels privileged to be related to,—"Uncle, uncle, how *is* it that you contrive to be so happy? Why is your face so cheerful, when so many thousands are craped over with a most uncomfortable gloominess?"

"My dear young friend," he answered, with his placid smile, "I am even as others, afflicted with infirmities; I have had my share of sorrow—some would say more—but I have found out the secret of being happy, and it is this:

"*Forget self.*"

"Until you do that, you can lay but little claim to a cheerful spirit. 'Forget what manner of man you are,' and think more with, rejoice more for, your neighbours. If I am poor, let me look upon my richer friend, and in estimating his blessings, forget my privations.

"If my neighbour is building a house, let me watch with him its progress, and think, 'Well, what a comfortable place it will be, to be sure; how much he may enjoy it with his family.' Thus I have a double pleasure—that of delight in noting the structure as it expands into beauty, and making my neighbour's weal mine. If he has planted a fine garden, I feast my eyes on the flowers, smell their fragrance: could I do more if it was my own?

"Another has a family of fine children; they bless him and are blessed by him; mine are all gone before me; I have none that bear my name; shall I, therefore, envy my neighbour his lovely children? No; let me enjoy their innocent smiles with him; let me *forget myself*—my tears when they were put away in darkness; or if I weep, may it be for joy that God took them untainted to dwell with His holy angels for ever.

"Believe an old man when he says there is great pleasure in living for others. The heart of the selfish man is like a city full of crooked lanes. If a generous thought from some glorious temple strays in there, wo to it—it is lost. It wanders about, and wanders about, until enveloped in darkness; as the mist of selfishness gathers around, it lies down upon some cold thought to die, and is shrouded in oblivion.

"So, if you would be happy, shun selfishness; do a kindly deed for this one, speak a kindly word for another. He who is constantly giving pleasure, is constantly receiving it. The little river gives to the great ocean, and the more it gives the faster it runs. Stop its flowing, and the hot sun would dry it up, till it would be but filthy mud, sending forth bad odours, and corrupting the fresh air of Heaven. Keep your heart constantly travelling on errands of mercy—it has feet that never tire, hands that cannot be overburdened, eyes that never sleep; freight its hands with blessings, direct its eyes—no matter how narrow your sphere—to the nearest object of suffering, and relieve it.

"I say, my dear young friend, take the word of an old man for it, who has tried every known panacea, and found all to fail, except this golden rule,

"*Forget self, and keep the heart busy for others.*"

CHARITY.—ITS OBJECTS

THE great Teacher, on being asked "Who is my neighbour?" replied "A man went down from Jerusalem to Jericho," and the parable which followed is the most beautiful which language has ever recorded. Story-telling, though often abused, is the medium by which truth can be most irresistibly conveyed to the majority of minds, and in the present instance we have a desire to portray in some slight degree the importance of Charity in every-day life.

A great deal has been said and written on the subject of indiscriminate giving, and many who have little sympathy with the needy or distressed, make the supposed unworthiness of the object an excuse for withholding their alms; while others, who really possess a large proportion of the milk of human kindness, in awaiting *great* opportunities to do good, overlook all in their immediate pathway, as beneath their notice. And yet it was the "widow's mite" which, amid the many rich gifts cast into the treasury, won the approval of the Searcher of Hearts; and we have His assurance that a cup of cold water given in a proper spirit shall not lose its reward.

Our design in the present sketch is to call the attention of the softer sex to a subject which has in too many instances escaped their attention; for our ideas of Charity embrace a wide field, and we hold that it should at all times be united with justice, when those less favoured than themselves are concerned.

"I do not intend hereafter to have washing done more than once in two weeks," said the rich Mrs. Percy, in reply to an observation of her husband, who was standing at the window, looking at a woman who was up to her knees in the snow, hanging clothes on a line in the yard. "I declare it is too bad, to be paying that poking old thing a half-a-dollar a week for our wash, and only six in the family. There she has been at it since seven o'clock this morning, and now it is almost four. It will require but two or three hours longer if I get her once a fortnight, and I shall save twenty-five cents a week by it."

"When your own sex are concerned, you women are the *closest* beings," said Mr. P., laughing. "Do just as you please, however," he continued, as he observed a brown gather on the brow of his wife; "for my part I should be glad if washing-days were blotted entirely from the calendar."

At this moment the washerwoman passed the window with her stiffened skirts and almost frozen hands and arms. Some emotions of pity stirring in his breast at the sight, he again asked, "Do you think it will be exactly right, my dear, to make old Phoebe do the same amount of labour for half the wages?"

"Of course it will," replied Mrs. Percy, decidedly; "we are bound to do the best we can for ourselves. If she objects, she can say so. There are plenty of poor I can get who will be glad to come, and by this arrangement I shall save thirteen dollars a year."

"So much," returned Mr. P., carelessly; "how these things do run up!" Here the matter ended as far as they were concerned. Not so with "old Phoebe," as she was called. In reality, however, Phoebe was not yet forty; it was care and hardship which had seamed her once blooming face, and brought on prematurely the appearance of age. On going to Mrs. Percy in the evening after she had finished her wash, for the meagre sum she had earned, that lady had spoken somewhat harshly about her being so slow, and mentioned the new arrangement she intended to carry into effect, leaving it optional with the poor woman to accept or decline. After a moment's hesitation, Phoebe, whose necessities allowed her no choice, agreed to her proposal, and the lady, who had been fumbling in her purse, remarked:—

"I have no change, nothing less than this three-dollar bill. Suppose I pay you by the month hereafter; it will save me a great deal of trouble, and I will try to give you your dollar a month regularly."

Phoebe's pale cheek waxed still more ghastly as Mrs. Percy spoke, but it was not within that lady's province to notice the colour of a washerwoman's face. She did, however, observe her lingering, weary steps as she proceeded through the yard, and conscience whispered some reproaches, which were so unpleasant and unwelcome, that she endeavoured to dispel them by turning to the luxurious supper which was spread before her. And here I would pause to observe, that whatever method may be adopted to reconcile the conscience to withholding money so justly due, so hardly earned, she disobeyed the positive injunction of that God who has not left the time of payment optional with ourselves, but who has said—"The wages of him that is hired, shall not abide with thee all night until the morning."—Lev. 19 chap. 13th verse.

The husband of Phoebe was a day labourer; when not intoxicated he was kind; but this was of rare occurrence, for most of his earnings went for ardent spirits, and the labour of the poor wife and mother was the main support of herself and four children—the eldest nine years, the youngest only eighteen months old. As she neared the wretched hovel she had left early in the morning, she saw the faces of her four little ones pressed close against the window.

"Mother's coming, mother's coming!" they shouted, as they watched her approaching through the gloom, and as she unlocked the door, which she had been obliged to fasten to keep them from straying away, they all sprang to her arms at once.

"God bless you, my babes!" she exclaimed, gathering them to her heart, "you have not been a minute absent from my mind this day. And what have *you* suffered," she added, clasping the youngest, a sickly, attenuated-looking object, to her breast. "Oh! it is hard, my little Mary, to leave you to the tender mercies of children hardly able to take care of themselves." And as the baby nestled its head closer to her side, and lifted its pale, imploring face, the anguished mother's fortitude gave way, and she burst into an agony of tears and sobbings. By-the-by, do some mothers, as they sit by the softly-lined cradles of their own beloved babes, ever think upon the sufferings of those hapless little ones, many times left with a scanty supply of food, and no fire, on a cold winter day, while the parent is earning the pittance which is to preserve them from starvation? And lest some may suppose that we are drawing largely upon our imagination, we will mention, in this place, that we knew of a child left under such circumstances, and half-perishing with cold, who was nearly burned to death by some hops (for there was no fuel to be found), which it scraped together in its ragged apron, and set on fire with a coal found in the ashes.

Phoebe did not indulge long in grief, however she forgot her weary limbs, and bustling about, soon made up a fire, and boiled some potatoes, which constituted their supper—after which she nursed the children, two at a time, for a while, and then put them tenderly to bed. Her husband had not come home, and as he was nearly always intoxicated, and sometimes ill-treated her sadly, she felt his absence a relief. Sitting over a handful of coals, she attempted to dry her wet feet; every bone in her body ached, for she was not naturally strong, and leaning her head on her hand, she allowed the big tears to course slowly down her cheeks, without making any attempt to wipe them away, while she murmured:

"Thirteen dollars a year gone! What is to become of us? I cannot get help from those authorized by law to assist the poor, unless I agree to put out my children, and I cannot live and see them abused and over-worked at their tender age. And people think their father might support us; but how can I help it that he spends all his earnings in drink? And rich as Mrs. Percy is, she did not pay me my wages to-night, and now I cannot get the yarn for my baby's stockings, and her little limbs must remain cold awhile longer; and I must do without the flour, too, that I was going to make into bread, and the potatoes are almost gone."

Here Phoebe's emotions overcame her, and she ceased speaking. After a while, she continued—

"Mrs. Percy also blamed me for being so slow; she did not know that I was up half the night, and that my head has ached ready to split all day. Oh! dear, oh! dear, oh! dear, if it were not for my babes, I should yearn for the quiet of the grave!"

And with a long, quivering sigh, such as one might heave at the rending of soul and body, Phoebe was silent.

Daughters of luxury! did it ever occur to you that we are all the children of one common Parent? Oh, look hereafter with pity on those faces where the records of suffering are deeply graven, and remember "*Be ye warmed and filled,*" will not suffice, unless the hand executes the promptings of the heart. After awhile, as the fire died out, Phoebe crept to her miserable pallet, crushed with the prospect of the days of toil which were still before her, and haunted by the idea of sickness and death, brought on by over-taxation of her bodily powers, while in case of such an event, she was tortured by the reflection—"what is to become of my children?"

Ah, this anxiety is the true bitterness of death, to the friendless and poverty-stricken parent. In this way she passed the night, to renew, with the dawn, the toils and cares which were fast closing their work on her. We will not say what Phoebe, under other circumstances, might have been. She possessed every noble attribute common to woman, without education, or training, but she was not prepossessing in her appearance; and Mrs. Percy, who never studied character, or sympathized with menials, or strangers, would have laughed at the idea of dwelling with compassion on the lot of her washerwoman with a drunken husband. Yet her feelings sometimes became interested for the poor she heard of abroad, the poor she read of, and she would now and then descant largely on the few cases of actual distress which had chanced to come under her notice, and the little opportunity she enjoyed of bestowing alms. Superficial in her mode of thinking and observation, her ideas of charity were limited, forgetful that to be true it must be a pervading principle of life, and can be exercised even in the bestowal of a gracious word or smile, which, under peculiar circumstances, may raise a brother from the dust—and thus win the approval of Him, who, although the Lord of angels, was pleased to say of her who brought but the "box of spikenard"—with tears of love—"*She hath done what she could.*"

THE VISION OF BOATS

ONE morn, when the Day-god, yet hidden
By the mist that the mountain enshrouds,
Was hoarding up hyacinth blossoms,
And roses, to fling at the clouds;
I saw from the casement, that northward
Looks out on the Valley of Pines,
(The casement, where all day in summer,
You hear the drew drop from the vines),

White shapes 'mid the purple wreaths glancing,
Like the banners of hosts at strife;
But I knew they were silvery pennons
Of boats on the River of Life.
And I watched, as the, mist cleared upward,
Half hoping, yet fearing to see
On that rapid and rock-sown River,
What the fate of the boats might be.

There were some that sped cheerily onward,
With white sails gallantly spread
Yet ever there sat at the look-out,
One, watching for danger ahead.
No fragrant and song-haunted island,
No golden and gem-studded coast
Could win, with its ravishing beauty,
The watcher away from his post.

When the tempest crouched low on the waters,
And fiercely the hurricane swept,
With furled sails, cautiously wearing,
Still onward in safety they kept.
And many sailed well for a season,
When river and sky were serene,
And leisurely swung the light rudder,
'Twixt borders of blossoming green.

But the Storm-King came out from his caverns,
With whirlwind, and lightning, and rain;
And my eyes, that grew dim for a moment,
Saw but the rent canvas again.
Then sorely I wept the ill-fated!
Yea, bitterly wept, for I knew
They had learned but the fair-weather wisdom,
That a moment of trial o'erthrew.

And one in its swift sinking, parted
A placid and sun-bright wave;
Oh, deftly the rock was hidden,
That keepeth that voyager's grave!
And I sorrowed to think how little
Of aid from, a kindly hand,
Might have guided the beautiful vessel
Away from the treacherous strand.

And I watched with a murmur of, blessing,
The few that on either shore
Were setting up signals of warning,
Where many had perished before.
But now, as the sunlight came creeping
Through the half-opened lids of the morn,
Fast faded that wonderful pageant,
Of shadows and drowsiness born.

And no sound could I hear but the sighing
Of winds, in the Valley of Pines;
And the heavy, monotonous dropping
Of dew from the shivering vines.
But all day, 'mid the clashing of Labour,
And the city's unmusical notes,
With thoughts that went seeking the hidden,
I pondered that Vision of Boats.

REGULATION OF THE TEMPER

THERE is considerable ground for thinking that the opinion very generally prevails that the temper is something beyond the power of regulation, control, or government. A good temper, too, if we may judge from the usual excuses for the want of it, is hardly regarded in the light of an attainable quality. To be slow in taking offence, and moderate in the expression of resentment, in which things good temper consists, seems to be generally reckoned rather among the gifts of nature, the privileges of a happy constitution, than among the possible results of careful self-discipline. When we have been fretted by some petty grievance, or, hurried by some reasonable cause of offence into a degree of anger far beyond what the occasion required, our subsequent regret is seldom of a kind for which we are likely to be much better. We bewail ourselves for a misfortune, rather than condemn ourselves for a fault. We speak of our unhappy temper as if it were something that entirely removed the blame from us, and threw it all upon the peculiar and unavoidable sensitiveness of our frame. A peevish and irritable temper is, indeed, an *unhappy* one; a source of misery to ourselves and to others; but it is not, in *all* cases, so valid an excuse for being easily provoked, as it is usually supposed to be.

A good temper is too important a source of happiness, and an ill temper too important a source of misery, to be treated with indifference or hopelessness. The false excuses or modes of regarding this matter, to which we have referred, should be exposed; for until their invalidity and incorrectness are exposed, no efforts, or but feeble ones, will be put forth to regulate an ill temper, or to cultivate a good one.

We allow that there are great differences of natural constitution. One who is endowed with a poetical temperament, or a keen sense of beauty, or a great love of order, or very large ideality, will be pained by the want or the opposites of these qualities, where one less amply endowed would suffer no provocation whatever. What would grate most harshly on the ear of an eminent musician, might not be noticed at all by one whose musical faculties were unusually small. The same holds true in regard to some other, besides musical deficiencies or discords. A delicate and sickly frame will feel annoyed by what would not at all disturb the same frame in a state of vigorous health. Particular circumstances, also, may expose some to greater trials and vexations than others. But, after all this is granted, the only reasonable conclusion seems to be, that the attempt to govern the temper is more difficult in some cases than in others; not that it is, in any case, impossible. It is, at least, certain that an opinion of its impossibility is an effectual bar against entering upon it. On the other hand, "believe that you will succeed, and you will succeed," is a maxim which has nowhere been more frequently verified than in the moral world. It should be among the first maxims admitted, and the last abandoned, by every earnest seeker of his own moral improvement.

Then, too, facts demonstrate that much has been done and can be done in regulating the worst of tempers. The most irritable or peevish temper has been restrained by company; has been subdued by interest; has been awed by fear; has been softened by grief; has been soothed by kindness. A bad temper has shown itself, in the same individuals, capable of increase, liable to change, accessible to motives. Such facts are enough to encourage, in every case, an attempt to govern the temper. All the miseries of a bad temper, and all the blessings of a good one, may be attained by an habitual tolerance, concern, and kindness for others—by an habitual restraint of considerations and feelings entirely selfish.

To those of our readers who feel moved or resolved by the considerations we have named to attempt to regulate their temper, or to cultivate one of a higher order of excellence, we would submit a few suggestions which may assist them in their somewhat difficult undertaking.

See, first of all, that you set as high a value on the comfort of those with whom you have to do as you do on your own. If you regard your own comfort *exclusively*, you will not make the allowances which a *proper* regard to the happiness of others would lead you to do.

Avoid, particularly in your intercourse with those to whom it is of most consequence that your temper should be gentle and forbearing—avoid raising into undue importance the little failings which you may perceive in them, or the trifling disappointments which they may occasion you. If we make it a subject of vexation, that the beings among whom we tire destined to live, are not perfect, we must give up all hope of attaining a temper not easily provoked. A habit of trying everything by the standard of perfection vitiates the temper more than it improves the understanding, and disposes the mind to discern faults with an unhappy penetration. I would not have you shut your eyes to the errors or follies, or thoughtlessnesses of your friends, but only not to magnify them or view them microscopically. Regard them in others as you would have them regard the same things in you, in an exchange of circumstances.

Do not forget to make due allowances for the original constitution and the manner of education or bringing up, which has been the lot of those with whom you have to do. Make such excuses for Others as the circumstances of their constitution, rearing, and youthful associations, do fairly demand.

Always put the best construction on the motives of others, when their conduct admits of more than one way of understanding it. In many cases, where neglect or ill intention seems evident at first sight, it may prove true that "second thoughts are best." Indeed, this common slaying is never more likely to prove true than in cases in which the *first* thoughts were the dictates of anger And even when the first thoughts are confirmed by further evidence, yet the habit of always waiting for complete evidence before we condemn, must have a calming; and moderating effect upon the temper, while it will take nothing from the authority of our just censures.

It will further, be a great help to our efforts, as well as our desires, for the government of the temper, if we consider frequently and seriously the natural consequences of hasty resentments, angry replies, rebukes impatiently given or impatiently received, muttered discontents, sullen looks, and harsh words. It may safely be asserted that the consequences of these and other ways in which ill-temper may show itself, are *entirely* evil. The feelings, which accompany them in ourselves, and those which they excite in others, are unprofitable as well as painful. They lessen our own comfort, and tend often rather to prevent than to promote the improvement of those with whom we find fault. If we give even friendly and judicious counsels in a harsh and pettish tone, we excite against *them* the repugnance naturally felt to *our manner*. The consequence is, that the advice is slighted, and the peevish adviser pitied, despised, or hated.

When we cannot succeed in putting a restraint on our *feelings* of anger or dissatisfaction, we can at least check the *expression* of those feelings. If our thoughts are not always in our power, our words and actions and looks may be brought under our command; and a command over these expressions of our thoughts and feelings will be found no mean help towards obtaining an increase of power over our thoughts and feelings themselves. At least, one great good will be effected: time will be gained; time for reflection; time for charitable allowances and excuses.

Lastly, seek the help of religion. Consider how you may most certainly secure the approbation of God. For a good temper, or a well-regulated temper, *may be* the constant homage of a truly religious man to that God, whose love and long-suffering forbearance surpass all human love and forbearance.

MANLY GENTLENESS

WHO is the most wretched man living? This question might constitute a very fair puzzle to those of our readers whose kind hearts have given them, in their own experience, no clue to the true answer. It is a species of happiness to be rich; to have at one's command an abundance of the elegancies and luxuries of life. Then he, perhaps, is the most miserable of men who is the poorest. It is a species of happiness to be the possessor of learning, fame, or power; and therefore, perhaps, he is the most miserable man who is the most ignorant, despised, and helpless. No; there is a man more wretched than these. We know not where he may be found; but find him where you will, in a prison or on a throne, steeped in poverty or surrounded with princely affluence; execrated, as he deserves to be, or crowned with world-wide applause; that man is the most miserable whose heart contains the least love for others.

It is a pleasure to be beloved. Who has not felt this? Human affection is priceless. A fond heart is more valuable than the Indies. But it is a still greater pleasure to love than to be loved; the emotion itself is of a higher kind; it calls forth our own powers into more agreeable exercise, and is independent of the caprice of others. Generally speaking, if we deserve to be loved, others will love us, but this is not always the case. The love of others towards us, is not always in proportion to our real merits; and it would be unjust to make our highest happiness dependent on it. But our love for others will always be in proportion to our real goodness; the more amiable, the more excellent we become, the more shall we love others; it is right, therefore, that this love should be made capable of bestowing upon us the largest amount of happiness. This is the arrangement which the Creator has fixed upon. By virtue of our moral constitution, to love is to be happy; to hate is to be wretched.

Hatred is a strong word, and the idea it conveys is very repulsive. We would hope that few of our readers know by experience what it is in its full extent. To be a very demon, to combine in ourselves the highest possible degree of wickedness and misery, nothing more is needful than to hate with sufficient intensity. But though, happily, comparatively few persons are fully under the influence of this baneful passion, how many are under it more frequently and powerfully than they ought to be? How often do we indulge in resentful, revengeful feelings, with all of which hatred more or less mixes itself? Have we not sometimes entertained sentiments positively malignant towards those who have wounded our vanity or injured our interests, secretly wishing them ill, or not heartily wishing them happiness? If so, we need only consult our own experience to ascertain that such feelings are both sinful and foolish; they offend our Maker, and render us wretched.

We know a happy man; one who in the midst of the vexations and crosses of this changing world, is always happy. Meet him anywhere, and at any time, his features beam with pleasure. Children run to meet him, and contend for the honour of touching his hand, or laying hold of the skirt of his coat, as he passes by, so cheerful and benevolent does he always look. In his own house he seems to reign absolute, and yet he never uses any weapon more powerful than a kind word. Everybody who knows him is aware, that, in point of intelligence, ay, and in physical prowess, too—for we know few men who can boast a more athletic frame—he is strong as a lion, yet in his demeanour he is gentle as a lamb. His wife is not of the most amiable temper, his children are not the most docile, his business brings him into contact with men of various dispositions; but he conquers all with the same weapons. What a contrast have we often thought he presents to some whose physiognomy looks like a piece of harsh handwriting, in which we can decipher nothing but *self, self, self*; who seem, both at home and abroad, to be always on the watch against any infringement of their dignity. Poor men! their dignity can be of little value if it requires so much care in order to be maintained. True manliness need take but little pains to procure respectful recognition. If it is genuine, others will see it, and respect it. The lion will always be acknowledged as the king of the beasts; but the ass, though clothed in the lion's skin, may bray loudly and perseveringly indeed, but he will never keep the forest in awe.

From some experience in the homes of working-men, and other homes too, we are led to think that much of the harsh and discordant feeling which too often prevails there may be ascribed to a false conception of what is truly great. It is a very erroneous impression that despotism is manly. For our part we believe that despotism is inhuman, satanic, and that wherever it is found—as much in the bosom of a family, as on the throne of a kingdom. We cannot bring ourselves to tolerate the inconsistency with which some men will inveigh against some absolute sovereign, and straight-way enact the pettiest airs of absolutism in their little empire at home. We have no private intimacy with "the autocrat of all the Russias," and may, with all humility, avow that we do not desire to have any; but this we believe, that out of the thousands who call him a tyrant, it would be no difficult matter to pick scores who are as bad, if not worse. Let us remember that it is not a great empire which constitutes a great tyrant. Tyranny must be measured by the strength of those imperious and malignant passions from which it flows, and carrying this rule along with us, it would not surprise us, if we found the greatest tyrant in the world in some small cottage, with none to oppress but a few unoffending children, and a helpless woman. O! when shall we, be just!—when shall we cease to prate about wrongs inflicted by others, and magnified by being beheld through the haze of distance, and seek to redress those which lie at our own doors, and to redress which we shall only have to prevail upon ourselves to be just and gentle! Arbitrary power is always associated either with cruelty, or conscious weakness. True greatness is above the petty arts of tyranny. Sometimes much domestic suffering may arise from a cause which is easily confounded with a tyrannical disposition—we refer to an exaggerated sense of justice. This is the abuse of a right feeling, and requires to be kept in vigilant check. Nothing is easier than to be one-sided in judging of the actions of others. How agreeable the task of applying the line and plummet! How quiet and complete the assumption of our own superior excellence which we make in doing it! But if the task is in some respects easy, it is most difficult if we take into account the necessity of being just in our decisions. In domestic life especially, in which so much depends on circumstances, and the highest questions often relate to mere matters of expediency, how easy it is to be "always finding fault," if we neglect to take notice of explanatory and extenuating circumstances! Anybody with a tongue and a most moderate complement of brains can call a thing stupid, foolish, ill-advised, and so forth; though it might require a larger amount of wisdom than the judges possessed to have done the thing better. But what do we want with captious judges in the bosom of a family? The scales of household polity are the scales of love, and he who holds them should be a sympathizing friend; ever ready to make allowance for failures, ingenious in contriving apologies, more lavish of counsels than rebukes, and less anxious to overwhelm a person with a sense of deficiency than to awaken in the bosom, a conscious power of doing better. One thing is certain: if any member of a family conceives it his duty to sit continually in the censor's chair, and weigh in the scales of justice all that happens in the domestic commonwealth, domestic happiness is out of the question. It is manly to extenuate and forgive, but a crabbed and censorious spirit is contemptible.

There is much more misery thrown into the cup of life by domestic unkindness than we might at first suppose. In thinking of the evils endured by society from malevolent passions of individuals, we are apt to enumerate only the more dreadful instances of crime: but what are the few murders which unhappily pollute the soil of this Christian land—what, we ask, is the suffering they occasion, what their demoralizing tendency—when compared with the daily effusions of ill-humour which sadden, may we not fear, many thousand homes? We believe that an incalculably greater number are hurried to the grave by habitual unkindness than by sudden violence; the slow poison of churlishness and neglect, is of all poisons the most destructive. If this is true, we want a new definition for the most flagrant of all crimes: a definition which shall leave out the element of time, and call these actions the same—equally hateful, equally diabolical, equally censured by the righteous government of Heaven—which proceed from the same motives, and lead to the same result, whether they be done in a moment, or spread out through a series of years. Habitual unkindness is demoralizing as well as cruel. Whenever it fails to break the heart, it hardens it. To take a familiar illustration: a wife who is never addressed by her husband in tones of kindness, must cease to love him if she wishes to be happy. It is her only alternative. Thanks to the nobility of our nature, she does not always take it. No; for years she battles with cruelty, and still presses with affection the hand which smites her, but it is fearfully at her own expense. Such endurance preys upon her health, and hastens her exit to the asylum of the grave. If this is to be avoided, she must learn to forget, what woman should never be tempted to forget, the vows, the self-renunciating devotedness of impassioned youth; she must learn to oppose indifference, to neglect and repel him with a heart as cold as his own. But what a tragedy lies involved in a career like this! We gaze on something infinitely more terrible than murder; we see our nature abandoned to the mercy of malignant passions, and the sacred susceptibilities which were intended to fertilize with the waters of charity the pathway of life, sending forth streams of bitterest gall. A catalogue of such cases, faithfully compiled, would eclipse, in turpitude and horror, all the calendars of crime that have ever sickened the attention of the world.

The obligations of gentleness and kindness are extensive as the claims to manliness; these three qualities must go together. There are some cases, however, in which such obligations are of special force. Perhaps a precept here will be presented most appropriately under the guise of an example. We have now before our mind's eye a couple, whose marriage tie was, a few months since, severed by death. The husband was a strong, hale, robust sort of a man, who probably never knew a day's illness in the course of his life, and whose sympathy on behalf of weakness or suffering in others it was exceedingly difficult to evoke; while his partner was the very reverse, by constitution weak and ailing, but withal a woman of whom any man might and ought to have been proud. Her elegant form, her fair transparent skin, the classical contour of her refined and expressive face, might have led a Canova to have selected her as a model of feminine beauty. But alas! she was weak; she could not work like other women; her husband could not *boast* among his shopmates how much she contributed to the maintenance of the family, and how largely she could afford to dispense with the fruit of his labours. Indeed, with a noble infant in her bosom, and the cares of a household resting entirely upon her, she required help herself, and at least she needed, what no wife can dispense with, but she least of all—*sympathy*, forbearance, and all those tranquilizing virtues which flow from a heart of kindness. She least of all could bear a harsh look; to be treated daily with cold, disapproving reserve, a petulant dissatisfaction could not but be death to her. We will not say it *was*—enough that she is dead. The lily bent before the storm, and at last was crushed by it. We ask but one question, in order to point the moral:—In the circumstances we have delineated, what course of treatment was most consonant with a manly spirit; that which was actually pursued, or some other which the reader can suggest?

Yes, to love is to be happy and to make happy, and to love is the very spirit of true manliness. We speak not of exaggerated passion and false sentiment; we speak not of those bewildering, indescribable feelings, which under that name, often monopolize for a time the guidance of the youthful heart; but we speak of that pure emotion which is benevolence intensified, and which, when blended with intelligence, can throw the light of joyousness around the manifold relations of life. Coarseness, rudeness, tyranny, are so many forms of brute power; so many manifestations of what it is man's peculiar glory not to be; but kindness and gentleness can never cease to be MANLY.

> Count not the days that have lightly flown,
> The years that were vainly spent;
> Nor speak of the hours thou must blush to own,
> When thy spirit stands before the Throne,
> To account for the talents lent.
>
> But number the hours redeemed from sin,
> The moments employed for Heaven;—
> Oh few and evil thy days have been,
> Thy life, a toilsome but worthless scene,
> For a nobler purpose given.

Will the shade go back on the dial plate?
Will thy sun stand still on his way?
Both hasten on; and thy spirit's fate
Rests on the point of life's little date:—
Then live while 'tis called to-day.

Life's waning hours, like the Sibyl's page,
As they lessen, in value rise;
Oh rouse thee and live! nor deem that man's age
Stands on the length of his pilgrimage,
But in days that are truly wise.

SILENT INFLUENCE

"HOW finely she looks!" said Margaret Winne, as a lady swept by them in the crowd; "I do not see that time wears upon her beauty at all."

"What, Bell Walters!" exclaimed her companion. "Are you one of those who think her such a beauty?"

"I think her a very fine-looking woman, certainly," returned Mrs. Winne; "and, what is more, I think her a very fine woman."

"Indeed!" exclaimed Mrs. Hall; "I thought you were no friends?"

"No," replied the first speaker; "but that does not make us enemies."

"But I tell you she positively dislikes you, Margaret," said Mrs. Hall. "It is only a few days since I knew of her saying that you were a bold, impudent woman, and she did not like you at all."

"That is bad," said Margaret, with a smile; "for I must confess that I like her."

"Well," said her companion, "I am sure I could never like any one who made such unkind speeches about me."

"I presume she said no more than she thought," said Margaret, quietly.

"Well, so much the worse!" exclaimed Mrs. Hall, in surprise. "I hope you do not think that excuses the matter at all?"

"Certainly, I do. I presume she has some reason for thinking as she does; and, if so, it was very natural she should express her opinion."

"Well, you are very cool and candid about it, I must say. What reason have you given her, pray, for thinking you were bold and impudent?"

"None, that I am aware of," replied Mrs. Winne, "but I presume she thinks I have. I always claim her acquaintance, when we meet, and I have no doubt she would much rather I would let it drop."

"Why don't you, then? I never knew her, and never had any desire for her acquaintance. She was no better than you when you were girls, and I don't think her present good fortune need make her so very scornful."

"I do not think she exhibits any more haughtiness than most people would under the same circumstances. Some would have dropped the acquaintance at once, without waiting for me to do it. Her social position is higher than mine, and it annoys her to have me meet her as an equal, just I used to do."

"You do it to annoy her, then?"

"Not by any means. I would much rather she would feel, as I do, that the difference between us is merely conventional, and might bear to be forgotten on the few occasions when accident throws us together. But she does not, and I presume it is natural. I do not know how my head might be turned, if I had climbed up in the world as rapidly as she has done. As it is, however, I admire her too much to drop her acquaintance just yet, as long as she leaves it to me."

"Really, Margaret, I should have supposed you had too much spirit to intrude yourself upon a person that you knew wished to shake you off; and I do not see how you can admire one that you know to be so proud."

"I do not admire her on account of her pride, certainly, though it is a quality that sits very gracefully upon her," said Margaret Winne; and she introduced another topic of conversation, for she did not hope to make her companion understand the motives that influenced her.

"Bold and impudent!" said Margaret, to herself, as she sat alone, in her own apartment. "I knew she thought it, for I have seen it in her looks; but she always treats me well externally, and I hardly thought she would say it. I know she was vexed with herself for speaking to me, one day, when she was in the midst of a circle of her fashionable acquaintances. I was particularly ill-dressed, and I noticed that they stared at me; but I had no intention, then, of throwing myself in her way. Well," she continued, musingly, "I am not to be foiled with one rebuff. I know her better than she knows me, for the busy world has canvassed her life, while they have never meddled with my own: and I think there are points of contact enough between us for us to understand each other, if we once found an opportunity. She stands in a position which I shall never occupy, and she has more power and strength than I; else she had never stood where she does, for she has shaped her fortunes by her own unaided will. Her face was not her fortune, as most people suppose, but her mind. She has accomplished whatever she has undertaken, and she can accomplish much more, for her resources are far from being developed. Those around her may remember yet that she was not always on a footing with them; but they will not do so long. She will be their leader, for she was born to rule. Yes; and she queens it most proudly among them. It were a pity to lose sight of her stately, graceful dignity. I regard her very much as I would some beautiful exotic, and her opinion of me affects me about as much as if she were the flower, and not the mortal. And yet I can never see her without wishing that the influence she exerts might be turned into a better channel. She has much of good about her, and I think that it needs but a few hints to make life and its responsibilities appear to her as they do to me. I have a message for her ear, but she must not know that it was intended for her. She has too much pride of place to receive it from me, and too much self-confidence to listen knowingly to the suggestions of any other mind than her own. Therefore, I will seek the society of Isabel Walters whenever I can, without appearing intrusive, until she thinks me worthy her notice, or drops me altogether. My talent lies in thinking, but she has all the life and energy I lack, and would make an excellent actor to my thought, and would need no mentor when her attention was once aroused. My usefulness must lie in an humble sphere, but hers—she can carry it wherever she will. It will be enough for my single life to accomplish, if, beyond the careful training of my own family, I can incite her to a development of her powers of usefulness. People will listen to her who will pay no attention to me; and, besides, she has the time and means to spare, which I have not."

"Everywhere, in Europe, they were talking of you, Mrs. Walters," said a lady, who had spent many years abroad, "and adopting your plans for vagrant and industrial schools, and for the management of hospitals and asylums. I have seen your name in the memorials laid before government in various foreign countries. You have certainly achieved a world-wide reputation. Do tell me how your attention came first to be turned to that sort of thing? I supposed you were one of our fashionable women, who sought simply to know how much care and responsibility they could lawfully avoid, and how high a social station it was possible to attain. I am sure something must have happened to turn your life into so different a channel."

"Nothing in particular, I assure you," returned Mrs. Walters. "I came gradually to perceive the necessity there was that some one should take personal and decisive action in those things that it was so customary to neglect. Fond as men are of money, it was far easier to reach their purses than their minds. Our public charities were quite well endowed, but no one gave them that attention that they needed, and thus evils had crept in that were of the highest importance. My attention was attracted to it in my own vicinity at first; and others saw it as well as I, but it was so much of everybody's business that everybody let it alone. I followed the example for awhile, but it seemed as much my duty to act as that of any other person; and though it is little I have done, I think that, in that little, I have filled the place designed for me by Providence."

"Well, really, Mrs. Walters, you were one of the last persons I should have imagined to be nicely balancing a point of duty, or searching out the place designed for them by Providence. I must confess myself at fault in my judgment of character for once."

"Indeed, madam," replied Mrs. Walters, "I have no doubt you judged me very correctly at the time you knew me. My first ideas of the duties and responsibilities of life were aroused by Margaret Winne; and I recollect that my intimacy with her commenced after you left the country."

"Margaret Winne? Who was she? Not the wife of that little Dr. Winne we used to hear of occasionally? They attended the same church with us, I believe?"

"Yes; she was the one. We grew up together, and were familiar with each other's faces from childhood; but this was about all. She was always in humble circumstances, as I had myself been in early life; and, after my marriage, I used positively to dislike her, and to dread meeting her, for she was the only one of my former acquaintances who met me on the same terms as she had always done. I thought she wished to remind me that we were once equals in station; but I learned, when I came to know her well, how far she was above so mean a thought. I hardly know how I came first to appreciate her, but we were occasionally thrown in contact, and her sentiments were so beautiful—so much above the common stamp—that I could not fail to be attracted by her. She was a noble woman. The world knows few like her. So modest and retiring—with an earnest desire to do all the good in the world of which she was capable, but with no ambition to shine. Well fitted as she was, to be an ornament in any station of society, she seemed perfectly content to be the idol of her own family, and known to few besides. There were few subjects on which she had not thought, and her clear perceptions went at once to the bottom of a subject, so that she solved simply many a question on which astute philosophers had found themselves at fault. I came at last to regard her opinion almost as an oracle. I have often thought, since her death, that it was her object to turn my life into that channel to which it has since been devoted, but I do not know. I had never thought of the work that has since occupied me at the time of her death, but I can see now how cautiously and gradually she led me among the poor, and taught me to sympathize with their sufferings, and gave me, little by little, a clue to the evils that had sprung up in the management of our public charities. She was called from her family in the prime of life, but they who come after her do assuredly rise up and call her blessed. She has left a fine family, who will not soon forget, the instructions of their mother."

"Ah! yes, there it is, Mrs. Walters. A woman's sphere, after all, is at home. One may do a great deal of good in public, no doubt, as you have done; but don't you think that, while you have devoted yourself so untiringly to other affairs, you have been obliged to neglect your own family in order to gain time for this? One cannot live two lives at once, you know."

"No, madam, certainly we cannot live two lives at once, but we can glean a much larger harvest from the one which is, bestowed upon us than we are accustomed to think. I do not, by any means, think that I have ever neglected my own family in the performance of other duties, and I trust my children are proving, by their hearty co-operation with me, that I am not mistaken. Our first duty, certainly is at home, and I determined, at the outset, that nothing should call me from the performance of this first charge. I do not think anything can excuse a mother from devoting a large portion of her life in personal attention to the children God has given her. But I can assure you that, to those things which I have done of which the world could take cognisance, I have given far less time than I used once to devote to dress and amusement, I found, by systematizing everything, that my time was more than doubled; and, certainly, I was far better fitted to attend properly to my own family, when my eyes, were opened to the responsibilities of life, than when my thoughts were wholly occupied by fashion and display."

ANTIDOTE FOR MELANCHOLY

"AH, friend K——, good-morning to you; I'm really happy to see you looking so cheerful. Pray, to what unusual circumstance may we be indebted for this happy, smiling face of yours, this morning?" (Our friend K——had been, unfortunately, of a very desponding and somewhat of a choleric turn of mind, previously.)

"Really, is the change so perceptible, then? Well, my dear sir, you shall have the secret; for, happy as I appear—and be assured, my appearances are by no means deceptive, for I never felt more happy in my life—it will still give me pleasure to inform you, and won't take long, either. It is simply this; I have made a whole family happy!"

"Indeed! Why, you have discovered a truly valuable: recipe for blues, then, which may be used *ad libitum*, eh, K——?"

"You may well say that. But, really, my friend, I feel no little mortification at not making so simple and valuable a discovery at an earlier period of my life, Heaven knows," continued K——, "I have looked for contentment everywhere else. First, I sought for wealthy in the gold mines of California, thinking that was the true source of all earthly joys; but after obtaining it, I found myself with such a multiplicity of cares and anxieties, that I was really more unhappy than ever. I then sought for pleasure in travelling. This answered somewhat the purpose of dissipating cares, &c., so long as it lasted; but, dear me, it gave no permanent satisfaction. After seeing the whole world, I was as badly off as Alexander the Great. He cried for another world to *conquer*, and I cried for another world to *see*."

The case of our friend, I imagine, differs not materially from that of a host of other seekers of contentment in this productive world. Like "blind leaders of the blind," our invariable fate is to go astray in the universal race for happiness. How common is it, after seeking for it in every place but the right one, for the selfish man to lay the whole blame upon this fine world—as if anybody was to blame but himself. Even some professors of religion are too apt to libel the world. "Well, this is a troublesome world, to make the best of it," is not an uncommon expression; neither is it a truthful one. "Troubles, disappointments, losses, crosses, sickness, and death, make up the sum and substance of our existence here," add they, with tremendous emphasis, as if they had no hand in producing the sad catalogue. The trouble is, we set too high a value on our own merits; we imagine ourselves deserving of great favours and privileges, while we are doing nothing to merit them. In this respect, we are not altogether unlike the young man in the parable, who, by-the-by, was also a professor—he professed very loudly of having done all those good things "from his youth up." But when the command came, "go sell all thou hast, and give to the poor," &c., it soon took the conceit out of him.

In this connexion, there are two or three seemingly important considerations, which I feel some delicacy in touching upon here. However, in the kindest possible spirit, I would merely remark, that there is a very large amount of wealth in the Church—by this I include its wealthy members, of course; and refer to no particular denomination; by Church, I mean all Christian denominations. Now, in connexion with this fact, such a question as this arises in my mind—and I put it, not, for the purpose of fault-finding, for I don't know that I have a right view of the matter, but merely for the consideration of those who are fond of hoarding up their earthly gains, viz.: Suppose the modern Church was composed of such professors as the self-denying disciples of our Saviour,—with their piety, simplicity, and this wealth; what, think you, would be the consequence? Now I do not intend to throw out any such flings as, "comparisons are odious"—"this is the modern Christian age"—"the age of Christian privileges," and all that sort of nonsense. Still, I am rather inclined to the opinion, that if we were all—in and out of the Church—disposed to live up to, or carry out what we professedly know to be right, it would be almost as difficult to find real trouble, as it is now to find real happiness.

The sources of contentment and discontentment are discoverable, therefore, without going into a metaphysical examination of the subject. Just in proportion as we happen to discharge, or neglect known duties, are we, according to my view, happy or miserable on earth. Philosophy tells us that our happiness and well-being depends upon a conformity to certain unalterable laws—moral, physical, and organic—which act upon the intellectual, moral, and material universe, of which man is a part, and which determine, or regulate the growth, happiness, and well-being of all organic beings. These views, when reduced to their simple meaning, amount to the same thing, call it by what name we will. Duties, of course, imply legal or moral obligations, which we are certainly legally or morally bound to pay, perform, or discharge. And certain it is, there is no getting over them—they are as irresistible as Divine power, as universal as Divine presence, as permanent as Divine existence, and no art nor cunning of man can disconnect unhappiness from transgressing them. How necessary to our happiness, then, is it, not only to know, but to perform our whole duty?

One of the great duties of man in this life, and, perhaps, the most neglected, is that of doing good, or benefiting one another. That doing good is clearly a duty devolving upon man, there can be no question. The benevolent Creator, in placing man in the world, endowed him with mental and physical energies, which clearly denote that he is to be active in his day and generation.

Active in what? Certainly not in mischief, for that would not be consistent with Divine goodness. Neither should we suppose that we are here for our own sakes simply. Such an idea would be presumptuous. For what purpose, then, was man endowed with all these facilities of mind and body, but to do good and glorify his Maker? True philosophy teaches that benevolence was not only the design of the Creator in all His works, but the fruits to be expected from them. The whole infinite contrivances of everything above, around, and within us, are directed to certain benevolent issues, and all the laws of nature are in perfect harmony with this idea.

That such is the design of man may also be inferred from the happiness which attends every good action, and the misery of discontentment which attends those who not only do wrong, but are useless to themselves and to society. Friend K——'s case, above quoted, is a fair illustration of this truth.

Now, then, if it is our duty to do all the good we can, and I think this will be admitted, particularly by the Christian, and this be measured by our means and opportunity, then there are many whom Providence has blessed with the means and opportunity of doing a very great amount of good. And if it be true, as it manifestly is, that "it is more blessed to give than receive," then has Providence also blessed them with very great privileges. The privilege of giving liberally, and thus obtaining for themselves the greater blessing, which is the result of every benevolent action, the simple satisfaction with ourselves which follows a good act, or consciousness of having done our duty in relieving a fellow-creature, are blessings indeed, which none but the good or benevolent can realize. Such kind spirits are never cast down. Their hearts always light and cheerful—rendered so by their many kind offices,—they can always enjoy their neighbours, rich or poor, high or low, and love them too; and with a flow of spirits which bespeak a heart all right within, they make all glad and happy around them.

Doing good is an infallible antidote for melancholy. When the heart seems heavy, and our minds can light upon nothing but little naughty perplexities, everything going wrong, no bright spot or relief anywhere for our crazy thoughts, and we are finally wound up in a web of melancholy, depend upon it there is nothing, nothing which can dispel this angry, ponderous, and unnatural cloud from our *rheumatic minds* and *consciences* like a charity visit—to give liberally to those in need of succour, the poor widow, the suffering, sick, and poor, the aged invalid, the lame, the blind, &c., &c.; all have a claim upon your bounty, and how they will bless you and love you for it—anyhow, they will thank kind Providence for your mission of love. He that makes one such visit will make another and another; he can't very well get weary in such well-doing, for his is the greater blessing. It is a blessing indeed: how the heart is lightened, the soul enlarged, the mind improved, and even health; for the mind being liberated from perplexities, the body is at rest, the nerves in repose, and the blood, equalized, courses freely through the system, giving strength, vigour, and equilibrium to the whole complicated machinery. Thus we can think clearer, love better, enjoy life, and be thankful for it.

What a beautiful arrangement it is that we can, by doing good to others, do so much good to ourselves! The wealthy classes, who "rise above society like clouds above the earth, to diffuse an abundant dew," should not forget this fact. The season has now about arrived, when the good people of all classes will be most busily engaged in these delightful duties. The experiment is certainly worth trying by all. If all those desponding individuals, whose chief comfort is to growl at this "troublesome world," will but take the hint, look trouble full in the face, and relieve it, they will, like friend K——, feel much better.

It may be set down as a generally correct axiom, (with some few exceptions, perhaps, such as accidents, and the deceptions and cruelties of those whom we injudiciously select for friends and confidants, from our want of discernment), that life is much what we make it, and so is the world.

THE SORROWS OF A WEALTHY CITIZEN

AH me! Am I really a rich man, or am I not? That is the question. I am sure I don't feel rich; and yet, here I am written down among the "wealthy citizens" as being worth seventy thousand dollars! How the estimate was made, or who furnished the data, is all a mystery to me. I am sure I wasn't aware of the fact before. "Seventy thousand dollars!" That sounds comfortable, doesn't it? Seventy thousand dollars!—But where is it? Ah! There is the rub! How true it is that people always know more about you than you do yourself.

Before this unfortunate book came out ("The Wealthy Citizens of Philadelphia"), I was jogging on very quietly. Nobody seemed to be aware of the fact that I was a rich man, and I had no suspicion of the thing myself. But, strange to tell, I awoke one morning and found myself worth seventy thousand dollars! I shall never forget that day. Men who had passed me in the street with a quiet, familiar nod, now bowed with a low salaam, or lifted their hats deferentially, as I encountered them on the *pave*.

"What's the meaning of all this?" thought I. "I haven't stood up to be shot at, nor sinned against innocence and virtue. I haven't been to Paris. I don't wear moustaches. What has given me this importance?"

And, musing thus, I pursued my way in quest of money to help me out with some pretty heavy payments. After succeeding, though with some difficulty in obtaining what I wanted, I returned to my store about twelve o'clock. I found a mercantile acquaintance awaiting me, who, without many preliminaries, thus stated his business:

"I want," said he, with great coolness, "to get a loan of six or seven thousand dollars; and I don't know of any one to whom I can apply with more freedom and hope of success than yourself. I think I can satisfy you, fully, in regard to security.

"My dear sir," replied I, "if you only wanted six or seven hundred dollars, instead of six or seven thousand dollars, I could not accommodate you. I have just come in from a borrowing expedition myself."

I was struck with the sudden change in the man's countenance. He was not only disappointed, but offended. He did not believe my statement. In his eyes, I had merely resorted to a subterfuge, or, rather, told a lie, because I did not wish to let him have my money. Bowing with cold formality, he turned away and left my place of business. His manner to me has been reserved ever since.

On the afternoon of that day, I was sitting in the back part of my store musing on some, matter of business, when I saw a couple of ladies enter. They spoke to one of my clerks, and he directed them back to where I was taking things comfortably in an old arm-chair.

"Mr. G— —, I believe?" said the elder of the two ladies, with a bland smile.

I had already arisen, and to this question, or rather affirmation, I bowed assent.

"Mr. G— —," resumed the lady, producing a small book as she spoke, "we are a committee, appointed to make collections in this district for the purpose of setting up a fair in aid of the funds of the Esquimaux Missionary Society. It is the design of the ladies who have taken this matter in hand to have a very large collection of articles, as the funds of the society are entirely exhausted. To the gentlemen of our district, and especially to those who leave been liberally *blessed with this world's goods*"—this was particularly emphasized—"we look for important aid. Upon you, sir, we have called first, in order that you may head the subscription, and thus set an example of liberality to others."

And the lady handed me the book in the most "of course" manner in the world, and with the evident expectation that I would put down at least fifty-dollars.

Of course I was cornered, and must do something, I tried to be bland and polite; but am inclined to think that I failed in the effort. As for fairs, I never did approve of them. But that was nothing. The enemy had boarded me so suddenly and so completely, that nothing, was left for me but to surrender at discretion, and I did so with as good grace as possible. Opening my desk, I took out a five dollar bill and presented it; to the elder of the two ladies, thinking that I was doing very well indeed. She took the money, but was evidently disappointed; and did not even ask me to head the list with my name.

"How money does harden the heart!" I overheard one of my fair visitors say to the other, in a low voices but plainly intended for my edification, as they walked off with their five dollar bill.

"Confound your impudence!" I said to myself, thus taking my revenge out of them. "Do you think I've got nothing else to do with my money but scatter it to the four winds?"

And I stuck my thumbs firmly in the armholes of my waistcoat, and took a dozen turns up and down my store, in order to cool off.

"Confound your impudence!" I then repeated, and quietly sat down again in the old arm-chair.

On the next day I had any number of calls from money-hunters. Business men, who had never thought of asking me for loans, finding that I was worth seventy thousand dollars, crowded in upon me for temporary favours, and, when disappointed in their expectations, couldn't seem to understand it. When I spoke of being "hard up" myself, they looked as if they didn't clearly comprehend what I meant.

A few days after the story of my wealth had gone abroad, I was sitting, one evening, with my family, when I was informed that a lady was in the parlour, and wished to see me.

"A lady!" said I.

"Yes, sir," replied the servant.

"Is she alone?"

"Yes, sir."

"What does she want?"

"She did not say, sir."

"Very well. Tell her I'll be down in a few moments."

When I entered the parlour, I found a woman, dressed in mourning, with her veil closely drawn.

"Mr. G——?" she said, in a low, sad voice.

I bowed, and took a place upon the sofa where she was sitting, and from which she had not risen upon my entrance.

"Pardon the great liberty I have taken," she began, after a pause of embarrassment, and in an unsteady voice. "But, I believe I have not mistaken your character for sympathy and benevolence, nor erred in believing that your hand is ever ready to respond to the generous impulses of our heart."

I bowed again, and my visitor went on.

"My object in calling upon you I will briefly state. A year ago my husband died. Up to that time I had never known the want of anything that money could buy. He was a merchant of this city, and supposed to be in good circumstances. But he left an insolvent estate; and now, with five little ones to care for, educate, and support, I have parted with nearly my last dollar, and have not a single friend to whom I can look for aid."

There was a deep earnestness and moving pathos in the tones of the woman's voice, that went to my heart. She paused for a few moments, overcome with her feelings, and then resumed:—

"One in an extremity like mine, sir, will do many things from which, under other circumstances she should shrink. This is my only excuse for troubling you at the present time. But I cannot see my little family in want without an effort to sustain them; and, with a little aid, I see my way clear to do so. I was well educated, and feel not only competent, but willing to undertake a school. There is one, the teacher of which being in bad health, wishes to give it up, and if I can get the means to buy out her establishment, will secure an ample and permanent income for my family. To aid me, sir, in doing this, I now make an appeal to you. I know you are able, and I believe you are willing to put forth your hand and save my children from want, and, it may be, separation."

The woman still remained closely veiled; I could not, therefore, see her face. But I could perceive that she was waiting with trembling suspense for my answer. Heaven knows my heart responded freely to her appeal.

"How much will it take to purchase this establishment?" I inquired.

"Only a thousand dollars," she replied.

I was silent. A thousand dollars!

"I do not wish it, sir, as a gift," she said "only as a loan. In a year or two I will be able to repay it."

"My dear madam," was my reply, "had I the ability most gladly would I meet your wishes. But, I assure you I have not. A thousand dollars taken from my business would destroy it."

A deep sigh, that was almost a groan, came up from the breast of the stranger, and her head dropped low upon her bosom. She seemed to have fully expected the relief for which she applied; and to be stricken to the earth by my words! We were both unhappy.

"May I presume to ask your name, madam?" said I, after a pause.

"It would do no good to mention it," she replied, mournfully. "It has cost me a painful effort to come to you; and now that my hope has proved, alas! in vain, I must beg the privilege of still remaining a stranger."

She arose, as she said this. Her figure was tall and dignified. Dropping me a slight courtesy, she was turning to go away, when I said,

"But, madam, even if I have not the ability to grant your request, I may still have it in my power to aid you in this matter. I am ready to do all I can; and, without doubt, among the friends of your husband will be found numbers to step forward and join in affording you the assistance so much desired, when they are made aware of your present extremity."

The lady made an impatient gesture, as if my words were felt as a mockery or an insult, and turning from me, again walked from the room with a firm step. Before I could recover myself, she had passed into the street, and I was left standing alone. To this day I have remained in ignorance of her identity. Cheerfully would I have aided her to the extent of my ability to do so. Her story touched my feelings and awakened my liveliest sympathies, and if, on learning her name and making proper inquiries into her circumstances, I had found all to be as she had stated, I would have felt it a duty to interest myself in her behalf, and have contributed in aid of the desired end to the extent of my ability. But she came to me under the false idea that I had but to put my hand in my pocket, or write a check upon the bank, and lo! a thousand dollars were forthcoming. And because I did not do this, she believed me unfeeling, selfish, and turned from me mortified, disappointed, and despairing.

I felt sad for weeks after this painful interview. On the very next morning I received a letter from an artist, in which he spoke of the extremity of his circumstances, and begged me to purchase a couple of pictures. I called at his rooms, for I could not resist his appeal. The pictures did not strike me as possessing much artistic value.

"What do you ask for them?" I inquired.

"I refused a hundred dollars for the pair. But I am compelled to part with them now, and you shall have them for eighty."

I had many other uses for eighty dollars, and therefore shook my head. But, as he looked disappointed, I offered to take one of the pictures at forty dollars. To this he agreed. I paid the money, and the picture was sent home. Some days afterward, I was showing it to a friend.

"What did you pay for it?" he asked.

"Forty dollars," I replied.

The friend smiled strangely.

"What's the matter?" said I.

"He offered it to me for twenty-five."

"That picture?"

"Yes."

"He asked me eighty for this and another, and said he had refused a hundred for the pair."

"He lied though. He thought, as you were well off, that he must ask you a good stiff price, or you wouldn't buy."

"The scoundrel!"

"He got ahead of you, certainly."

"But it's the last time," said I, angrily.

And so things went on. Scarcely a day passed in which my fame as a wealthy citizen did not subject me to some kind of experiment from people in want of money. If I employed a porter for any service and asked what was to pay, after the work was done, ten chances to one that he didn't touch his hat and reply,

"Anything that you please, sir," in the hope that I, being a rich man, would be ashamed to offer him less than about four times his regular price. Poor people in abundance called upon me for aid; and all sorts of applications to give or lend money met me at every turn. And when I, in self-defence, begged off as politely as possible, hints gentle or broad, according to the characters or feelings of those who came, touching the hardening and perverting influence of wealth, were thrown out for my especial edification.

And still the annoyance continues. Nobody but myself doubts the fact that I am worth from seventy to a hundred thousand dollars, and I am, therefore, considered allowable game for all who are too idle or prodigal to succeed in the world; or as Nature's almoner to all who are suffering from misfortunes.

Soon after the publication to which I have alluded was foisted upon our community as a veritable document, I found myself a secular dignitary in the church militant. Previously I had been only a pew-holder, and an unambitious attendant upon the Sabbath ministrations of the Rev. Mr— —. But a new field suddenly opened before me; I was a man of weight and influence, and must be used for what I was worth. It is no joke, I can assure the reader, when I tell them that the way my pocket suffered was truly alarming. I don't know, but I have seriously thought, sometimes, that if I hadn't kicked loose from my dignity, I would have been gazetted as a bankrupt long before this time.

Soon after sending in my resignation as vestryman or deacon, I will not say which, I met the Rev. Mr— —, and the way he talked to me about the earth being the "Lord's and the fullness thereof;" about our having the poor always with us; about the duties of charity, and the laying up of treasure in heaven, made me ashamed to go to church for a month to come. I really began to fear that I was a doomed man and that the reputation of being a "wealthy citizen" was going to sink me into everlasting perdition. But I am getting over that feeling now. My cash-book, ledger, and bill-book set me right again; and I can button up my coat and draw my purse-strings, when guided by the dictates of my own judgment, without a fear of the threatened final consequences before my eyes. Still, I am the subject of perpetual annoyance from all sorts of people, who will persist in believing that I am made of money; and many of these approach me in, such a way as to put it almost entirely out of my power to say "no." They come with appeals for small amounts, as loans, donations to particular charities, or as the price of articles that I do not want, but which I cannot well refuse to take. I am sure that, since I have obtained my present unenviable reputation, it hasn't cost me a cent less than two thousand, in money given away, loaned never to be returned, and in the purchase of things that I never would have thought of buying.

And, with all this, I have made more enemies than I ever before had in my life, and estranged half of my friends and acquaintances.

Seriously, I have it in contemplation to "break" one of these days, in order to satisfy the world that I am not a rich man. I see no other effectual remedy for present grievances.

"WE'VE ALL OUR ANGEL SIDE"

DESPAIR not of the better part
That lies in human kind—
A gleam of light still flickereth
In e'en the darkest mind;
The savage with his club of war,
The sage so mild and good,
Are linked in firm, eternal bonds
Of common brotherhood.
Despair not! Oh despair not, then,
For through this world so wide,
No nature is so demon-like,
But there's an angel side.

The huge rough stones from out the mine,
Unsightly and unfair,
Have veins of purest metal hid
Beneath the surface there;
Few rocks so bare but to their heights
Some tiny moss-plant clings,
And round the peaks, so desolate,
The sea-bird sits and sings.
Believe me, too, that rugged souls,
Beneath their rudeness hide
Much that is beautiful and good—
We've all our angel side.

In all there is an inner depth—
A far off, secret way,
Where, through dim windows of the soul,
God sends His smiling ray;
In every human heart there is
A faithful sounding chord,
That may be struck, unknown to us,
By some sweet loving word;
The wayward heart in vain may try
Its softer thoughts to hide,
Some unexpected tone reveals
It has its angel side.

Despised, and low, and trodden down,
Dark with the shade of sin:
Deciphering not those halo lights
Which God hath lit within;
Groping about in utmost night,
Poor prisoned souls there are,
Who guess not what life's meaning is,
Nor dream of heaven afar;
Oh! that some gentle hand of love
Their stumbling steps would guide,
And show them that, amidst it all,
Life has its angel side.

Brutal, and mean, and dark enough,
God knows, some natures are,
But He, compassionate, comes near—
And shall we stand afar?
Our cruse of oil will not grow less,

If shared with hearty hand,
And words of peace and looks of love
Few natures can withstand.
Love is the mighty conqueror—
Love is the beauteous guide—
Love, with her beaming eye, can see
We've all our angel side.

BLIND JAMES

IN the month of December, in the neighbourhood of Paris, two men, one young, the other rather advanced in years, were descending the village street, which was made uneven and almost impassable by stones and puddles.

Opposite to them, and ascending this same street, a labourer, fastened to a sort of dray laden with a cask, was slowly advancing, and beside him a little girl, of about eight years old, who was holding the end of the barrow. Suddenly the wheel went over an enormous stone, which lay in the middle of the street, and the car leaned towards the side of the child.

"The man must be intoxicated," cried the young man, stepping forward to prevent the overturn of the dray. When he reached the spot, he perceived that the man was blind.

"Blind!" said he, turning towards his old friend. But the latter, making him a sign to be silent, placed his hand, without speaking, on that of the labourer, while the little girl smiled. The blind man immediately raised his head, his sightless eyes were turned towards the two gentlemen, his face shone with an intelligent and natural pleasure, and, pressing closely the hand which held his own, he said, with an accent of tenderness,

"Mr. Desgranges!"

"How!" said the young man, moved and surprised; "he knew you by the touch of your hand."

"I do not need even that," said the blind man; "when he passes me in the street, I say to myself, 'That is his step.'" And, seizing the hand of Mr. Desgranges, he kissed it with ardour. "It was indeed you, Mr. Desgranges, who prevented my falling—always you."

"Why," said the young man, "do you expose yourself to such accidents, by dragging this cask?"

"One must attend to his business, sir," replied he, gayly.

"Your business?"

"Undoubtedly," added Mr. Desgranges. "James is our water-carrier. But I shall scold him for going out without his wife to guide him."

"My wife was gone away. I took the little girl. One must be a little energetic, must he not? And, you see, I have done very well since I last saw you, my dear Mr. Desgranges; and you have assisted me."

"Come, James, now finish serving your customers, and then you can call and see me. I am going home."

"Thank you, sir. Good-by, sir; good-by, sir."

And he started again, dragging his cask, while the child turned towards the gentlemen her rosy and smiling face.

"Blind, and a water-carrier!" repeated the young man, as they walked along.

"Ah! our James astonishes you, my young friend. Yes, it is one of those miracles like that of a paralytic who walks. Should you like to know his story?"

"Tell it to me."

"I will do so. It does not abound in facts or dramatic incidents, but it will interest you, I think, for it is the history of a soul, and of a good soul it is—a man struggling against the night. You will see the unfortunate man going step by step out of a bottomless abyss to begin his life again—to create his soul anew. You will see how a blind man, with a noble heart for a stay, makes his way even in this world."

While they were conversing, they reached the house of Mr. Desgranges, who began in this manner:—

"One morning, three years since, I was walking on a large dry plain, which separates our village from that of Noiesemont, and which is all covered with mill-stones just taken from the quarry. The process of blowing the rocks was still going on. Suddenly a violent explosion was heard. I looked. At a distance of four or five hundred paces, a gray smoke, which seemed to come from a hole, rose from the ground. Stones were then thrown up in the air, horrible cries were heard, and springing from this hole appeared a man, who began to run across the plain as if mad. He shook his arms, screamed, fell down, got up again, disappeared in the great crevices of the plain, and appeared again. The distance and the irregularity of his path prevented me from distinguishing anything clearly; but, at the height of his head, in the place of his face, I saw a great, red mark. In alarm, I approached him, while from the other side of the plain, from Noiesemont, a troop of men and women were advancing, crying aloud. I was the first to reach the poor creature. His face was all one wound, and torrents of blood were streaming over his garments, which were all in rags.

"Scarcely had I taken hold of him, when a woman, followed by twenty peasants, approached, and threw herself before him.

"'James, James, is it you? I did not know you, James.'

"The poor man, without answering, struggled furiously in our hands.

"'Ah!' cried the woman, suddenly, and with a heart-rending voice, 'it is he!'

"She had recognised a large silver pin, which fastened his shirt, which was covered with blood.

"It was indeed he, her husband, the father of three children, a poor labourer, who, in blasting a rock with powder, had received the explosion in his face, and was blind, mutilated, perhaps mortally wounded.

"He was carried home. I was obliged to go away the same day, on a journey, and was absent a month. Before my departure, I sent him our doctor, a man devoted to his profession as a country physician, and as learned as a city physician. On my return—

"'Ah! well, doctor,' said I, 'the blind man?'

"'It is all over with him. His wounds are healed, his head is doing well, he is only blind; but he will die; despair has seized him, and he will kill himself. I can do nothing more for him, This is all,' he said; 'an internal inflammation is taking place. He must die.'

"I hastened to the poor man. I arrived. I shall never forget the sight. He was seated on a wooden stool, beside a hearth on which there was no fire, his eyes covered with a white bandage. On the floor an infant of three months was sleeping; a little girl of four years old was playing in the ashes; one, still older, was shivering opposite to her; and, in front of the fireplace, seated on the disordered bed, her arms hanging down, was the wife. What was left to be imagined in this spectacle was more than met the eye. One felt that for several hours, perhaps, no word had been spoken in this room. The wife was doing nothing, and seemed to have no care to do anything. They were not merely unfortunate, they seemed like condemned persons. At the sound of my footsteps they arose, but without speaking.

"'You are the blind man of the quarry?'

"'Yes, sir.'

"'I have come to see you.'

"'Thank you, sir.'

"'You met with a sad misfortune there.'

"'Yes, sir.'

"His voice was cold, short, without any emotion. He expected nothing from any one. I pronounced the words 'assistance,' 'public compassion.'

"'Assistance!' cried his wife, suddenly, with a tone of despair; 'they ought to give it to us; they must help us; we have done nothing to bring upon us this misfortune; they will not let my children die with hunger.'

"She asked for nothing—begged for nothing. She claimed help. This imperative beggary touched me more than the common lamentations of poverty, for it was the voice of despair; and I felt in my purse for some pieces of silver.

"The man then, who had till now been silent, said, with a hollow tone,

"'Your children must die, since I can no longer see.'

"There is a strange power in the human voice. My money fell back into my purse. I was ashamed of the precarious assistance. I felt that here was a call for something more than mere almsgiving—the charity of a day. I soon formed my resolution."

"But what could you do?" said the young man, to Mr. Desgranges.

"What could I do?" replied he, with animation. "Fifteen days after, James was saved. A year after, he gained his own living, and might be heard singing at his work."

"Saved! working! singing! but how?"

"How! by very natural means. But wait, I think I hear him. I will make him tell you his simple story. It will touch you more from his lips. It will embarrass me less, and his cordial and ardent face will complete the work."

In fact, the noise of some one taking off his wooden shoes was heard at the door, and then a little tap.

"Come in, James;" and he entered with his wife,

"I have brought Juliana, my dear Mr. Desgranges, the poor woman—she must see you sometimes, must she not?"

"You did right, James. Sit down."

He came forward, pushing his stick before him, that he might not knock against a chair. He found one, and seated himself. He was young, small, vigorous, with black hair, a high and open forehead, a singularly expansive face for a blind man, and, as Rabelais says, a magnificent smile of thirty-two teeth. His wife remained standing behind him.

"James," said Mr. Desgranges to him, "here is one of my good friends, who is very desirous to see you."

"He is a good man, then, since he is your friend."

"Yes. Talk with him; I am going to see my geraniums. But do not be sad, you know I forbid you that."

"No, no, my dear friend, no!"

This tender and simple appellation seemed to charm the young man; and after the departure of his friend, approaching the blind man, he said,

"You are very fond of Mr. Desgranges?"

"Fond of him!" cried the blind man, with impetuosity; "he saved me from ruin, sir. It was all over with me; the thought of my children consumed me; I was dying because I could not see. He saved me."

"With assistance—with money?"

"Money! what is money? Everybody can give that. Yes, he clothed us, he fed us, he obtained a subscription of five hundred francs (about one hundred dollars) for me; but all this was as nothing; he did more—he cured my heart!"

"But how?"

"By his kind words, sir. Yes, he, a person of so much consequence in the world, he came every day into my poor house, he sat on my poor stool, he talked with me an hour, two hours, till I became quiet and easy."

"What did he say to you?"

"I do not know; I am but a foolish fellow, and he must tell you all he said to me; but they were things I had never heard before. He spoke to me of the good God better than a minister; and he brought sleep back to me."

"How was that?"

"It was two months since I had slept soundly. I would just doze, and then start up, saying,

"'James, you are blind,' and then my head would go round—round, like a madman; and this was killing me. One morning he came in, this dear friend, and said to me,

"'James, do you believe in God?'

"'Why do you ask that, Mr. Desgranges?'

"'Well, this night, when you wake, and the thought of your misfortune comes upon you, say aloud a prayer—then two—then three—and you will go to sleep.'"

"Yes," said the wife, with her calm voice, "the good God, He gives sleep."

"This is not all, sir. In my despair I would have killed myself. I said to myself, 'You are useless to your family, you are the woman of the house, and others support you.' But he was displeased—'Is it not you who support your family? If you had not been blind, would any one have given you the five hundred francs?'

"'That is true, Mr. Desgranges.'

"'If you were not blind, would any one provide for your children?'

"'That is true, Mr. Desgranges.'

"'If you were not blind, would every one love you, as we love you?'

"'It is true, Mr. Desgranges, it is true.'

"'You see, James, there are misfortunes in all families. Misfortune is like rain; it must fall a little on everybody. If you were not blind, your wife would, perhaps, be sick; one of your children might have died. Instead of that, you have all the misfortune, my poor man; but they—they have none.'

"'True, true.' And I began to feel less sad. I was even happy to suffer for them. And then he added,

"'Dear James, misfortune is either the greatest enemy or the greatest friend of men. There are people whom it makes wicked; there are others made better by it. For you, it must make you beloved by everybody; you must become so grateful, so affectionate, that when they wish to speak of any one who is good, they will say, good as the blind man of the Noiesemont. That will serve for a dowry to your daughter.' This is the way he talked to me, sir: and it gave me heart to be unfortunate."

"Yes; but when he was not here?"

"Ah, when he was not here, I had, to be sure, some heavy moments. I thought of my eyes—the light is so beautiful! Oh, God! cried I, in anguish, if ever I should see clearly again, I would get up at three o'clock in the morning, and I would, not go to bed till ten at night, that I might gather up more light."

"James, James!" said his wife.

"You are right, Juliana; he has forbidden me to be sad. He would perceive it, sir. Do you think that when my head had gone wrong in the night, and he came in the morning, and merely looked at me, he would say—'James, you have been thinking that;' and then he would scold me, this dear friend. Yes," added he, with an expression of joy—"he would scold me, and that would give me pleasure, because he tried to make his words cross, but he could not do it."

"And what gave you the idea of becoming a water-carrier?"

"He gave me that, also. Do you suppose I have ideas? I began to lose my grief, but my time hung heavy on my hands. At thirty-two years old, to be sitting all day in a chair! He then began to instruct me, as he said, and he told me beautiful stories. The Bible—the history of an old man, blind like me, named Tobias; the history of Joseph; the history of David; the history of Jesus Christ. And then he made me repeat them after him. But my head, it was hard—it was hard; it was not used to learning, and I was always getting tired in my arms and my legs."

"And he tormented us to death," said his wife, laughing.

"True, true," replied he, laughing also; "I became cross. He came again, and said,

"'James, you must go to work.'

"I showed him my poor, burned hands.

"'It is no matter; I have bought you a capital in trade.'

"'Me, Mr. Desgranges?'

"'Yes, James, a capital into which they never put goods, and where they always find them.'

"'It must have cost you a great deal, sir.'

"'Nothing at all, my lad.'

"'What is then this fund?'

"'The river.'

"'The river? Do you wish me to become a fisherman?'

"'Not all; a water-carrier.'

"'Water-carrier! but eyes?'

"'Eyes; of what use are they? do the dray-horses have eyes? If they do, they make use of them; if they do not, they do without them. Come, you must be a water-carrier.'

"'But a cask?'

"'I will give you one.'

"'A cart?'

"'I have ordered one at the cart-maker's.'

Friends and Neighbors | 131

"'But customers?'

"I will give you my custom, to begin with, eighteen francs a month; (my dear friend pays for water as dearly as for wine.) Moreover, you have nothing to say, either yes or no. I have dismissed my water-carrier, and you would not let my wife and me die with thirst. This dear Madame Desgranges, just think of it. And so, my boy, in three days—work. And you, Madam James, come here;' and he carried off Juliana."

"Yes, sir," continued the wife, "he carried me off, ordered leather straps, made me buy the wheels, harnessed me; we were all astonishment, James and I; but stop, if you can, when Mr. Desgranges drives you. At the end of three days, here we are with the cask, he harnessed and drawing it, I behind, pushing; we were ashamed at crossing the village, as if we were doing something wrong; it seemed as if everybody would laugh at us. But Mr. Desgranges was there in the street.

"'Come on, James,' said he, 'courage.'

"We came along, and in the evening he put into our hands a piece of money, saying," continued the blind man, with emotion—

"'James, here are twenty sous you have earned to-day.'

"Earned, sir, think of that! earned, it was fifteen months that I had only eaten what had been given to me. It is good to receive from good people, it is true; but the bread that one earns, it is as we say, half corn, half barley; it nourishes better, and then it was done, I was no longer the woman, I was a labourer—a labourer—James earned his living."

A sort of pride shone from his face.

"How!" said the young man, "was your cask sufficient to support you?"

"Not alone, sir; but I have still another profession."

"Another profession!"

"Ha, ha, yes, sir; the river always runs, except when it is frozen, and, as Mr. Desgranges says, 'water-carriers do not make their fortune with ice,' so he gave me a Winter trade and Summer trade."

"Winter trade!"

Mr. Desgranges returned at this moment—James heard him—"Is it not true, Mr. Desgranges, that I have another trade besides that of water-carrier?"

"Undoubtedly."

"What is it then?"

"Wood-sawyer."

"Wood-sawyer? impossible; how could you measure the length of the sticks? how could you cut wood without cutting yourself?"

"Cut myself, sir," replied the blind man, with a pleasant shade of confidence; "I formerly was a woodsawyer, and the saw knows me well; and then one learns everything—I go to school, indeed. They put a pile of wood at my left side, my saw and saw horse before me, a stick that is to be sawed in three; I take a thread, I cut it the size of the third of the stick—this is the measure. Every place I saw, I try it, and so it goes on till now there is nothing burned or drunk in the village without calling upon me."

"Without mentioning," added Mr. Desgranges, "that he is a commissioner."

"A commissioner!" said the young man, still more surprised.

"Yes, sir, when there is an errand to be done at Melun, I put my little girl on my back, and then off I go. She sees for me, I walk for her; those who meet me, say, 'Here is a gentleman who carries his eyes very high;' to which I answer, 'that is so I may see the farther.' And then at night I have twenty sous more to bring home."

"But are you not afraid of stumbling against the stones?"

"I lift my feet pretty high; and then I am used to it; I come from Noiesemont here all alone."

"All alone! how do you find your way?"

"I find the course of the wind as I leave home, and this takes the place of the sun with me."

"But the holes?"

"I know them all."

"And the walls?"

"I feel them. When I approach anything thick, sir, the air comes with less force upon my face; it is but now and then that I get a hard knock, as by example, if sometimes a little handcart is left on the road, I do not suspect it—whack! bad for you, poor five-and-thirty, but this is soon over. It is only when I get bewildered, as I did day before yesterday. O then—-"

"You have not told me of that, James," said Mr. Desgranges.

"I was, however, somewhat embarrassed, my dear friend. While I was here the wind changed, I did not perceive it; but at the end of a quarter of an hour, when I had reached the plain of Noiesemont, I had lost my way, and I felt so bewildered that I did not dare to stir a step. You know the plain, not a house, no passersby. I sat down on the ground, I listened; after a moment I heard at, as I supposed, about two hundred paces distant, a noise of running water. I said, 'If this should be the stream which is at the bottom of the plain?' I went feeling along on the side from which the noise came—I reached the stream; then I reasoned in this way: the water comes down from the side of Noiesemont and crosses it. I put in my hand to feel the current."

"Bravo, James."

"Yes, but the water was so low and the current so small, that my hand felt nothing. I put in the end of my stick, it was not moved. I rubbed my head finally, I said, 'I am a fool, here is my handkerchief;' I took it, I fastened it to the end of my cane. Soon I felt that it moved gently to the right, very gently. Noiesemont is on the right. I started again and I get home to Juliana, who began to be uneasy."

"O," cried the young man, "this is admir——"

But Mr. Desgranges stopped him, and leading him to the other end of the room,

"Silence!" said he to him in a low voice. "Not admirable—do not corrupt by pride the simplicity of this man. Look at him, see how tranquil his face is, how calm after this recital which has moved you so much. He is ignorant of himself, do not spoil him."

"It is so touching," said the young man, in a low tone.

"Undoubtedly, and still his superiority does not lie there. A thousand blind men have found out these ingenious resources, a thousand will find them again; but this moral perfection—this heart, which opens itself so readily to elevated consolations—this heart which so willingly takes upon it the part of a victim—this heart which has restored him to life. For do not be deceived, it is not I who have saved him, it is his affection for me; his ardent gratitude has filled his whole soul, and has sustained—he has lived because he has loved!"

At that moment, James, who had remained at the other end of the room, and who perceived that we were speaking low, got up softly, and with a delicate discretion, said to his wife,

"We will go away without making any noise."

"Are you going, James?"

"I am in the way, my dear Mr. Desgranges."

"No, pray stay longer."

His benefactor retained him, reaching out to him cordially his hand. The blind man seized the hand in his turn, and pressed it warmly against his heart.

"My dear friend, my dear good friend, you permit me to stay a little longer. How glad I am to find myself near you. When I am sad I say—'James, the good God will, perhaps, of His mercy, put you in the same paradise with Mr. Desgranges,' and that does me good."

The young man smiled at this simple tenderness, which believed in a hierarchy in Heaven. James heard him.

"You smile, sir. But this good man has re-created James. I dream of it every night—I have never seen him, but I shall know him then. Oh my God, if I recover my sight I will look at him for ever—for ever, like the light, till he shall say to me, James, go away. But he will not say so, he is too good. If I had known him four years ago, I would have served him, and never have left him."

"James, James!" said Mr. Desgranges; but the poor man could not be silenced.

"It is enough to know he is in the village; this makes my heart easy. I do not always wish to come in, but I pass before his house, it is always there; and when he is gone a journey I make Juliana lead me into the plain of Noiesemont, and I say—'turn me towards the place where he is gone, that I may breathe the same air with him.'"

Mr. Desgranges put his hand before his mouth. James stopped.

"You are right, Mr. Desgranges, my mouth is rude, it is only my heart which is right. Come, wife," said he, gayly, and drying his great tears which rolled from his eyes, "Come, we must give our children their supper. Good-by, my dear friend, good-by, sir."

He went away, moving his staff before him. Just as he laid his hand upon the door, Mr. Desgranges called him back.

"I want to tell you a piece of news which will give you pleasure. I was going to leave the village this year; but I have just taken a new lease of five years of my landlady."

"Do you see, Juliana," said James to his wife, turning round, "I was right when I said he was going away."

"How," replied Mr. Desgranges, "I had told them not to tell you of it."

"Yes; but here," putting his hand on his heart, "everything is plain here. I heard about a month since, some little words, which had begun to make my head turn round; when, last Sunday, your landlady called me to her, and showed me more kindness than usual, promising me that she would take care of me, and that she would never abandon me. When I came home, I said to Juliana, 'Wife, Mr. Desgranges is going to quit the village; but that lady has consoled me.'"

In a few moments the blind man had returned to his home.

DEPENDENCE

"WELL, Mary," said Aunt Frances, "how do you propose to spend the summer? It is so long since the failure and death of your guardian, that I suppose you are now familiar with your position, and prepared to mark out some course for the future."

"True, aunt; I have had many painful thoughts with regard to the loss of my fortune, and I was for a time in great uncertainty about my future course, but a kind offer, which I received, yesterday, has removed that burden. I now know where to find a respectable and pleasant home."

"Is the offer you speak of one of marriage?" asked Aunt Frances, smiling.

"Oh! dear, no; I am too young for that yet. But Cousin Kate is happily married, and lives a few miles out of the city, in just the cosiest little spot, only a little too retired; and she has persuaded me that I shall do her a great kindness to accept a home with her."

"Let me see. Kate's husband is not wealthy, I believe?"

"No: Charles Howard is not wealthy, but his business is very good, and improving every year; and both he and Kate are too whole-souled and generous to regret giving an asylum to an unfortunate girl like me. They feel that 'it is more blessed to give than to receive.'"

"A very noble feeling, Mary; but one in which I am sorry to perceive that you are a little wanting."

"Oh! no, Aunt Frances, I do feel it deeply; but it is the curse of poverty that one must give up, in some measure, the power of benefiting others. And, then, I mean to beguile Kate of so many lonely hours, and perform so many friendly offices for her husband, that they will think me not a burden but a treasure."

"And you really think you can give them as much comfort as the expense of your maintenance could procure them in any other way?"

"Yes, aunt; it may sound conceited, perhaps, but I do really think I can. I am sure, if I thought otherwise, I would never consent to become a burden to them."

"Well, my dear, then your own interest is all that remains to be considered. There are few blessings in life that can compensate for the loss of self-reliance. She who derives her support from persons upon whom she has no natural claim, finds the effect upon herself to be decidedly narrowing. Perpetually in debt, without the means of reimbursement, barred from any generous action which does not seem like 'robbing Peter to pay Paul,' she sinks too often into the character of a sponge, whose only business is absorption. But I see you do not like what I am saying, and I will tell you something which I am sure you *will* like—my own veritable history.

"I was left an orphan in childhood, like yourself, and when my father's affairs were settled, not a dollar remained for my support. I was only six years of age, but I had attracted the notice of a distant relative, who was a man of considerable wealth. Without any effort of my own, I became an inmate of his family, and his only son, a few years my elder, was taught to consider me as a sister.

"George Somers was a generous, kind-hearted boy, and I believe he was none the less fond of me, because I was likely to rob him of half his fortune. Mr. Somers often spoke of making a will, in which I was to share equally with his son in the division of his property, but a natural reluctance to so grave a task led him to defer it from one year to another. Meantime, I was sent to expensive schools, and was as idle and superficial as any heiress in the land.

"I was just sixteen when my kind benefactor suddenly perished on board the ill-fated Lexington, and, as he died without a will, I had no legal claim to any farther favours. But George Somers was known as a very open-handed youth, upright and honourable, and, as he was perfectly well acquainted with the wishes of his father, I felt no fears with regard to my pecuniary condition. While yet overwhelmed with grief at the loss of one whom my heart called father, I received a very kind and sympathizing letter from George, in which he said he thought I had better remain at school for another year, as had been originally intended.

"'Of course,' he added, 'the death of my father does not alter our relation in the least; you are still my dear and only sister.'

"And, in compliance with his wishes, I passed another year at a very fashionable school—a year of girlish frivolity, in which my last chance of acquiring knowledge as a means of future independence was wholly thrown away. Before the close of this year I received another letter from George, which somewhat surprised, but did not at all dishearten me. It was, in substance, as follows:—

"'MY own dear Sister:—I wrote you, some months ago, from Savannah, in Georgia told you how much I was delighted with the place and people; how charmed with Southern frankness and hospitality. But I did not tell you that I had there met with positively the most bewitching creature in the world—for I was but a timid lover, and feared that, as the song says, the course of true love never would run smooth. My charming Laura was a considerable heiress, and, although no sordid considerations ever had a feather's weight upon her own preferences, of course, yet her father was naturally and very properly anxious that the guardian of so fair a flower should be able to shield it from the biting winds of poverty. Indeed, I had some difficulty in satisfying his wishes on this point, and in order to do so, I will frankly own that I assumed to myself the unencumbered possession of my father's estate, of which so large a share belongs of right to you. I am confident that when you know my Laura you will forgive me this merely nominal injustice. Of course, this connexion can make no sort of difference in your rights and expectations. You will always have a home at my house. Laura is delighted, with the idea of such a companion, and says she would on no account dispense with that arrangement. And whenever, you marry as girls do and will, I shall hold myself bound to satisfy any reasonable wishes on the part of the happy youth that wins you. Circumstances hastened my marriage somewhat unexpectedly, or I should certainly have informed you previously, and requested your presence at the nuptial ceremony. We have secured a beautiful house in Brooklyn, and shall expect you to join us as soon as your present year expires, Laura sends her kindest regards, and I remain, as always, your sincere and affectionate brother, GEORGE SOMERS.'

"Not long after the receipt of this letter, one of the instructresses, in the institution where I resided requested the favour of a private interview. She then said she knew something generally of my position and prospects, and, as she had always felt an instinctive interest in my fortunes, she could not see me leave the place without seeking my confidence, and rendering me aid, if aid was in her power. Though surprised and, to say the truth, indignant, I simply inquired what views, had occurred to her with regard to my future life.

"She said, then, very kindly, that although I was not very thorough in, any branch of study, yet she thought I had a decided taste for the lighter and more ornamental parts of female education. That a few months earnest attention to these would fit me for a position independent of my connexions, and one of which none of my friends would have cause to be ashamed.

"I am deeply pained to own to you how I answered her. Drawing myself up, I said, coldly,

"'I am obliged to you, madam, for your quite unsolicited interest in my affairs. When I leave this place, it will be to join my brother and sister in Brooklyn, and, as we are all reasonably wealthy, I must try to make gold varnish over any defects in my neglected education.'

"I looked to see my kind adviser entirely annihilated by these imposing words, but she answered with perfect calmness,

"'I know Laura Wentworth, now Mrs. Somers. She was educated at the North, and was a pupil of my own for a year. She is wealthy and beautiful, and I hope you will never have cause to regret assuming a position with regard to her that might be mistaken for dependence.'

"With these words, my well-meaning, but perhaps injudicious friend, took leave, and I burst into a mocking laugh, that I hoped she might linger long enough to hear. 'This is too good!' I repeated to myself—but I could not feel perfectly at ease. However, I soon forgot all thoughts of the future, in the present duties of scribbling in fifty albums, and exchanging keepsakes, tears, and kisses, with a like number of *very* intimate friends.

"It was not until I had finally left school, and was fairly on the way to the home of my brother, that I found a moment's leisure to think seriously of the life that was before me. I confess that I felt some secret misgivings, as I stood at last upon the steps of the very elegant house that was to be my future home. The servant who obeyed my summons, inquired if I was Miss Rankin, a name I had never borne since childhood.

"I was about to reply in the negative, when she added, 'If you are the young lady that Mr. Somers is expecting from the seminary, I will show you to your room.'

"I followed mechanically, and was left in a very pretty chamber, with the information that Mrs. Somers was a little indisposed, but would meet me at dinner. The maid added that Mr. Somers was out of town, and would not return till evening. After a very uncomfortable hour, during which I resolutely suspended my opinion with regard to my position, the dinner-bell rang, and the domestic again appeared to show me to the dining-room.

"Mrs. Somers met me with extended hand. 'My dear Miss Rankin!' she exclaimed, 'I am most happy to see you. I have heard George speak of you so often and so warmly that I consider you quite as a relative. Come directly to the table. I am sure you must be famished after your long ride. I hope you will make yourself one of us, at once, and let me call you Fanny. May I call you Cousin Fanny?' she pursued, with an air of sweet condescension that was meant to be irresistible.

"'As you please,' I replied coldly.

"To which she quickly responded, 'Oh, that will be delightful.'

"She then turned to superintend the carving of a fowl, and I had time to look at her undisturbed. She was tall and finely formed, with small delicate features, and an exquisite grace in every movement; a haughty sweetness that was perfectly indescribable. She had very beautiful teeth, which she showed liberally when she smiled, and in her graver moments her slight features wore an imperturbable serenity, as if the round world contained nothing that was really worth her attention. An animated statue, cold, polished, and pitiless! was my inward thought, as I bent over my dinner.

"When the meal was over, Mrs. Somers said to me, in a tone of playful authority,

"'Now, Cousin Fanny, I want you to go to your room and rest, and not do an earthly thing until teatime. After that I have a thousand things to show you.'

"At night I was accordingly shown a great part of the house; a costly residence, and exquisitely furnished, but, alas! I already wearied of this icy splendour. Every smile of my beautiful hostess (I could not now call her sister), every tone of her soft voice, every movement of her superb form, half queen-like dignity, half fawn-like grace—seemed to place an insurmountable barrier between herself and me. It was not that I thought more humbly of myself—not that I did not even consider myself her equal—but her dainty blandishments were a delicate frost-work, that almost made me shiver and when, she touched her cool lips to mine, and said 'Good-night, dear,' I felt as if even then separated from her real, living self, by a wall of freezing marble.

"'Poor George!' I said, as I retired to rest—'You have wedded this soulless woman, and she will wind you round her finger.'

"I did not sit up for him, for he was detained till a late hour, but I obeyed the breakfast-bell with unfashionable eagerness, as I was becoming nervous about our meeting, and really anxious to have it over. After a delay of some minutes, I heard the wedded pair coming leisurely down the stairs, in, very amicable chatter.

"'I am glad you like her, Laura,' said a voice which I knew in a moment as that of George. How I shivered as I caught the smooth reply, 'A nice little thing. I am very glad of the connexion. It will be such a relief not to rely entirely upon servants. There should be a middle class in every family.'

"With these words she glided through the door, looked with perfect calmness in my flashing eyes, and said,

"'Ah, Fanny! I, was just telling George here how much I shall like you.'

"The husband came forward with an embarrassed air; I strove to meet him with dignity, but my heart failed me, and I burst into tears.

"'Forgive me, madam,' I said, on regaining my composure—'This is our first meeting since the death of *our father*.'

"'I understand your feelings perfectly,' she quietly replied. 'My father knew the late Mr. Somers well, and thought very highly of him, He was charitable to a fault, and yet remarkable for discernment. His bounty was seldom unworthily bestowed.'

"His bounty! I had never been thought easy to intimidate, but I quailed before this unapproachable ice-berg. It made no attempt from that moment to vindicate what I was pleased to call my rights, but awaited passively the progress of events.

"After breakfast, Mrs. Somers said to the maid in attendance,

"'Dorothy, bring some hot water and towels for Miss Rankin.'

"She then turned to me and continued, 'I shall feel the china perfectly safe in your hands, cousin. These servants are so very unreliable.'

"And she followed George to the parlour above, where their lively tones and light laughter made agreeable music.

"In the same easy way, I was invested with a variety of domestic cares, most of them such as I would willingly have accepted, had she waited for me to manifest such a willingness. But a few days after my arrival, we received a visit from little Ella Grey, a cousin of Laura's, who was taken seriously ill on the first evening of her stay. A physician was promptly summoned, and, after a conference with him, Mrs. Somers came to me, inquiring earnestly,

"'Cousin Fanny, have you ever had the measles?'

"I replied in the affirmative.

"'Oh, I am very glad!' was her response; 'for little Ella is attacked with them, and very severely; but, if you will take charge of her, I shall feel no anxiety. It is dreadful in sickness to be obliged to depend upon hirelings.'

"So I was duly installed as little Ella's nurse, and, as she was a spoiled child, my task was neither easy nor agreeable.

"No sooner was the whining little creature sufficiently improved to be taken to her own home, than the house was thrown into confusion by preparations for a brilliant party. Laura took me with her on a shopping excursion, and bade me select whatever I wished, and send the bill with hers to Mr. Somers. I purchased a few indispensable articles, but I felt embarrassed by her calm, scrutinizing gaze, and by the consciousness that every item of my expenditures would be scanned by, perhaps, censorious eyes.

"What with my previous fatigue while acting as Ella's nurse, and the laborious preparations for the approaching festival, I felt, as the time drew near, completely exhausted. Yet I was determined not to so far give way to the depressing influences that surrounded me, as to absent myself from the party. So, after snatching an interval of rest, to relieve my aching head, I dressed myself with unusual care, and repaired to the brilliantly lighted rooms. They were already filled, and murmuring like a swarm of bees, although, as one of the guests remarked, there were more drones than workers in the hive. I was now no drone, certainly, and that was some consolation. When I entered, Laura was conversing with a group of dashing young men, who were blundering over a book of charades. Seeing me enter, she came towards me immediately.

"'Cousin Fanny, you who help everybody, I want you to come to the aid of these stupid young men. Gentlemen, this is our Cousin Fanny, the very best creature in the world.' And with this introduction she left me, and turned to greet some new arrivals. After discussing the charades till my ears were weary of empty and aimless chatter, I was very glad to find my group of young men gradually dispersing, and myself at liberty to look about me, undisturbed. George soon came to me, gave me his arm, and took me to a room where were several ladies, friends of his father, and who had known me very well as a child.

"'You remember Fanny,' he said to them; and then left me, and devoted himself to the courteous duties of the hour. While I was indulging in a quiet chat with a very kind old friend, she proposed to go with me to look at the dancers, as the music was remarkably fine, and it was thought the collected beauty and fashion of the evening would make a very brilliant show. We left our seats, accordingly, but were soon engaged in the crowd, and while waiting for an opportunity to move on, I heard one of my young men ask another,

"'How do you like *la cousine*?'

"I lost a part of the answer, but heard the closing words distinctly—'*et un peu passee.*' '*Oui, decidement!*' was the prompt response, and a light laugh followed, while, shrinking close to my kind friend, I rejoiced that my short stature concealed me from observation. I was not very well taught, but, like most school-girls, I had a smattering of French, and I knew the meaning of the very ordinary phrases that had been used with regard to me. Before the supper-hour, my headache became so severe that I was glad to take refuge in my own room. There I consulted my mirror, and felt disposed to forgive, the young critics for their disparaging remarks. *Passee!* I looked twenty-five at least, and yet I was not eighteen, and six months before I had fancied myself a beauty and an heiress!

"But I will not weary you with details. Suffice it to say; that I spent only three months of this kind of life, and then relinquished the protection of Mr. and Mrs. Somers, and removed to a second-rate boarding-house, where I attempted to maintain myself by giving lessons in music. Every day, however, convinced me of my unfitness for this task, and, as I soon felt an interest in the sweet little girls who looked up to me for instruction, my position with regard to them became truly embarrassing. One day I had been wearying myself by attempting the impossible task of making clear to another mind, ideas that lay confusedly in my own, and at last I said to my pupil,

"'You may go home now, Clara, dear, and practise the lesson of yesterday. I am really ill to-day, but to-morrow I shall feel better, and I hope I shall then be able to make you understand me.'

"The child glided out, but a shadow still fell across the carpet. I looked up, and saw in the doorway a young man, whose eccentricities sometimes excited a smile among his fellow-boarders, but who was much respected for his sense and independence.

"'To make yourself understood by others, you must first learn to understand yourself,' said he, as he came forward. Then, taking my hand, he continued,—'What if you should give up all this abortive labour, take a new pupil, and, instead of imparting to others what you have not very firmly grasped yourself, try if you can make a human being of me?'

"I looked into his large gray eyes, and saw the truth and earnestness shining in their depths, like pebbles at the bottom of a pellucid spring. I never once thought of giving him a conventional reply. On the contrary, I stammered out,

"'I am full, of faults and errors; I could never do you any good.'

"'I have studied your character attentively,' returned he, 'and I know you have faults, but they are unlike mine; and I think that you might be of great service to me; or, if the expression suits you better, that we might be of great aid to each other. Become my wife, and I will promise to improve more rapidly than any pupil in your class.'

"And I did become his wife, but not until a much longer acquaintance had convinced me, that in so doing, I should not exchange one form of dependence for another, more galling and more hopeless."

"Then this eccentric young man was Uncle Robert?"

"Precisely. But you see he has made great improvement, since."

"Well, Aunt Frances, I thank you for your story; and now for the moral. What do you think I had better do?"

"I will tell you what you can do, if you choose. Your uncle has just returned from a visit to his mother. He finds her a mere child, gentle and amiable, but wholly unfit to take charge of herself. Her clothes have taken fire repeatedly, from her want of judgment with regard to fuel and lights, and she needs a companion for every moment of the day. This, with their present family, is impossible, and they are desirous to secure some one who will devote herself to your grandmother during the hours when your aunt and the domestics are necessarily engaged. You were always a favourite there, and I know they would be very much relieved if you would take this office for a time, but they feel a delicacy in making any such proposal. You can have all your favourites about you—books, flowers, and piano; for the dear old lady delights to hear reading or music, and will sit for hours with a vacant smile upon her pale, faded face. Then your afternoons will be entirely your own, and Robert is empowered to pay any reliable person a salary of a fixed and ample amount, which will make you independent for the time."

"But, aunt, you will laugh at me, I know, yet I do really fear that Kate will feel this arrangement as a disappointment."

"Suppose I send her a note, stating that you have given me some encouragement of assuming this important duty, but that you could not think of deciding without showing a grateful deference to her wishes?"

"That will be just the thing. We shall get a reply to-morrow." With to-morrow came the following note:—

"*My Dear Aunt Frances:*—Your favour of yesterday took us a little by surprise, I must own I had promised myself a great deal of pleasure in the society of our Mary; but since she is inclined (and I think it is very noble in her) to foster with the dew of her youth the graceful but fallen stem that lent beauty to us all, I cannot say a word to prevent it. Indeed, it has occurred to me, since the receipt of your note, that we shall need the room we had reserved for Mary, to accommodate little Willie, Mr. Howard's pet nephew, who has the misfortune to be lame. His physicians insist upon country air, and a room upon the first floor. So tell Mary I love her a thousand times better for her self-sacrifice, and will try to imitate it by doing all in my power for the poor little invalid that is coming.

"With the kindest regards, I remain

"Your affectionate niece,

"KATE HOWARD."

"Are you now decided, Mary?" asked Aunt Frances, after their joint perusal of the letter.

"Not only decided, but grateful. I have lost my fortune, it is true; but while youth and health remain, I shall hardly feel tempted to taste the luxuries of dependence."

TWO RIDES WITH THE DOCTOR

JUMP in, if you would ride with the doctor. You have no time to lose, for the patient horse, thankful for the unusual blessing which he has enjoyed in obtaining a good night's rest, stands early at the door this rainy morning, and the worthy doctor himself is already in his seat, and is hastily gathering up the reins, for there have been no less than six rings at his bell within as many minutes, and immediate attendance is requested in several different places.

It is not exactly the day one might select for a ride, for the storm is a regular north-easter, and your hands and feet are benumbed with the piercing cold wind, while you are drenched with the driving rain.

But the doctor is used to all this, and, unmindful of wind and rain, he urges his faithful horse to his utmost speed, eager to reach the spot where the most pressing duty calls. He has at least the satisfaction of being welcome. Anxious eyes are watching for his well-known vehicle from the window; the door is opened ere he puts his hand upon the lock, and the heartfelt exclamation,

"Oh, doctor, I am so thankful you have come!" greets him as he enters.

Hastily the anxious father leads the way to the room where his half-distracted wife is bending in agony over their first-born, a lovely infant of some ten months, who is now in strong convulsions. The mother clasps her hands, and raises her eyes in gratitude to heaven, as the doctor enters,-he is her only earthly hope. Prompt and efficient remedies are resorted to, and in an hour the restored little one is sleeping tranquilly in his mother's arms.

The doctor departs amid a shower of blessings, and again urging his horse to speed, reaches his second place of destination. It is a stately mansion. A spruce waiter hastens to answer his ring, but the lady herself meets him as he enters the hall.

"We have been expecting you anxiously, doctor. Mr. Palmer is quite ill, this morning. Walk up, if you please."

The doctor obeys, and is eagerly welcomed by his patient.

"Do exert your utmost skill to save me from a fever, doctor. The symptoms are much the same which I experienced last year, previous to that long siege with the typhoid. It distracts me to think of it. At this particular juncture I should lose thousands by absence from my business."

The doctor's feelings are enlisted,—his feelings of humanity and his feelings of self-interest, for doctors must live as well as other people; and the thought of the round sum which would find its way to his own purse, if he could but succeed in preventing the loss of thousands to his patient, was by no means unpleasing.

The most careful examination of the symptoms is made, and well-chosen prescriptions given. He is requested to call as often as possible through the day, which he readily promises to do, although press of business and a pouring rain render it somewhat difficult.

The result, however, will be favourable to his wishes. His second and third call give him great encouragement, and on the second day after the attack, the merchant returns to his counting-room exulting in the skill of his physician.

But we must resume our ride. On, on goes the doctor; rain pouring, wind blowing, mud splashing. Ever and anon he checks his horse's speed, at his various posts of duty. High and low, rich and poor anxiously await his coming. He may not shrink from the ghastly spectacle of human suffering and death. Humanity, in its most loathsome forms, is presented to him.

The nearest and dearest may turn away in grief and horror, but the doctor blenches not.

Again we are digressing. The doctor's well-known tap is heard at the door of a sick-room, where for many days he has been in constant attendance. Noiselessly he is admitted. The young husband kneels at the side of the bed where lies his dearest earthly treasure. The calm but deeply-afflicted mother advances to the doctor, and whispers fearfully low,

"There is a change. She sleeps. Is it—oh! can it be the sleep of death?"

Quickly the physician is at the bedside, and anxiously bending over his patient.

Another moment and he grasps the husband's hand, while the glad words "She will live," burst from his lips.

We may not picture forth their joy. On, on, we are riding with the doctor. Once more we are at his own door. Hastily he enters, and takes up the slate containing the list of calls during his absence. At half a dozen places his presence is requested without delay.

A quick step is heard on the stairs, and his gentle wife hastens to welcome him.

"I am so glad you have come; how wet you must be!"

The parlour door is thrown open. What a cheerful fire, and how inviting look the dressing-gown and the nicely warmed slippers!

"Take off your wet clothes, dear; dinner will soon be ready," urges the wife.

"It is impossible, Mary. There are several places to visit yet. Nay, never look so sad. Have not six years taught you what a doctor's wife must expect?"

"I shall never feel easy when you are working so hard, Henry; but surely you will take a cup of hot coffee; I have it all ready. It will delay you but a moment."

The doctor consents; and while the coffee is preparing, childish voices are heard, and little feet come quickly through the hall.

"Papa has come home!" shouts a manly little fellow of four years, as he almost drags his younger sister to the spot where he has heard his father's voice.

The father's heart is gladdened by their innocent joy, as they cling around him; but there is no time for delay. A kiss to each, one good jump for the baby, the cup of coffee is hastily swallowed, the wife receives her embrace with tearful eyes, and as the doctor springs quickly into his chaise, and wheels around the corner, she sighs deeply as she looks at the dressing-gown and slippers, and thinks of the favourite dish which she had prepared for dinner; and now it may be night before he comes again. But she becomes more cheerful as she remembers that a less busy season will come, and then they will enjoy the recompense of this hard labour.

The day wears away, and at length comes the happy hour when gown and slippers may be brought into requisition. The storm still rages without, but there is quiet happiness within. The babies are sleeping, and father and mother are in that snug little parlour, with its bright light and cheerful fire. The husband is not too weary to read aloud, and the wife listens, while her hands are busied with woman's never-ending work.

But their happiness is of short duration. A loud ring at the bell.

"Patient in the office, sir," announces the attendant.

The doctor utters a half-impatient exclamation; but the wife expresses only thankfulness that it is an office patient.

"Fine night for a sick person to come out!" muttered the doctor, as he unwillingly lays down his book, and rises from the comfortable lounge.

But he is himself again by the time his hand is on the door of the office, and it is with real interest that he greets his patient.

"Tooth to be extracted? Sit down, sir. Here, Biddy, bring water and a brighter lamp. Have courage, sir; one moment will end it."

The hall door closes on the relieved sufferer, and the doctor throws himself again on the lounge, and smilingly puts the bright half dollar in his pocket.

"That was not so bad, after all, Mary. I like to make fifty cents in that way."

"Cruel creature! Do not mention it."

"Cruel! The poor man blessed me in his heart. Did I not relieve him from the most intense suffering?"

"Well, never mind. I hope there will be no more calls to-night."

"So do I. Where is the book? I will read again." No more interruptions. Another hour, and all, are sleeping quietly.

Midnight has passed, when the sound of the bell falls on the doctor's wakeful ear. As quickly as possible he answers it in person, but another peal is heard ere he reaches the door.

A gentleman to whose family he has frequently been called, appears.

"Oh! doctor, lose not a moment; my little Willie is dying with the croup!"

There is no resisting this appeal. The still wet overcoat and boots are drawn on; medicine case hastily seized, and the doctor rushes forth again into the storm.

Pity for his faithful horse induces him to traverse the distance on foot, and a rapid walk of half a mile brings him to the house.

It was no needless alarm. The attack was a severe one, and all his skill was required to save the life of the little one. It was daylight ere he could leave him with safety. Then, as he was about departing for his own home, an express messenger arrived to entreat him to go immediately to another place nearly a mile in an opposite direction.

Breakfast was over ere he reached his own house. His thoughtful wife suggested a nap; but a glance at the already well-filled slate showed this to be out of the question. A hasty toilet, and still hastier breakfast, and the doctor is again seated in his chaise, going on his accustomed rounds; but we will not now accompany him.

Let us pass over two or three months, and invite ourselves to another ride. One pleasant morning, when less pressed with business, he walks leisurely from the house to the chaise, and gathering up the reins with a remarkably thoughtful air, rides slowly down the street.

But few patients are on his list, and these are first attended to.

The doctor then pauses for consideration. He has set apart this day for *collecting*. Past experience has taught him that the task is by no means an agreeable one. It is necessary, however—absolutely so—for, as we have said before, doctors must live as well as other people; their house-rent must be paid, food and clothing must be supplied.

A moment only pauses the doctor, and then we are again moving onward. A short ride brings us to the door of a pleasantly-situated house. We remember it well. It is where the little one lay in fits when we last rode out with the doctor. We recall the scene: the convulsed countenance of the child; the despair of the parents, and the happiness which succeeded when their beloved one was restored to them.

Surely they will now welcome the doctor. Thankfully will they pay the paltry sum he claims as a recompense for his services. We are more confident than the doctor. Experience is a sure teacher. The door does not now fly open at his approach. He gives his name to the girl who answers the bell, and in due time the lady of the house appears.

"Ah! doctor, how do you do? You are quite a stranger! Delightful weather," &c.

The doctor replies politely, and inquires if her husband is in.

"Yes, he is in; but I regret to say he is exceedingly engaged this morning. His business is frequently of a nature which cannot suffer interruption. He would have been pleased to have seen you."

The doctor's pocket-book is produced, and the neatly drawn bill is presented.

"If convenient to Mr. Lawton, the amount would be acceptable."

"I will hand it to him when he is at leisure. He will attend to it, no doubt."

The doctor sighs involuntarily as he recalls similar indefinite promises; but it is impossible to insist upon interrupting important business. He ventures another remark, implying that prompt payment would oblige him; bows, and retires.

On, on goes the faithful horse. Where is to be our next stopping-place? At the wealthy merchant's, who owed so much to the doctor's skill some two months since. Even the doctor feels confidence here. Thousands saved by the prevention of that fever. Thirty dollars is not to be thought of in comparison.

All is favourable. Mr. Palmer is at home, and receives his visiter in a cordial manner. Compliments are passed. Now for the bill.

"Our little account, Mr. Palmer."

"Ah! I recollect; I am a trifle in your debt. Let us see: thirty dollars! So much? I had forgotten that we had needed medical advice, excepting in my slight indisposition a few weeks since."

Slight indisposition! What a memory some people are blessed with!

The doctor smothers his rising indignation.

"Eight visits, Mr. Palmer, and at such a distance. You will find the charge a moderate one."

"Oh! very well; I dare say it is all right. I am sorry I have not the money for you to-day, doctor. Very tight just at present; you know how it is with men of business."

"It would be a great accommodation if I could have it at once."

"Impossible, doctor! I wish I could oblige you. In a week, or fortnight, at the farthest, I will call at your office."

A week or fortnight! The disappointed doctor once more seats himself in his chaise, and urges his horse to speed. He is growing desperate now, and is eager to reach his next place of destination. Suddenly he checks the horse. A gentleman is passing whom he recognises as the young husband whose idolized wife has so lately been snatched from the borders of the grave.

"Glad to see you, Mr. Wilton; I was about calling at your house."

"Pray, do so, doctor; Mrs. Wilton will be pleased to see you."

"Thank you; but my call was on business, to-day. I believe I must trouble you with my bill for attendance during your wife's illness."

"Ah! yes; I recollect. Have you it with you? Fifty dollars! Impossible! Why, she was not ill above three weeks."

"Very true; but think of the urgency of the case. Three or four calls during twenty-four hours were necessary, and two whole nights I passed at her bedside."

"And yet the charge appears to me enormous. Call it forty, and I will hand you the amount at once."

The doctor hesitates. "I cannot afford to lose ten dollars, which is justly my due, Mr. Wilton."

"Suit yourself, doctor. Take forty, and receipt the bill, or stick to your first charge, and wait till I am ready to pay it. Fifty dollars is no trifle, I can tell you."

And this is the man whose life might have been a blank but for the doctor's skill!

Again we are travelling onward. The unpaid bill is left in Mr. Wilton's hand, and yet the doctor half regrets that he had not submitted to the imposition. Money is greatly needed just now, and there seems little prospect of getting any.

Again and again the horse is stopped at some well-known post. A poor welcome has the doctor to-day. Some bills are collected, but their amount is discouragingly small. Everybody appears to feel astonishingly healthy, and have almost forgotten that they ever had occasion for a physician. There is one consolation, however: sickness will come again, and then, perhaps, the unpaid bill may be recollected. Homeward goes the doctor. He is naturally of a cheerful disposition; but now he is seriously threatened with a fit of the blues. A list of calls upon his slate has little effect to raise his spirits. "All work and no pay," he mutters to himself, as he puts on his dressing-gown and slippers; and, throwing himself upon the lounge, turns a deaf ear to the little ones, while he indulges in a revery as to the best mode of paying the doctor.

KEEP IN STEP

Those who would walk together must keep in step.
—OLD PROVERB.

AY, the world keeps moving forward,
Like an army marching by;
Hear you not its heavy footfall,
That resoundeth to the sky?
Some bold spirits bear the banner—
Souls of sweetness chant the song,—
Lips of energy and fervour
Make the timid-hearted strong!
Like brave soldiers we march forward;
If you linger or turn back,
You must look to get a jostling
While you stand upon our track.
Keep in step.

My good neighbour, Master Standstill,
Gazes on it as it goes;
Not quite sure but he is dreaming,
In his afternoon's repose!
"Nothing good," he says, "can issue
From this endless moving on;
Ancient laws and institutions
Are decaying, or are gone.
We are rushing on to ruin,
With our mad, new-fangled ways."

While he speaks a thousand voices,
As the heart of one man, says—
"Keep in step!"

Gentle neighbour, will you join us,
Or return to *"good old ways?"*
Take again the fig-leaf apron
Of Old Adam's ancient days;—
Or become a hardy Briton—
Beard the lion in his lair,
And lie down in dainty slumber
Wrapped in skins of shaggy bear,—
Rear the hut amid the forest,
Skim the wave in light canoe?
Ah, I see! you do not like it.
Then if these "old ways" won't do,
Keep in step.

Be assured, good Master Standstill,
All-wise Providence designed
Aspiration and progression
For the yearning human mind.
Generations left their blessings,
In the relies of their skill,
Generations yet are longing
For a greater glory still;
And the shades of our forefathers
Are not jealous of our deed—
We but follow where they beckon,
We but go where they do lead!
Keep in step.

One detachment of our army
May encamp upon the hill,
While another in the valley

May enjoy its own sweet will;
This, may answer to one watchword,
That, may echo to another;
But in unity and concord,
They discern that each is brother!
Breast to breast they're marching onward,
In a good now peaceful way;
You'll be jostled if you hinder,
So don't offer let or stay—
Keep in step.

JOHNNY COLE

"I GUESS we will have to put out our Johnny," said Mrs. Cole, with a sigh, as she drew closer to the fire, one cold day in autumn. This remark was addressed to her husband, a sleepy, lazy-looking man, who was stretched on a bench, with his eyes half closed. The wife, with two little girls of eight and ten, were knitting as fast as their fingers could fly; the baby was sound asleep in the cradle; while Johnny, a boy of thirteen, and a brother of four, were seated on the wide hearth making a snare for rabbits. The room they occupied was cold and cheerless; the warmth of the scanty fire being scarcely felt; yet the floor, and every article of furniture, mean as they were, were scrupulously neat and clean.

The appearance of this family indicated that they were very poor. They were all thin and pale, really for want of proper food, and their clothes had been patched until it was difficult to decide what the original fabric had been; yet this very circumstance spoke volume in favour of the mother. She was, a woman of great energy of character, unfortunately united to a man whose habits were such, that, for the greater part of the time, he was a dead weight upon her hands; although not habitually intemperate, he was indolent and good-for-nothing to a degree, lying in the sun half his time, when the weather was warm, and never doing a stroke of work until driven to it by the pangs of hunger.

As for the wife, by taking in sewing, knitting, and spinning for the farmers' families in the neighbourhood, she managed to pay a rent of twenty dollars for the cabin in which they lived; while she and Johnny, with what assistance they could occasionally get from Jerry, her husband, tilled the half acre of ground attached; and the vegetables thus obtained, were their main dependance during the long winter just at hand. Having thus introduced the Coles to our reader, we will continue the conversation.

"I guess we will have to put out Johnny, and you will try and help us a little more, Jerry, dear."

"Why, what's got into the woman now?" muttered Jerry, stretching his arms, and yawning to the utmost capacity of his mouth. The children laughed at their father's uncouth gestures, and even Mrs. Cole's serious face relaxed into a smile, as she answered,

"Don't swallow us all, and I will tell you. The winter is beginning early, and promises to be cold. Our potatoes didn't turn out as well as I expected, and the truth is, we cannot get along so. We won't have victuals to last us half the time; and, manage as I will, I can't much more than pay the rent, I get so little for the kind of work I do. Now, if Johnny gets a place, it will make one less to provide for; and he will be learning to do something for himself."

"Yes, but mother," said the boy, moving close to her side, and laying his head on her knee, "yes, but who'll help you when I am gone? Who'll dig the lot, and hoe, and cut the wood, and carry the water? You can't go away down to the spring in the deep snow. And who'll make the fire in the cold mornings?"

The mother looked sorry enough, as her darling boy—for he was the object around which the fondest affections of her heart had entwined themselves—she looked sorry enough, as he enumerated the turns he was in the habit of doing for her; but, woman-like, she could suffer and be still; so she answered cheerfully,

"May be father will, dear; and when you grow bigger, and learn how to do everything, you'll be such a help to us all."

"Don't depend on me," said Jerry, now arousing himself and sauntering to the fire; "I hardly ever feel well,"—complaining was Jerry's especial forte, an excuse for all his laziness; yet his appetite never failed; and when, as was sometimes the case, one of the neighbours sent a small piece of meat, or any little article of food to his wife, under the plea of ill health he managed to appropriate nearly the whole of it. He was selfishness embodied, and a serious injury to his family, as few cared to keep him up in his laziness.

One evening, a few days later, Mrs. Cole, who had been absent several hours, came in looking very tired, and after laying aside her old bonnet and shawl, informed them that she had obtained a place for Johnny. It was four miles distant, and the farmer's man would stop for him on his way from town, the next afternoon. What a beautiful object was farmer Watkins's homestead, lying as it did on the sunny slope of a hill; its gray stone walls, peeping out from between the giant trees that overshadowed it, while everything around and about gave evidence of abundance and comfort. The thrifty orchard; the huge barn with its overflowing granaries; the sleek, well-fed cattle; even the low-roofed spring-house, with its superabundance of shining pails and pans, formed an item which could hardly be dispensed with, in the *tout ensemble* of this pleasant home.

Farmer Watkins was an honest, hard-working man, somewhat past middle age, with a heart not naturally devoid of kindness, but, where his hirelings were concerned, so strongly encrusted with a layer of habits, that they acted as an effectual check upon his better feelings. His family consisted of a wife, said to be a notable manager, and five or six children, the eldest, a son, at college. In this household, work, work, was the order of the day; the farmer himself, with his great brown fists, set the example, and the others, willing or unwilling, were obliged to follow his lead. He had agreed to take John Cole, as he said, more to get rid of his mother's importunities, than for any benefit he expected to derive from him; and when remonstrated with by his wife for his folly in giving her the trouble of another brat, he answered shortly: "Never fear, I'll get the worth of his victuals and clothes out of him." Johnny was to have his boarding, clothes, and a dollar a month, for two years. This dollar a month was the great item in Mrs. Cole's calculations; twelve dollars a year, she argued, would almost pay her rent, and when the tears stood in Johnny's great brown eyes (for he was a pretty, gentle-hearted boy), as he was bidding them all good-bye, and kissing the baby over and over again, she told him about the money he would earn, and nerved his little heart with her glowing representations, until he was able to choke back the tears, and leave home almost cheerfully.

Home—yes, it was home; for they had much to redeem the miseries of want within those bare cabin walls, for gentle hearts and kindly smiles were there. There

"The mother sang at the twilight fall,
To the babe half slumbering on her knee."

There his brother and sisters played; there his associations, his hopes, his wishes, were all centered. When he arrived at farmer Watkins's, and was sent into the large carpeted kitchen, everything was so unlike this home, that his fortitude almost gave way, and it was as much as he could do, as he told his mother afterwards, "to keep from bursting right out." Mrs. Watkins looked very cross, nor did she notice him, except to order him to stand out of the way of the red-armed girl who was preparing supper and placing it on a table in the ample apartment. Johnny looked with amazement at the great dishes of meat, and plates of hot biscuit, but the odour of the steaming coffee, and the heat, were almost too much for him, as he had eaten nothing since morning, for he was too sorry to leave home to care about dinner. The girl, noticing that his pale face grew paler, laughingly drew her mistress's attention to "master's new boy."

"Go out and bring in some wood for the stove," said Mrs. Watkins, sharply; "the air will do you good."

Johnny went out, and, in a few minutes, felt revived. Looking about, he soon found the wood-shed; there was plenty of wood, but none cut of a suitable length; it was all in cord sticks. Taking an axe, he chopped an armful, and on taking it into the house, found the family, had finished their suppers; the biscuits and meat were all eaten.

"Come on here to your supper," said the maid-servant, angrily. "What have you been doing?" and, without waiting for an answer, she filled a tin basin with mush and skimmed milk, and set it before him. The little boy did not attempt to speak, but sat down and ate what was given him. Immediately after, he was sent into a loft to bed, where he cried himself to sleep. Ah! when we count the thousand pulsations that yield pain or pleasure to the human mind, what a power to do good or evil is possessed by every one; and how often would a kind word, or one sympathizing glance, gladden the hearts of those thus prematurely forced upon the anxieties of the world! But how few there are who care to bestow them! The next morning, long before dawn, the farmer's family, with the exception of the younger children were astir. The cattle were to be fed and attended to, the horses harnessed, the oxen yoked, and great was the bustle until all hands were fairly at work. As for Johnny, he was taken into the field to assist in husking corn. The wind was keen, and the stalks, from recent rain, were wet, and filled with ice. His scanty clothing scarcely afforded any protection from the cold, and his hands soon became so numb that he could scarcely use them; but, if he stopped one moment to rap them, or breathe upon them, in the hope of imparting some warmth, the farmer who was close at hand, in warm woollen clothes and thick husking gloves, would call out,

"Hurry up, hurry up, my boy! no idle bread must be eaten here!"

And bravely did Johnny struggle not to mind the cold and pain, but it would not do; he began to cry, when the master, who never thought of exercising anything but severity towards those who laboured for him, told him sternly that if he did not stop his bawling in a moment, he would send him home. This was enough for Johnny; anything was better than to go back and be a burden on his mother; he worked to the best of his ability until noon. At noon, he managed to get thoroughly warm, behind the stove, while eating his dinner. Still, the sufferings of the child, with his insufficient clothing, were very great; but nobody seemed to think of the *hired boy* being an object of sympathy, and thus it continued. The rule seemed to be to get all that was possible out of him, and his little frame was so weary at night, that he had hardly time to feel rested, until called with the dawn to renew his labour. A monthly Sunday however, was the golden period looked forward to in his day-dreams, for it had been stipulated by his parent, that on Saturday evening every four weeks, he was to come home, and stay all the next day. And when the time arrived, how nimbly did he get over the ground that stretched between him and the goal of his wishes! How much he had to tell! But as soon as he began to complain, his mother would say cheerfully, although her heart bled for the hardships of her child,

"Never mind, you will get used to work, and after awhile, when you grow up, you can rent a farm, and take me to keep house for you."

This was the impulse that prompted to action. No one can be utterly miserable who has a hope, even a remote one, of bettering his condition; and with a motive such as this to cheer him, Johnny persevered; young as he was, he understood the necessity. But how often, during the four weary weeks that succeeded, did the memory of the Saturday night he had spent at home come up before his mental vision! The fresh loaf of rye bread, baked in honour of his arrival, and eaten for supper, with maple molasses—the very molasses he had helped to boil on shares with Farmer Thrifty's boys in the spring. What a feast they had! Then the long evening afterwards, when the blaze of the hickory fires righted up the timbers of the old cabin with a mellow glow, and mother looked so cheerful and smiled so kindly as she sat spinning in its warmth and light. And how even father had helped to pop corn in the iron pot.

Ah! that was a time long to be remembered; and he had ample opportunity to draw comparisons, for he often thought his master cared more for his cattle than he did for him, and it is quite probable he did; for while they were warmly housed he was needlessly exposed, and his comfort utterly disregarded. If there was brush to cut, or fence to make, or any outdoor labour to perform, a wet, cold, or windy day was sure to be selected, while in *fine weather* the wood was required to be chopped, and, generally speaking, all the work that could be done under shelter. Yet we dare say Farmer Watkins never thought of the inhumanity of this, or the advantage he would himself derive by arranging it otherwise.

John Cole had been living out perhaps a year. He had not grown much in this period; his frame had always been slight, and his sunken cheeks and wasted limbs spoke of the hard usage and suffering of his present situation. The family had many delicacies for themselves, but the *work boy* they knew never was used to such things, and they were indifferent, as to what his fare chanced to be. He generally managed to satisfy the cravings of hunger on the coarse food given him, but that was all. About this time it happened that the farmer was digging a ditch, and as he was afraid winter would set in before it was completed, Johnny and himself were at work upon it early and late, notwithstanding the wind whistled, and it was so cold they could hardly handle the tools. While thus employed, it chanced that they got wet to the skin with a drizzling rain, and on returning to the house the farmer changed his clothes, drank some hot mulled cider, and spent the remainder of the evening in his high-backed chair before a comfortable fire; while the boy was sent to grease a wagon in an open shed, and at night crept to his straw pallet, shaking as though in an ague fit. The next morning he was in a high fever, and with many a "wonder of what had got into him," but without one word of sympathy, or any other manifestation of goodwill, he was sent home to his mother. Late in the evening of the same day a compassionate physician was surprised to see a woman enter his office; her garments wet and travel-stained, and, with streaming eyes, she besought him to come and see her son.

"My Johnny, my Johnny, sir!" she cried, "he has been raving wild all day, and we are afraid he will die."

Mistaking the cause of the good man's hesitation, she added, with a fresh burst of grief, "Oh! I will work my fingers to the bone to pay you, sir, if you will only come. We live in the Gap."

A few inquiries were all that was necessary to learn the state of the case. The benevolent doctor took the woman in his vehicle, and proceeded, over a mountainous road of six miles, to see his patient. But vain was the help of man! Johnny continued delirious; it was work, work, always at work; and pitiful was it to hear his complaints of being cold and tired, while his heart-broken parent hung over him, and denied herself the necessaries of life to minister to his wants. After being ill about a fortnight, he awoke one evening apparently free from fever. His expression was natural, but he seemed so weak he could not speak. His mother, with a heart overflowing with joy at the change she imagined favourable, bent over him. With a great effort he placed his arms about her neck; she kissed his pale lips; a smile of strange meaning passed over his face, and ere she could unwind that loving clasp her little Johnny was no more. He had gone where the wicked cease from troubling, and the weary are at rest; but her hopes were blasted; her house was left unto her desolate; and as she watched, through the long hours of night, beside the dead body, it was to our Father who art in Heaven her anguished heart poured itself out in prayer. Think of this, ye rich! who morning and evening breathe the same petition by your own hearthstones. Think of it, ye who have authority to oppress! Do not deprive the poor man or woman of the "ewe lamb" that is their sole possession; and remember that He whose ear is ever open to the cry of the distressed, has power to avenge their cause.

THE THIEF AND HIS BENEFACTOR

"CIRCUMSTANCES made me what I am," said a condemned criminal to a benevolent man who visited him in prison. "I was driven by necessity to steal."

"Not so," replied the keeper, who was standing by. "Rather say, that your own character made the circumstances by which you were surrounded. God never places upon any creature the necessity of breaking his commandments. You stole, because, in heart, you were a thief."

The benevolent man reproved the keeper for what he called harsh words. He believed that, alone, by the force of external circumstances, men were made criminals. That, if society were differently arranged, there would be little or no crime in the world. And so he made interest for the criminal, and, in the end, secured his release from prison. Nor did his benevolence stop here. He took the man into his service, and intrusted to him his money and his goods.

"I will remove from him all temptation to steal," said he, "by a liberal supply of his wants."

"Have you a wife?" he asked of the man, when he took him from prison.

"No," was replied.

"Nor any one but yourself to support?"

"I am alone in the world."

"You have received a good education; and can serve me as a clerk. I therefore take you into my employment, at a fair salary. Will five hundred dollars be enough?"

"It will be an abundance," said the man, with evident surprise at an offer so unexpectedly liberal.

"Very well. That will place you above temptation."

"And I will be innocent and happy. You are my benefactor. You have saved me."

"I believe it," said the man of benevolence.

And so he intrusted his goods and his money to the man he had reformed by placing him in different circumstances.

But it is in the heart of man that evil lies; and from the heart's impulses spring all our actions. That must cease to be a bitter fountain before it can send forth sweet water. The thief was a thief still. Not a month elapsed ere he was devising the means to enable him to get from his kind, but mistaken friend, more than the liberal sum for which he had agreed to serve him. He coveted his neighbour's goods whenever his eyes fell upon them; and restlessly sought to acquire their possession. In order to make more sure the attainment of his ends, he affected sentiments of morality, and even went so far as to cover his purposes by a show of religion. And thus he was able to deceive and rob his kind friend.

Time went on; and the thief, apparently reformed by a change of relation to society, continued in his post of responsibility. How it was, the benefactor could not make out; but his affairs gradually became less prosperous. He made investigations into his business, but was unable to find anything wrong.

"Are you aware that your clerk is a purchaser of property to a considerable extent?" said a mercantile friend to him one day.

"My clerk! It cannot be. His income is only five hundred dollars a year."

"He bought a piece of property for five thousand last week."

"Impossible!"

"I know it to be true. Are you aware that he was once a convict in the State's Prison?"

"Oh yes. I took him from prison myself, and gave him a chance for his life. I do not believe in hunting men down for a single crime, the result of circumstances rather than a bad heart."

"A truly honest man, let me tell you," replied the merchant, "will be honest in any and all circumstances. And a rogue will be a rogue, place him where you will. The evil is radical, and must be cured radically. Your reformed thief has robbed you, without doubt."

"I have reason to fear that he has been most ungrateful," replied the kind-hearted man, who, with the harmlessness of the dove, did not unite the wisdom of the serpent.

And so it proved. His clerk had robbed him of over twenty thousand dollars in less than five years, and so sapped the foundations of his prosperity, that he recovered with great difficulty.

"You told me, when in prison," said the wronged merchant to his clerk, "that circumstances made you what you were. This you cannot say now."

"I can," was the reply. "Circumstances made me poor, and I desired to be rich. The means of attaining wealth were placed in my hands, and I used them. Is it strange that I should have done so? It is this social inequality that makes crime. Your own doctrine, and I subscribe to it fully."

"Ungrateful wretch!" said the merchant, indignantly, "it is the evil of your own heart that prompts to crime. You would be a thief and a robber if you possessed millions."

And he again handed him over to the law, and let the prison walls protect society from his depredations.

No, it is not true that in external circumstances lie the origins of evil. God tempts no man by these. In the very extremes of poverty we see examples of honesty; and among the wealthiest, find those who covet their neighbour's goods, and gain dishonest possession thereof. Reformers must seek to elevate the personal character, if they would regenerate society. To accomplish the desired good by a different external arrangement, is hopeless; for in the heart of man lies the evil,—there is the fountain from which flow forth the bitter and blighting waters of crime.

JOHN AND MARGARET GREYLSTON

"AND you will really send Reuben to cut down that clump of pines?"

"Yes, Margaret. Well, now, it is necessary, for more reasons than" — —

"Don't tell me so, John," impetuously interrupted Margaret Greylston. "I am sure there is no necessity in the case, and I am sorry to the very heart that you have no more feeling than to order *those* trees to be cut down."

"Feeling! well, maybe I have more than you think; yet I don't choose to let it make a fool of me, for all that. But I wish you would say no more about those trees, Margaret; they really must come down; I have reasoned with you on this matter till I am sick of it."

Miss Greylston got up from her chair, and walked out on the shaded porch; then she turned and called her brother.

"Will you come here, John?"

"And what have you to say?"

"Nothing, just now; I only want you to stand here and look at the old pines."

And so John Greylston did; and he saw the distant woods grave and fading beneath the autumn wind—while the old pines upreared their stately heads against the blue sky, unchanged in beauty, fresh and green as ever.

"You see those trees, John, and so do I; and standing here, with them full in view, let me plead for them; they are very old, those pines, older than either of us; we played beneath them when we were children; but there is still a stronger tie: our mother loved them—our dear, sainted mother. Thirty years it has been since she died, but I can never forget or cease to love anything she loved. Oh! John, you remember just as well as I do, how often she would sit beneath those trees and read or talk sweetly to us; and of the dear band who gathered there with her, only we are left, and the old pines. Let them stand, John; time enough to cut them down when I have gone to sit with those dear ones beneath the trees of heaven;" and somewhat breathless from long talking, Miss Margaret paused.

John Greylston was really touched, and he laid his hand kindly on his sister's shoulder.

"Come, come, Madge, don't talk so sadly. I remember and love those things as well as you do, but then you see I cannot afford to neglect my interests for weak sentiment. Now the road must be made, and that clump of trees stand directly in its course, and they must come down, or the road will have to take a curve nearly half a mile round, striking into one of my best meadows, and a good deal more expense this will be, too. No, no," he continued, eagerly, "I can't oblige you in this thing. This place is mine, and I will improve it as I please. I have kept back from making many a change for your sake, but just here I am determined to go on." And all this was said with a raised voice and a flushed face.

"You never spoke so harshly to me in your life before, John, and, after all, what have I done? Call my feelings on this matter weak sentiment, if you choose, but it is hard to hear such words from your lips;" and, with a reproachful sigh, Miss Margaret walked into the house.

They had been a large family, those Greylstons, in their day, but now all were gone; all but John and Margaret, the two eldest—the twin brother and sister. They lived alone in their beautiful country home; neither had ever been married. John had once loved a fair young creature, with eyes like heaven's stars, and rose-tinged cheeks and lips, but she fell asleep just one month before her wedding-day, and John Greylston was left to mourn over her early grave, and his shivered happiness. Dearly Margaret loved her twin brother, and tenderly she nursed him through the long and fearful illness which came upon him after Ellen Day's death. Margaret Greylston was radiant in the bloom of young womanhood when this great grief first smote her brother, but from that very hour she put away from her the gayeties of life, and sat down by his side, to be to him a sweet, unselfish controller for evermore, and no lover could ever tempt her from her post.

"John Greylston will soon get over his sorrow; in a year or two Ellen will be forgotten for a new face."

So said the world; Margaret knew better. Her brother's heart lay before her like an open book, and she saw indelible lines of grief and anguish there. The old homestead, with its wide lands, belonged to John Greylston. He had bought it years before from the other heirs; and Margaret, the only remaining one, possessed neither claim nor right in it. She had a handsome annuity, however, and nearly all the rich plate and linen with which the house was stocked, together with some valuable pieces of furniture, belonged to her. And John and Margaret Greylston lived on in their quiet and beautiful home, in peace and happiness; their solitude being but now and then invaded by a flock of nieces and nephews, from the neighbouring city—their only and well-beloved relatives.

It was long after sunset. For two full hours the moon and stars had watched John Greylston, sitting so moodily alone upon the porch. Now he got up from his chair, and tossing his cigar away in the long grass, walked slowly into the house. Miss Margaret did not raise her head; her eyes, as well as her fingers, seemed intent upon the knitting she held. So her brother, after a hurried "Good-night," took a candle and went up to his own room, never speaking one gentle word; for he said to himself, "I am not going to worry and coax with Margaret any longer about the old pines. She is really troublesome with her sentimental notions." Yet, after all, John Greylston's heart reproached him, and he felt restless and ill at ease.

Miss Margaret sat very quietly by the low table, knitting steadily on, but she was not thinking of her work, neither did she delight in the beauty of that still autumn evening; the tears came into her eyes, but she hastily brushed them away; just as though she feared John might unawares come back and find her crying.

Ah! these *way-side* thorns are little, but sometimes they pierce as sharply as the gleaming sword.

"Good-morning, John!"

At the sound of that voice, Mr. Greylston turned suddenly from the book-case, and his sister was standing near him, her face lit up with a sweet, yet somewhat anxious smile. He threw down in a hurry the papers he had been tying together, and the bit of red tape, and holding out his hand, said fervently,

"I was very harsh last night. I am really sorry for it; will you not forgive me, Margaret?"

"To be sure I will; for indeed, John, I was quite as much to blame as you."

"No, Madge, you were not," he quickly answered; "but let it pass, now. We will think and say no more about it;" and, as though he were perfectly satisfied, and really wished the matter dropped, John Greylston turned to his papers again.

So Miss Margaret was silent. She was delighted to have peace again, even though she felt anxious about the pines, and when her brother took his seat at the breakfast table, looking and speaking so kindly, she felt comforted to think the cloud had passed away; and John Greylston himself was very glad. So the two went on eating their breakfast quite happily. But alas! the storm is not always over when the sky grows light. Reuben crossed the lawn, followed by the gardener, and Miss Margaret's quick eye caught the gleaming of the axes swung over their shoulders. She hurriedly set down the coffee-pot.

"Where are those men going? Reuben and Tom I mean."

"Only to the woods," was the careless answer.

"But what woods, John? Oh! I can tell by your face; you are determined to have the pines cut down."

"I am." And John Greylston folded his arms, and looked fixedly at his sister, but she did not heed him. She talked on eagerly—

"I love the old trees; I will do anything to save them. John, you spoke last night of additional expense, should the road take that curve. I will make it up to you; I can afford to do this very well. Now listen to reason, and let the trees stand."

"Listen to reason, yourself," he answered more gently. "I will not take a cent from you. Margaret, you are a perfect enthusiast about some things. Now, I love my parents and old times, I am sure, as well as you do, and that love is not one bit the colder, because I do not let it stand in the way of interest. Don't say anything more. My mind is made up in this matter. The place is mine, and I cannot see that you have any right to interfere in the improvements I choose to make on it."

A deep flush stole over Miss Greylston's face.

"I have indeed no legal right to counsel or plead with you about these things," she answered sadly, "but I have a sister's right, that of affection—you cannot deny this, John. Once again, I beg of you to let the old pines alone."

"And once again, I tell you I will do as I please in this matter," and this was said sharply and decidedly.

Margaret Greylston said not another word, but pushing back her chair, she arose from the breakfast-table and went quickly from the room, even before her brother could call to her. Reuben and his companion had just got in the last meadow when Miss Greylston overtook them.

"You, will let the pines alone to-day," she calmly said, "go to any other work you choose, but remember those trees are not to be touched."

"Very well, Miss Margaret," and Reuben touched his hat respectfully,

"Mr. John is very changeable in his notions," burst in Tom; "not an hour ago he was in such a hurry to get us at the pine."

"Never mind," authoritatively said Miss Greylston; "do just as you are bid, without any remarks;" and she turned away, and went down the meadow path, even as she came, within quick step, without a bonnet, shading her eyes from the morning sun with her handkerchief.

John Greylston still sat at the breakfast-table, half dreamily balancing the spoon across the saucer's edge. When his sister came in again, he raised his head, and mutely-inquiringly looked at her, and she spoke,—

"I left this room just to go after Reuben and Tom; I overtook them before they had crossed the last meadow, and I told them not to touch the pine trees, but to go, instead, to any other work they choose. I am sure you will be angry with me for all this; but, John, I cannot help it if you are."

"Don't say so, Margaret," Mr. Greylston sharply answered, getting up at the same time from his chair, "don't tell me you could not help it. I have talked and reasoned with you about those trees, until my patience is completely worn out; there is no necessity for you to be such an obstinate fool."

"Oh! John, hush, hush!"

"I will not," he thundered. "I am master here, and I will speak and act in this house as I see fit. Now, who gave you liberty to countermand my orders; to send my servants back from the work I had set for them to do? Margaret, I warn you; for, any more such freaks, you and I, brother and sister though we be, will live no longer under the same roof."

"Be still, John Greylston! Remember *her* patient, self-sacrificing love. Remember the past—be still."

But he would not; relentlessly, stubbornly, the waves of passion raged on in his soul.

"Now, you hear all this; do not forget it; and have done with your silly obstinacy as soon as possible, for I will be worried no longer with it;" and roughly pushing away the slight hand which was laid upon his arm, Mr. Greylston stalked out of the house.

For a moment, Margaret stood where her brother had left her, just in the centre of the floor. Her cheeks were very white, but quickly a crimson flush came over them, and her eyes filled with tears; then she sat down upon the white chintz-covered settle, and hiding her face in the pillows, wept violently for a long time.

"I have consulted Margaret's will always; in many things I have given up to it, but here, where reason is so fully on my side, I will go on. I have no patience with her weak stubbornness, no patience with her presumption in forbidding my servants to do as I have told them; such measures I will never allow in my house;" and John Greylston, in his angry musings, struck his cane smartly against a tall crimson dahlia, which grew in the grass-plat. It fell quivering across his path, but he walked on, never heeding what he had done. There was a faint sense of shame rising in his heart, a feeble conviction of having been himself to blame; but just then they seemed only to fan and increase his keen indignation. Yet in the midst of his anger, John Greylston had the delicate consideration for his sister and himself to repeat to the men the command she had given them.

"Do as Miss Greylston bade you; let the trees stand until further orders." But pride prompted this, for he said to himself, "If Margaret and I keep at this childish work of unsaying each other's commands, that sharp old fellow, Reuben, will suspect that we have quarrelled."

Mr. Greylston's wrath did not abate; and when he came home at dinner-time, and found the table so nicely set, and no one but the little servant to wait upon him, Margaret away, shut up with a bad headache, in her own room, he somehow felt relieved,—just then he did not want to see her. But when eventide came, and he sat down to supper, and missed again his sister's calm and pleasant face, a half-regretful feeling stole over him, and he grew lonely, for John Greylston's heart was the home of every kindly affection. He loved Margaret dearly. Still, pride and anger kept him aloof from her; still his soul was full of harsh, unforgiving thoughts. And Margaret Greylston, as she lay with a throbbing head and an aching heart upon her snowy pillow, thought the hours of that bright afternoon and evening very long and very weary. And yet those hours were full of light, and melody, and fragrance, for the sun shone, and the sky was blue, the birds sang, and the waters rippled; even the autumn flowers were giving their sweet, last kisses to the air. Earth was fair,—why, then, should not human hearts rejoice? Ah! *Nature's* loveliness *alone* cannot cheer the soul. There was once a day when the beauty even of *Eden* ceased to gladden two guilty tremblers who hid in its bowers.

"A soft answer turneth away wrath, but grievous words stir up anger." When Margaret Greylston came across that verse, she closed her Bible, and sat down beside the window to muse. "Ah," she thought, "how true is that saying of the wise man! If I had only from the first given John soft answers, instead of grievous words, we might now have been at peace. I knew his quick temper so well; I should have been more gentle with him." Then she recalled all John's constant and tender attention to her wishes; the many instances in which he had gone back from his own pleasure to gratify her; but whilst she remembered these things, never once did her noble, unselfish heart dwell upon the sacrifices, great and numerous, which she had made for his sake. Miss Margaret began to think she had indeed acted very weakly and unjustly towards her brother. She had half a mind just then to go to him, and make this confession. But she looked out and saw the dear old trees, so stately and beautiful, and then the memory of all John's harsh and cruel words rushed back upon her. She struggled vainly to banish them from her mind, she strove to quell the angry feelings which arose with those memories. At last she knelt and prayed. When she got up from her knees traces of tears were on her face, but her heart was calm. Margaret Greylston had been enabled, in the strength of "that grace which cometh from above," to forgive her brother freely, yet she scarcely hoped that he would give her the opportunity to tell him this.

"Good-morning," John Greylston said, curtly and chillingly enough to his sister. Somehow she was disappointed, even though she knew his proud temper so well, yet she had prayed that there would have been some kindly relentings towards her; but there seemed none. So she answered him sadly, and the two sat down to their gloomy, silent breakfast. And thus it was all that day. Mr. Greylston still mute and ungracious; his sister shrank away from him. In that mood she scarcely knew him; and her face was grave, and her voice so sad, even the servants wondered what was the matter. Margaret Greylston had fully overcome all angry, reproachful feelings against her brother. So far her soul had peace, yet she mourned for his love, his kind words, and pleasant smiles; and she longed to tell him this, but his coldness held her back. Mr. Greylston found his comfort in every way consulted; favourite dishes were silently placed before him; sweet flowers, as of old, laid upon his table. He knew the hand which wrought these loving acts. But did this knowledge melt his heart? In a little while we shall see.

And the third morning dawned. Yet the cloud seemed in no wise lifted. John Greylston's portrait hung in the parlour; it was painted in his young days, when he was very handsome. His sister could not weary of looking at it; to her this picture seemed the very embodiment of beauty. Dear, unconscious soul, she never thought how much it was like herself, or even the portrait of her which hung in the opposite recess—for brother and sister strikingly resembled each other. Both had the same high brows, the same deep blue eyes and finely chiselled features, the same sweet and pleasant smiles; there was but one difference: Miss Margaret's hair was of a pale golden colour, and yet unchanged; she wore it now put back very smoothly and plainly from her face. When John was young, his curls were of so dark a brown as to look almost black in the shade. They were bleached a good deal by time, but yet they clustered round his brow in the same careless, boyish fashion as of old.

Just now Miss Margaret could only look at her brother's picture with tears. On that very morning she stood before it, her spirit so full of tender memories, so crowded with sad yearnings, she felt as though they would crush her to the earth. Oh, weary heart! endure yet "a little while" longer. Even now the angel of reconciliation is on the wing.

Whilst John Greylston sat alone upon the foot of the porch at the front of the house, and his sister stood so sadly in the parlour, the city stage came whirling along the dusty turnpike. It stopped for a few minutes opposite the lane which led to John Greylston's place. The door was opened, and a grave-looking young man sprang out. He was followed by a fairy little creature, who clapped her hands, and danced for joy when she saw the white chimneys and vine-covered porches of "Greylston Cottage."

"Annie! Annie!" but she only laughed, and gathering up the folds of her travelling dress, managed to get so quickly and skilfully over the fence, that her brother, who was unfastening the gate, looked at her in perfect amazement.

"What in the world," he asked, with a smile on his grave face, "possessed you to get over the fence in that monkey fashion? All those people looking at you, too. For shame, Annie! Will you never be done with those childish capers?"

"Yes, maybe when I am a gray-haired old woman; not before. Don't scold now, Richard; you know very well you, and the passengers beside, would give your ears to climb a fence as gracefully as I did just now. There, won't you hand me my basket, please?"

He did so, and then, with a gentle smile, took the white, ungloved fingers in his.

"My darling Annie, remember"—

"Stage waits," cried the driver.

So Richard Bermon's lecture was cut short; he had only time to bid his merry young sister good-bye. Soon he was lost to sight.

Annie Bermon hurried down the lane, swinging her light willow basket carelessly on her arm, and humming a joyous air all the way. Just as she opened the outer lawn gate, the great Newfoundland dog came towards her with a low growl; it changed directly though into a glad bark.

"I was sure you would know me, you dear old fellow; but I can't stop to talk to you just now." And Annie patted his silken ears, and then went on to the house, the dog bounding on before her, as though he had found an old playmate.

John Greylston rubbed his eyes. No, it was not a dream. His darling niece was really by his side, her soft curls touching his cheek; he flung his arms tightly around her.

"Dear child, I was just dreaming about you; how glad I am to see your sweet face again."

"I was sure you would be, Uncle John," she answered gayly, "and so I started off from home this morning just, in a hurry. I took a sudden fancy that I would come, and they could not keep me. But where is dear Aunt Margaret? Oh, I know what I will do. I'll just run in and take her by surprise. How well you look, uncle—so noble and grand too; by the way, I always think King Robert Bruce must just have been such a man like you."

"No laughing at your old uncle, you little rogue," said John Greylston pleasantly, "but run and find your aunt. She is somewhere in the house." And he looked after her with a loving smile as she flitted by him. Annie Bermon passed quickly through the shaded sitting-room into the cool and matted hall, catching glimpses as she went of the pretty parlour and wide library; but her aunt was in neither of these rooms; so she hurried up stairs, and stealing on tiptoe, with gentle fingers she pushed open the door. Margaret Greylston was sitting by the table, sewing; her face was flushed, and her eyes red and swollen as with weeping. Annie stood still in wonder. But Miss Margaret suddenly looked up, and her niece sprang, with a glad cry, into her arms.

"You are not well, Aunt Margaret? Oh! how sorry I am to hear that, but it seems to me I could never get sick in this sweet place; everything looks so bright and lovely here. And I *would* come this morning, Aunt Margaret, in spite of everything Sophy and all of them could say. They told me I had been here once before this summer, and stayed a long time, and if I would, come again, my welcome would be worn out, just as if I was going to believe *such* nonsense;" and Annie tossed her head. "But I persevered, and you see, aunty dear, I am here, we will trust for some good purpose, as Richard would say."

A silent Amen to this rose up in Miss Margaret's heart, and with it came a hope dim and shadowy, yet beautiful withal; she hardly dared to cherish it. Annie went on talking,—

"I can only stay two weeks with you—school commences then, and I must hurry back to it; but I am always so glad to get here, away from the noise and dust of the city; this is the best place in the world. Do you know when we were travelling this summer, I was pining all the time to get here. I was so tired of Newport and Saratoga, and all the crowds we met."

"You are singular in your tastes, some would think, Annie," said Miss Greylston, smiling fondly on her darling.

"So Madge and Sophy were always saying; even Clare laughed at me, and my brothers, too,—only Richard,—Oh! by the way, I did torment him this morning, he is so grave and good, and he was just beginning a nice lecture at the gate, when the driver called, and poor Richard had only time to send his love to you. Wasn't it droll, though, that lecture being cut so short?" and Annie threw herself down in the great cushioned chair, and laughed heartily.

Annie Bermond was the youngest of John and Margaret Greylston's nieces and nephews. Her beauty, her sweet and sunny temper made her a favourite at home and abroad. John Greylston loved her dearly; he always thought she looked like his chosen bride, Ellen Day. Perhaps there was some likeness, for Annie had the same bright eyes, and the same pouting, rose-bud lips—but Margaret thought she was more like their own family. She loved to trace a resemblance in the smiling face, rich golden curls, and slight figure of Annie to her young sister Edith, who died when Annie was a little baby. Just sixteen years old was Annie, and wild and active as any deer, as her city-bred sisters sometimes declared half mournfully.

Somehow, Annie Bermond thought it uncommonly grave and dull at the dinner-table, yet why should it be so? Her uncle and aunt, as kind and dear as ever, were there; she, herself, a blithe fairy, sat in her accustomed seat; the day was bright, birds were singing, flowers were gleaming, but there was a change. What could it be? Annie knew not, yet her quick perception warned her of the presence of some trouble—some cloud. In her haste to talk and cheer her uncle and aunt, the poor child said what would have been best left unsaid.

"How beautiful those trees are; I mean those pines on the hill; don't you admire them very much, Uncle John?"

"Tolerably," was the rather short answer. "I am too well used to trees to go into the raptures of my little city niece about them;" and all this time Margaret looked fixedly down upon the floor.

"Don't you frown so, uncle, or I will run right home to-morrow," said Annie, with the assurance of a privileged pet; "but I was going to ask you about the rock just back of those pines. Do you and Aunt Margaret still go there to see the sunset? I was thinking about you these two past evenings, when the sunsets were so grand, and wishing I was with you on the rock; and you were both there, weren't you?"

This time John Greylston gave no answer, but his sister said briefly,

"No, Annie, we have not been at the rock for several evenings;" and then a rather painful silence followed.

Annie at last spoke:

"You both, somehow, seem so changed and dull; I would just like to know the reason. May be aunty is going to be married. Is that it, Uncle John?"

Miss Margaret smiled, but the colour came brightly to her face.

"If this is really so, I don't wonder you are sad and grave; you, especially, Uncle John; how lonely and wretched you would be! Oh! would you not be very sorry if Aunt Madge should leave you, never to come back again? Would not your heart almost break?"

John Greylston threw down his knife and fork violently upon the table, and pushing back his chair, went from the room.

Annie Bermond looked in perfect bewilderment at her aunt, but Miss Margaret was silent and tearful.

"Aunt! darling aunt! don't look so distressed;" and Annie put her arms around her neck; "but tell me what have I done; what is the matter?"

Miss Greylston shook her head.

"You will not speak now, Aunt Margaret; you might tell me; I am sure something has happened to distress you. Just as soon as I came here, I saw a change, but I could not understand it. I cannot yet. Tell me, dear aunt!" and she knelt beside her.

So Miss Greylston told her niece the whole story, softening, as far as truth would permit, many of John's harsh speeches; but she was, not slow to blame herself. Annie listened attentively. Young as she was, her heart took in with the deepest sympathy the sorrow which shaded her beloved friends.

"Oh! I am so very sorry for all this," she said half crying; "but aunty, dear, I do not think uncle will have those nice old trees cut down. He loves you too much to do it; I am sure he is sorry now for all those sharp things he said; but his pride keeps him back from telling you this, and maybe he thinks you are angry with him still. Aunt Margaret, let me go and say to him that your love is as warm as ever, and that you forgive him freely. Oh! it may do so much good. May I not go?"

But Miss Greylston tightened her grasp on the young girl's hand.

"Annie, you do not know your uncle as well as I do. Such a step can do no good,—love, you cannot help us."

"Only let me try," she returned, earnestly; "Uncle John loves me so much, and on the first day of my visit, he will not refuse to hear me. I will tell him all the sweet things you said about him. I will tell him there is not one bit of anger in your heart, and that you forgive and love him dearly. I am sure when he hears this he will be glad. Any way, it will not make matters worse. Now, do have some confidence in me. Indeed I am not so childish as I seem. I am turned of sixteen now, and Richard and Sophy often say I have the heart of a woman, even if I have the ways of a child. Let me go now, dear Aunt Margaret; I will soon come back to you with such good news."

Miss Greylston stooped down and kissed Annie's brow solemnly, tenderly. "Go, my darling, and may God be with you." Then she turned away.

And with willing feet Annie Bermond went forth upon her blessed errand. She soon found her uncle. He was sitting beneath the shade of the old pines, and he seemed to be in very deep thought. Annie got down on the grass beside him, and laid her soft cheek upon his sunburnt hand. How gently he spoke—

"What did you come here for, sweet bird?"

"Because I love you so much, Uncle John; that is the reason; but won't you tell me why you look so very sad and grave? I wish I knew your thoughts just now."

"And if you did, fairy, they would not make you any prettier or better than you are."

"I wonder if they do you any good, uncle?" she quickly replied; but her companion made no answer; he only smiled.

Let me write here what John Greylston's tongue refused to say. Those thoughts, indeed, had done him good; they were tender, self-upbraiding, loving thoughts, mingled, all the while, with touching memories, mournful glimpses of the past—the days of his sore bereavement, when the coffin-lid was first shut down over Ellen Day's sweet face, and he was smitten to the earth with anguish. Then Margaret's sympathy and love, so beautiful in its strength, and unselfishness, so unwearying and sublime in its sacrifices, became to him a stay and comfort. And had she not, for his sake, uncomplainingly given up the best years of her life, as it seemed? Had her love ever faltered? Had it ever wavered in its sweet endeavours to make him happy? These memories, these thoughts, closed round John Greylston like a circle of rebuking angels. Not for the first time were they with him when Annie found him beneath the old pines. Ever since that morning of violent and unjust anger they had been struggling in his heart, growing stronger, it seemed, every hour in their reproachful tenderness. Those loving, silent attentions to his wishes John Greylston had noted, and they rankled like sharp thorns in his soul. He was not worthy of them; this he knew. How he loathed himself for his sharp and angry words! He had it in his heart to tell his sister this, but an overpowering shame held him back.

"If I only knew how Madge felt towards me," he said many times to himself, "then I could speak; but I have been such a brute. She can do nothing else but repulse me;" and this threw around him that chill reserve which kept Margaret's generous and forgiving heart at a distance.

Even every-day life has its wonders, and perhaps not one of the least was that this brother and sister, so long fellow-pilgrims, so long readers of each other's hearts, should for a little while be kept asunder by mutual blindness. Yet the hand which is to chase the mists from their darkened eyes, even now is raised, what though it be but small? God in his wisdom and mercy will cause its strength to be sufficient.

When John Greylston gave his niece no answer, she looked intently in his face and said,

"You will not tell me what you have been thinking about; but I can guess, Uncle John. I know the reason you did not take Aunt Margaret to the rock to see the sunset."

"Do you?" he asked, startled from his composure, his face flushing deeply.

"Yes; for I would not rest until aunty told me the whole story, and I just came out to talk to you about it. Now, Uncle John, don't frown, and draw away your hand; just listen to me a little while; I am sure you will be glad." Then she repeated, in her pretty, girlish way, touching in its earnestness, all Miss Greylston had told her. "Oh, if you had only heard her say those sweet things, I know you would not keep vexed one minute longer! Aunt Margaret told me that she did not blame you at all, only herself; that she loved you dearly, and she is so sorry because you seem cold and angry yet, for she wants so very, very much to beg your forgiveness, and tell you all this, dear Uncle John, if you would only—"

"Annie," he suddenly interrupted, drawing her closely to his bosom; "Annie, you precious child, in telling me all this you have taken a great weight off of my heart. You have done your old uncle a world of good. God bless you a thousand times! If I had known this at once; if I had been sure, from the first, of Margaret's forgiveness for my cruel words, how quickly I would have sought it. My dear, noble sister!" The tears filled John Greylston's dark blue eyes, but his smile was so exceedingly tender and beautiful, that Annie drew closer to his side.

"Oh, that lovely smile!" she cried, "how it lights your face; and now you look so good and forgiving, dearer and better even than a king. Uncle John, kiss me again; my heart is so glad! shall I run now and tell Aunt Margaret all this sweet news?"

"No, no, darling little peace-maker, stay here; I will go to her myself;" and he hurried away.

Annie Bermond sat alone upon the hill, musingly platting the long grass together, but she heeded not the work of her fingers. Her face was bright with joy, her heart full of happiness. Dear child! in one brief hour she had learned the blessedness of that birthright which is for all God's sons and daughters, if they will but claim it. I mean *the privilege of doing good, of being useful.*

Miss Greylston sat by the parlour window, just where she could see who crossed the lawn. She was waiting with a kind of nervous impatience for Annie. She heard a footstep, but it was only Liddy going down to the dairy. Then Reuben went by on his way to the meadow, and all was silent again. Where was Annie?—but now quick feet sounded upon the crisp and faded leaves. Miss Margaret looked out, and saw her brother coming,—then she was sure Annie had in some way missed him, and she drew back from the window keenly disappointed, not even a faint suspicion of the blessed truth crossing her mind. As John Greylston entered the hall, a sudden and irresistible desire prompted Margaret to go and tell him all the loving and forgiving thoughts of her heart, no matter what his mood should be. So she threw down her work, and went quickly towards the parlour door. And the brother and sister met, just on the threshold.

"John—John," she said, falteringly, "I must speak to you; I cannot bear this any longer."

"Nor can I, Margaret."

Miss Greylston looked up in her brother's face; it was beaming with love and tenderness. Then she knew the hour of reconciliation had come, and with a quick, glad cry, she sprang into his arms and laid her head down upon his shoulder.

"Can you ever forgive me, Madge?"

She made no reply—words had melted into tears, but they were eloquent, and for a little while it was quite still in the parlour.

"You shall blame yourself no longer, Margaret. All along you have behaved like a sweet Christian woman as you are, but I have been an old fool, unreasonable and cross from the very beginning. Can you really forgive me all those harsh words, for which I hated myself not ten hours after they were said? Can you, indeed, forgive and forget these? Tell me so again."

"John," she said, raising her tearful face from his shoulder, "I do forgive you most completely, with my whole heart, and, O! I wanted so to tell you this two days ago, but your coldness kept me back. I was afraid your anger was not over, and that you would repel me."

"Ah, that coldness was but shame—deep and painful shame. I was needlessly harsh with you, and moments of reflection only served to fasten on me the belief that I had lost all claim to your love, that you could not forgive me. Yes! I did misjudge you, Madge, I know, but when I looked back upon the past, and all your faithful love for me, I saw you as I had ever seen you, the best of sisters, and then my shameful and ungrateful conduct rose up clearly before me. I felt so utterly unworthy."

Miss Greylston laid her finger upon her brother's lips. "Nor will I listen to you blaming yourself so heavily any longer. John, you had cause to be angry with me; I was unreasonably urgent about the trees," and she sighed; "I forgot to be gentle and patient; so you see I am to blame as well as yourself."

"But I forgot even common kindness and courtesy;" he said gravely. "What demon was in my heart, Margaret, I do not know. Avarice, I am afraid, was at the bottom of all this, for rich as I am, I somehow felt very obstinate about running into any more expense or trouble about the road; and then, you remember, I never could love inanimate things as you do. But from this time forth I will try—and the pines"—

"Let the pines go down, my dear brother, I see now how unreasonable I have been," suddenly interrupted Miss Greylston; "and indeed these few days past I could not look at them with any pleasure; they only reminded me of our separation. Cut them down: I will not say one word."

"Now, what a very woman you are, Madge! Just when you have gained your will, you want to turn about; but, love, the trees shall not come down. I will give them to you; and you cannot refuse my peace-offering; and never, whilst John Greylston lives, shall an axe touch those pines, unless you say so, Margaret."

He laughed when he said this, but her tears were falling fast.

"Next month will be November; then comes our birth-day; we will be fifty years old, Margaret. Time is hurrying on with us; he has given me gray locks, and laid some wrinkles on your dear face; but that is nothing if our hearts are untouched. O, for so many long years, ever since my Ellen was snatched from me,"—and here John Greylston paused a moment—"you have been to me a sweet, faithful comforter. Madge, dear twin sister, your love has always been a treasure to me; but you well know for many years past it has been my *only* earthly treasure. Henceforth, God helping me, I will seek to restrain my evil temper. I will be more watchful; if sometimes I fail, Margaret, will you not love me, and bear with me?"

Was there any need for that question? Miss Margaret only answered by clasping her brother's hand more closely in her own. As they stood there in the autumn sunlight, united so lovingly, hand in hand, each silently prayed that thus it might be with them always; not only through life's autumn, but in that winter so surely for them approaching, and which would give place to the fair and beautiful spring of the better land.

Annie Bermond's bright face looked in timidly at the open door.

"Come here, darling, come and stand right beside your old uncle and aunt, and let us thank you with all our hearts for the good you have done us. Don't cry any more, Margaret. Why, fairy, what is the matter with you?" for Annie's tears were falling fast upon his hand.

"I hardly know, Uncle John; I never felt so glad in my life before, but I cannot help crying. Oh, it is so sweet to think the cloud has gone."

"And whose dear hand, under God's blessing, drove the cloud away, but yours, my child?"

Annie was silent; she only clung the tighter to her uncle's arm, and Miss Greylston said, with a beaming smile,

"Now, Annie, we see the good purpose God had in sending you here to-day. You have done for us the blessed work of a peace-maker."

Annie had always been dear to her uncle and aunt, but from that golden autumn day, she became, if such a thing could be, dearer than ever—bound to them by an exceedingly sweet tie.

Years went by. One snowy evening, a merry Christmas party was gathered together in the wide parlour at Greylston Cottage,—nearly all the nephews and nieces were there. Mrs. Lennox, the "Sophy" of earlier days, with her husband; Richard Bermond and his pretty little wife were amongst the number; and Annie, dear, bright Annie—her fair face only the fairer and sweeter for time—sat, talking in a corner with young Walter Selwyn. John Greylston went slowly to the window, and pushed aside the curtains, and as he stood there looking out somewhat gravely in the bleak and wintry night, he felt a soft hand touch him, and he turned and found Annie Bermond by his side.

"You looked so lonely, my dear uncle."

"And that is the reason you deserted Walter?" he said, laughing. "Well, I will soon send you back to him. But, look out here first, Annie, and tell me what you see;" and she laid her face close to the window-pane, and, after a minute's silence, said,

"I see the ground white with snow, the sky gleaming with stars, and the dear old pines, tall and stately as ever."

"Yes, the pines; that is what I meant, my child. Ah, they have been my silent monitors ever since that day; you remember it, Annie! Bless you, child! how much good you did us then."

But Annie was silently crying beside him. John Greylton wiped his eyes, and then he called his sister Margaret to the window.

"Annie and I have been looking at the old pines, and you can guess what we were thinking about. As for myself," he added, "I never see those trees without feeling saddened and rebuked. I never recall that season of error, without the deepest shame and grief. And still the old pines stand. Well, Madge, one day they will shade our graves; and of late I have thought that day would dawn very soon."

Annie Bermond let the curtain fall very slowly forward, and buried her face in her hands; but the two old pilgrims by her side, John and Margaret Greylston, looked at each other with a smile of hope and joy. They had long been "good and faithful servants," and now they awaited the coming of "the Master," with a calm, sweet patience, knowing it would be well with them, when He would call them hence.

The pines creaked mournfully in the winter wind, and the stars looked down upon bleak wastes, and snow-shrouded meadows; yet the red blaze heaped blithely on the hearth, taking in, in its fair light, the merry circle sitting side by side, and the thoughtful little group standing so quietly by the window. And even now the picture fades, and is gone. The curtain falls—the story of John and Margaret Greylston is ended.

THE WORLD WOULD BE THE BETTER FOR IT

IF men cared less for wealth and fame,
And less for battle-fields and glory;
If, writ in human hearts, a name
Seemed better than in song and story;
If men, instead of nursing pride,
Would learn to hate and to abhor it—
If more relied
On Love to guide,
The world would be the better for it.

If men dealt less in stocks and lands,
And more in bonds and deeds fraternal;
If Love's work had more willing hands
To link this world to the supernal;
If men stored up Love's oil and wine,
And on bruised human hearts would pour it;
If "yours" and "mine"
Would once combine,
The world would be the better for it.

If more would act the play of Life,
And fewer spoil it in rehearsal;
If Bigotry would sheathe its knife
Till Good became more universal;
If Custom, gray with ages grown,
Had fewer blind men to adore it—
If talent shone

In truth alone,
The world would be the better for it.

If men were wise in little things—
Affecting less in all their dealings—
If hearts had fewer rusted strings
To isolate their kindly feelings;
If men, when Wrong beats down the Right,
Would strike together and restore it—
If Right made Might
In every fight,
The world would be the better for it.

TWO SIDES TO A STORY

"HAVE you seen much of your new neighbours, yet?" asked Mrs. Morris, as she stepped in to have an hour's social chat with her old friend, Mrs. Freeman.

"Very little," was the reply. "Occasionally I have seen the lady walking in her garden, and have sometimes watched the sports of the children on the side-walk, but this is all. It is not like the country, you know. One may live here for years, and not become acquainted with the next-door neighbours."

"Some may do so," replied Mrs. Morris, "but, for my part, I always like to know something of those around me. It is not always desirable to make the acquaintance of near neighbours, but by a little observation it is very easy to gain an insight into their characters and position in society. The family which has moved into the house next to yours, for instance, lived near to me for nearly two years, and although I never spoke to one of them, I can tell you of some strange transactions which took place in their house."

"Indeed!" replied Mrs. Freeman, with little manifestation of interest or curiosity; but Mrs. Morris was too eager to communicate her information to notice her friend's manner, and lowering her voice to a confidential tone, continued:—

"There is an old lady in their family whom they abuse in the most shocking manner. She is very rich, and they by threats and ill-treatment extort large sums of money from her."

"A singular way of inducing any one to bestow favours," replied Mrs. Freeman, dryly. "Why does not the old lady leave there?"

"Bless your heart, my dear friend, she cannot get an opportunity! They never suffer her to leave the house unattended. Once or twice, indeed, she succeeded in getting into the street, but they discovered her in a moment, and actually forced her into the house. You smile incredulously, but if you had been an eye-witness of their proceedings, as I have, or had heard the screams of the poor creature, and the heavy blows which they inflict, you would be convinced of the truth of what I tell you."

"I do not doubt the truth of your story in the least, my dear Mrs. Morris. I only think that in this case, as in most others, there must be two sides to the story. It is almost incredible that such barbarous treatment could continue for any great length of time without discovery and exposure."

"Oh, as to that, people are not fond of getting themselves into trouble by meddling with their neighbours' affairs. I am very cautious about it myself. I would not have mentioned this matter to any one but an old friend like yourself. It seemed best to put you on your guard."

"Thank you," was the smiling reply. "It is hardly probable that I shall be called upon to make any acquaintance with my new neighbours but if I am, I certainly shall not forget your caution."

Satisfied that she had succeeded, at least partially, in awakening the suspicions of her friend, Mrs. Morris took her departure, while Mrs. Freeman, quite undisturbed by her communications, continued her usual quiet round of domestic duties, thinking less of the affairs of her neighbours than of those of her own household.

Occasionally she saw the old lady whom Mrs. Morris had mentioned walking in the adjoining garden, sometimes alone, and sometimes accompanied by the lady of the house, or one of the children. There was nothing striking in her appearance. She looked cheerful and contented, and showed no signs of confinement or abuse. Once, when Mrs. Freeman was in her garden, she had looked over the fence, and praised the beauty of her flowers, and when a bunch was presented to her, had received them with that almost childish delight which aged people often manifest.

Weeks passed on, and the remarks of Mrs. Morris were almost forgotten, when Mrs. Freeman was aroused one night by loud cries, apparently proceeding from the adjoining house; and on listening intently could plainly distinguish the sound of heavy blows, and also the voice of the old lady in question, as if in earnest expostulation and entreaty.

Mrs. Freeman aroused her husband, and together they listened in anxiety and alarm. For nearly an hour the sounds continued, but at length all was again quiet. It was long, however, before they could compose themselves to rest. It was certainly strange and unaccountable, and there was something so inhuman in the thought of abusing an aged woman that their hearts revolted at the idea.

Still Mrs. Freeman maintained, as was her wont, that there must be two sides to the story; and after vainly endeavouring to imagine what the other side could be, she fell asleep, and was undisturbed until morning.

All seemed quiet the next day, and Mrs. Freeman had somewhat recovered from the alarm of the previous night, when she was again visited by her friend, Mrs. Morris. As usual, she had confidential communications to make, and particularly wished the advice of Mrs. Freeman in a matter which she declared weighed heavily upon her mind; and being assured that they should be undisturbed, began at once to impart the weighty secret.

"You remember Mrs. Dawson, who went with her husband to Europe, a year or two ago?"

"Certainly I do," was the reply. "I was well acquainted with her."

"Do you recollect a girl who had lived with her for several years? I think her name was Mary Berkly."

"Quite well. Mrs. Dawson placed great confidence in her, and wished to take her abroad, but Mary was engaged to an honest carpenter, in good business, and wisely preferred a comfortable house in her own country."

"She had other reasons, I suspect," replied Mrs. Morris, mysteriously, "but you will hear. This Mary Berkly, or as she is now called, Mary White, lives not far from my present residence. Her husband is comfortably off, and his wife is not obliged to work, excepting in her own family, but still she will occasionally, as a favour, do up a few muslins for particular persons. You know she was famous for her skill in those things. The other day, having a few pieces which I was particularly anxious to have look nice, I called upon her to see if she would wash them for me. She was not at home, but her little niece, who lives with her, a child of four years old, said that Aunt Mary would be in directly, and asked me to walk into the parlour. I did so, and the little thing stood by my side chattering away like a magpie. In reply to my questions as to whether she liked to live with her aunt, what she amused herself with, &c., &c., she entered into a long account of her various playthings, and ended by saying that she would show me a beautiful new doll which her good uncle had given her, if I would please to unlock the door of a closet near where I was sitting, as she could not turn the key.

"To please the child I unlocked the door. She threw it wide open, and to my astonishment I saw that it was filled with valuable silver plate, china, and other articles of similar kind, some of which I particularly remembered having seen at Mrs. Dawson's."

"Perhaps she gave them to Mary," suggested Mrs. Freeman. "She was quite attached to her."

"Impossible!" exclaimed Mrs. Morris. "Valuable silver plate is not often given to servants. But I have not yet finished. Just as the child had found the doll Mrs. White entered, and on seeing the closet-door open, said sternly to the child,

"'Rosy, you did very wrong to open that door without my leave. I shall not let you take your doll again for a week;' and looking very red and confused, she hastily closed it, and turned the key. Now, to my mind, these are suspicious circumstances, particularly as I recollect that Mr. and Mrs. Dawson were robbed of silver plate shortly before they went to Europe, and no trace could be found of the thieves."

"True," replied Mrs. Freeman, thoughtfully; "I recollect the robbery very well. Still I cannot believe that Mary had anything to do with it. I was always pleased with her modest manner, and thought her an honest, capable girl."

"She is very smooth-faced, I know," answered Mrs. Morris, "but appearances are certainly against her. I am confident that the articles I saw belonged to Mrs. Dawson."

"There may be another side to the story, however," remarked her friend; "but why not mention your suspicions to Mrs. Dawson? You know she has returned, and is boarding in the upper part of the city. I have her address, somewhere."

"I know where she lives; but would you really advise me to meddle with the affair? I shall make enemies of Mr. and Mrs. White, if they hear of it, and I like to have the good-will of all, both, rich and poor."

"I do not believe that Mary would take anything wrongfully," replied Mrs. Freeman; "but if my suspicions were as fully aroused as yours seem to be, I presume I should mention what I saw to Mrs. Dawson, if it were only for the sake of hearing the other side of the story, and thus removing such unpleasant doubts from my mind. And, indeed, if you really think that the articles which you saw were stolen, it becomes your duty to inform the owners thereof, or you become, in a measure, a partaker of the theft."

"That is true," said Mrs. Morris, rising, "and in that way I might ultimately gain the ill-will of Mrs. Dawson; therefore I think I will go at once and tell her my suspicions."

"Which, I am convinced, you will find erroneous," replied Mrs. Freeman.

"We shall see," was the answer of her friend, accompanied by an ominous shake of the head; and promising to call upon Mrs. Freeman on her return, she took leave.

During her absence, the alarming cries from the next house were again heard; and presently the old lady appeared on the side-walk, apparently in great agitation and alarm, and gazing wildly about her, as if seeking a place of refuge; but she was instantly seized in the forcible manner Mrs. Morris had described, and carried into the house.

"This is dreadful!" exclaimed Mrs. Freeman. "What excuse can there be for such treatment?" and for a moment her heart was filled with indignation toward her supposed barbarous neighbours; but a little reflection caused her still to suspend her judgment, and endeavour to learn both sides of the story.

As she sat ruminating on this singular occurrence, and considering what was her duty in regard to it, she was aroused by the entrance of Mrs. Morris, who, with an air of vexation and disappointment, threw herself upon the nearest chair, exclaiming,

"A pretty piece of work I have been about! It is all owing to your advice, Mrs. Freeman. If it had not been for you I should not have made such a fool of myself."

"Why, what has happened to you?" asked Mrs. Freeman, anxiously. "What advice have I given you which has caused trouble?"

"You recommended my calling upon Mrs. Dawson, did you not?"

"Certainly: I thought it the easiest way to relieve your mind from painful suspicions. What did she say?"

"Say! I wish you could have seen the look she gave me when I told her what I saw at Mrs. White's. You know her haughty manner? She thanked me for the trouble I had taken on her account, and begged leave to assure me that she had perfect confidence in the honesty of Mrs. White. The articles which had caused me so much unnecessary anxiety were intrusted to her care when they went to Europe, and it had not yet been convenient to reclaim them. I cannot tell you how contemptuously she spoke. I never felt so mortified in my life."

"There is no occasion for feeling so, if your intentions were good," answered Mrs. Freeman; "and certainly it must be a relief to you to hear the other side of the story. Nothing less would have convinced you of Mrs. White's honesty."

Mrs. Morris was prevented from replying by the sudden and violent ringing of the bell, and an instant after the door was thrown open, and the old lady, whose supposed unhappy condition had called forth their sympathies, rushed into the room.

"Oh, save me! save me!" she exclaimed, frantically. "I am pursued,— protect me, for the love of Heaven!"

"Poor creature!" said Mrs. Morris. "You see that I was not mistaken in this story, at least. There can be no two sides to this."

"Depend upon it there is," replied Mrs. Freeman; but she courteously invited her visitor to be seated, and begged to know what had occasioned her so much alarm.

The poor lady told a plausible and piteous tale of ill-treatment, and, indeed, actual abuse. Mrs. Morris listened with a ready ear, and loudly expressed her horror and indignation. Mrs. Freeman was more guarded. There was something in the old lady's appearance and manners that excited an undefinable feeling of fear and aversion. Mrs. Freeman felt much perplexed as to the course she ought to pursue, and looked anxiously at the clock to see if the time for her husband's return was near.

It still wanted nearly two hours, and after a little more consideration she decided to go herself into the next door, ask for an interview with the lady of the house, frankly state what had taken place, and demand an explanation. This resolution she communicated in a low voice to Mrs. Morris, who opposed it as imprudent and ill-judged.

"Of course they will deny the charge," she argued, "and by letting them know where the poor creature has taken shelter, you will again expose her to their cruelty. Besides, you will get yourself into trouble. My advice to you is to keep quiet until your husband returns, and then to assist the poor lady secretly to go to her friends in the country, who she says will gladly receive her."

"But I am anxious to hear both sides of the story before I decide to assist her," replied Mrs. Freeman.

"Nonsense!" exclaimed her friend. "Even you must see that there cannot be two sides to this story. There is no possible excuse for cruelty, and to an inoffensive, aged woman."

While they were thus consulting together, their visitor regarded them with a troubled look, and a fierce gleaming eye, which did not, escape Mrs. Freeman's observation; and just as Mrs. Morris finished speaking, the maniac sprang upon her, like a tiger on his prey, and, seizing her by the throat, demanded what new mischief was plotting against her.

The screams of the terrified women drew the attention of the son of the old lady, who had just discovered her absence, and was hastening in search of her. At once suspecting the truth, he rushed without ceremony into his neighbour's house, and speedily rescued Mrs. Morris from her unpleasant and somewhat dangerous situation. After conveying his mother to her own room, and consigning her to strict custody, he returned, and respectfully apologized to Mrs. Freeman for what had taken place.

"His poor mother," he said, "had for several years been subject to occasional fits of insanity. Generally she had appeared harmless, excepting as regarded herself. Unless prevented by force, she would sometimes beat her own flesh in a shocking manner, uttering at the same time loud cries and complaints of the abuse of those whom she supposed to be tormenting her.

"In her lucid intervals she had so earnestly besought them not to place her in the asylum for the insane, but to continue to bear with her under their own roof, that they had found it impossible to refuse their solemn promise to comply with her wishes.

"For themselves, their love for her rendered them willing to bear with her infirmities, but it should be their earnest care that their neighbours should not again be disturbed."

Mrs. Freeman kindly expressed her sympathy and forgiveness for the alarm which she had experienced, and the gentleman took leave.

Poor Mrs. Morris had remained perfectly silent since her release; but as the door closed on their visiter, and her friend kindly turned to inquire how she found herself, she recovered her speech, and exclaimed, energetically,

"I will never, never say again that there are not two sides to a story. If I am ever tempted to believe one side without waiting to hear the other, I shall surely feel again the hands of that old witch upon my throat."

"Old witch!" repeated Mrs. Freeman. "Surely she demands our sympathy as much as when we thought her suffering under ill-treatment. It is indeed a sad thing to be bereft of reason. But this will be a useful lesson to both of us: for I will readily acknowledge that in this instance I was sometimes tempted to forget that there are always 'two sides to a story.'"

LITTLE KINDNESSES

NOT long since, it was announced that a large fortune had been left to a citizen of the United States by a foreigner, who, some years before, had "become ill" while travelling in this country, and whose sick-bed was watched with the utmost care and kindness by the citizen referred to. The stranger recovered, continued his journey, and finally returned to his own country. The conduct of the American at a moment so critical, and when, without relatives or friends, the invalid was languishing in a strange land, was not forgotten. He remembered it in his thoughtful and meditative moments, and when about to prepare for another world, his gratitude was manifested in a truly signal manner. A year or two ago, an individual in this city was labouring under great pecuniary difficulty. He was unexpectedly called upon for a considerable sum of money; and, although his means were abundant, they were not at that time immediately available. Puzzled and perplexed, he hesitated as to his best course, when, by the merest chance, he met an old acquaintance, and incidentally mentioned the facts of the case. The other referred to an act of kindness that he had experienced years before, said that he had never forgotten it, and that nothing would afford him more pleasure than to extend the relief that was required, and thus show, his grateful appreciation of the courtesy of former years! The kindness alluded to was a mere trifle, comparatively speaking, and its recollection had passed entirely from the memory of the individual who had performed it. Not so, however, with the obliged. He had never forgotten it, and the result proved, in the most conclusive manner, that he was deeply grateful.

We have mentioned the two incidents with the object of inculcating the general policy of courtesy and kindness, of sympathy and assistance, in our daily intercourse with our fellow-creatures. It is the true course under all circumstances. "Little kindnesses" sometimes make an impression that "lingers and lasts" for years. This is especially the case with the sensitive, the generous, and the high-minded. And how much may be accomplished by this duty of courtesy and humanity! How the paths of life may be smoothed and softened! How the present may be cheered, and the future rendered bright and beautiful!

There are, it is true, some selfish spirits, who can neither appreciate nor reciprocate a courteous or a generous act. They are for themselves—"now and for ever"—if we may employ such a phrase—and appear never to be satisfied. You can never do enough for them. Nay, the deeper the obligation, the colder the heart. They grow jealous, distrustful, and finally begin to hate their benefactors. But these, we trust, are "the exceptions," not "the rule." Many a heart has been won, many a friendship has been secured, many a position has been acquired, through the exercise of such little kindnesses and courtesies as are natural to the generous in spirit and the noble of soul—to all, indeed, who delight, not only in promoting their own prosperity, but in contributing to the welfare of every member of the human family. Who cannot remember some incident of his own life, in which an individual, then and perhaps now a stranger—one who has not been seen for years, and never may be seen again on this side the grave, manifested the true, the genuine, the gentle spirit of a gentleman and a Christian, in some mere trifle—some little but impulsive and spontaneous act, which nevertheless developed the whole heart, and displayed the real character! Distance and time may separate, and our pursuits and vocations may be in paths distinct, dissimilar, and far apart. Yet, there are moments—quiet, calm, and contemplative, when memory will wander back to the incidents referred to, and we will feel a secret bond of affinity, friendship, and brotherhood. The name will be mentioned with respect if not affection, and a desire will be experienced to repay, in some way or on some occasion, the generous courtesy of the by-gone time. It is so easy to be civil and obliging, to be kindly and humane! We not only thus assist the comfort of others, but we promote our own mental enjoyment. Life, moreover, is full of chance's and changes. A few years, sometimes, produce extraordinary revolutions in the fortunes of men. The haughty of to-day may be the humble of to-morrow; the feeble may be the powerful; the rich may be the poor, But, if elevated by affluence or by position, the greater the necessity, the stronger the duty to be kindly, courteous, and conciliatory to those less fortunate. We can afford to be so; and a proper appreciation of our position, a due sympathy for the misfortunes of others, and a grateful acknowledge to Divine Providence, require that we should be so. Life is short at best. We are here a few years—we sink into the grave—and even our memory is phantom-like and evanescent. How plain, then, is our duty! It is to be true to our position, to our conscience, and to the obligations imposed upon us by society, by circumstances, and by our responsibility to the Author of all that is beneficent and good.

LEAVING OFF CONTENTION BEFORE IT BE MEDDLED WITH

WE are advised to leave off contention before it be meddled with, by one usually accounted a very wise man. Had he never given the world any other evidence of superior wisdom, this admonition alone would have been sufficient to have established his claims thereto. It shows that he had power to penetrate to the very root of a large share of human misery. For what is the great evil in our condition here? Is it not misunderstanding, disagreement, alienation, contention, and the passions and results flowing from these? Are not contempt, and hatred, and strife, and alteration, and slander, and evil-speaking, the things hardest to bear, and most prolific of suffering, in the lot of human life? The worst woes of life are such as spring from, these sources.

Is there any cure for these maladies? Is there anything to prevent or abate these exquisite sufferings? The wise man directs our attention to a remedial preventive in the advice above referred to. His counsel to those whose lot unites them in the same local habitations and name to those who are leagued in friendship or business, in the changes of sympathy and the chances of collision, is, to suppress anger or dissatisfaction, to be candid and charitable in judging, and, by all means, to leave off contention before it be meddled with. His counsel to all is to endure injury meekly, not to give expression to the sense of wrong, even when we might seem justified in resistance or complaint. His counsel is to yield something we might fairly claim, to pardon when we might punish, to sacrifice somewhat of our rights for the sake of peace and friendly affection. His counsel is not to fire at every provocation, not to return evil for evil, not to cherish any fires of revenge, burning to be even with the injurious person. His counsel is to curb our imperiousness, to repress our impatience, to pause in the burst of another's feeling, to pour water upon the kindling flames, or, at the very least, to abstain from adding any fresh fuel thereto.

One proof of the superior wisdom of this counsel is, that few seem to appreciate or perceive it. To many it seems no great virtue or wisdom, no great and splendid thing, in some small issue of feeling or opinion, in the family or among friends, to withhold a little, to tighten the rein upon some headlong propensity, and await a calm for fair adjustment. Such a course is not usually held to be a proof of wisdom or virtue; and men are much more ready to praise and think well of smartness, and spirit, and readiness for an encounter. To leave off contention before it is meddled with does not command any very general admiration; it is too quiet a virtue, with no striking attitudes, and with lips which answer nothing. This is too often mistaken for dullness, and want of proper spirit. It requires discernment and superior wisdom to see a beauty in such repose and self-control, beyond the explosions of anger and retaliation. With the multitude, self-restraining meekness under provocation is a virtue which stands quite low in the catalogue. It is very frequently set down as pusillanimity and cravenness of spirit. But it is not so; for there is a self-restraint under provocation which is far from being cowardice, or want of feeling, or shrinking from consequences; there is a victory over passionate impulses which is more difficult and more meritorious than a victory on the bloody battle-field. It requires more power, more self-command, often, to leave off contention, when provocation and passion are causing the blood to boil, than to rush into it.

Were this virtue more duly appreciated, and the admonition of the Wise Man more extensively heeded, what a change would be effected in human life! How many of its keenest sufferings would be annihilated! The spark which kindles many great fires would be withheld; and, great as are the evils and sufferings caused by war, they are not as great, probably, as those originating in impatience and want of temper. The fretfulness of human life, it seems not hard to believe, is a greater evil, and destroys more happiness, than all the bloody scenes of the battle-field. The evils of war have generally something to lighten the burden of them in a sense of necessity, or of rights or honour invaded; but there is nothing of like importance to alleviate the sufferings caused by fretfulness, impatience, want of temper. The excitable peevishness which kindles at trifles, that roughens the daily experience of a million families, that scatters its little stings at the table and by the hearth-stone, what does this but unmixed harm? What ingredient does it furnish but of gall? Its fine wounding may be of petty consequence in any given case, and its tiny darts easily extracted; but, when habitually carried into the whole texture of life, it destroys more peace than plague and famine and the sword. It is a deeper anguish than grief; it is a sharper pang than the afflicted moan with; it is a heavier pressure from human hands than when affliction lays her hand upon you. All this deduction from human comfort, all this addition to human suffering, may be saved, by heeding the admonition of wisdom given by one of her sons. When provoked by the follies or the passions, the offences or neglects, the angry words or evil-speaking of others, restrain your propensity to complain or contend; leave off contention before you take the first step towards it. You will then be greater than he that taketh a city. You will be a genial companion in your family and among your neighbours. You will be loved at home and blessed abroad. You will be a source of comfort to others, and carry a consciousness of praiseworthiness in your own bosom. On the contrary, an acrid disposition, a readiness to enter into contention, is like vinegar to the teeth, like caustic to an open sore. It eats out all the beauty, tenderness, and affection of domestic and social life. For all this the remedy is simple. Put a restraint upon your feelings; give up a little; take less than belongs to you; endure more than should be put upon you; make allowance for another's judgment or educational defects; consider circumstances and constitution; leave off contention before it be meddled with. If you do otherwise, quick resentment and stiff maintenance of your position will breed endless disputes and bitterness. But happy will be the results of the opposite course, accomplished every day and every hour in the family, with friends, with companions, with all with whom you have any dealings or any commerce in life.

Let any one set himself to the cultivation of this virtue of meekness and self-restraint, and he will find that it cannot be secured by one or a few efforts, however resolute; by a few struggles, however severe. It requires industrious culture; it requires that he improve every little occasion to quench strife and fan concord, till a constant sweetness smooths the face of domestic life, and kindness and tenderness become the very expression of the countenance. This virtue of self-control must grow by degrees. It must grow by a succession of abstinences from returning evil for evil, by a succession of leaving off contention before the first angry word escapes.

It may help to cultivate this virtue, to practise some forethought. When tempted to irritable, censorious speech, one might with advantage call to recollection the times, perhaps frequent, when words uttered in haste have caused sorrow or repentance. Then, again, the fact might be called to mind, that when we lose a friend, every harsh word we may have spoken rises to condemn us. There is a resurrection, not for the dead only, but for the injuries we have fixed in their hearts—in hearts, it may be, bound to our own, and to which we owed gentleness instead of harshness. The shafts of reproach, which come from the graves of those who have been wounded by our fretfulness and irritability, are often hard to bear. Let meek forbearance and self-control prevent such suffering, and guard us against the condemnations of the tribunal within.

There is another tribunal, also, which it were wise to think of. The rule of that tribunal is, that if we forgive not those who trespass against us, we ourselves shall not be forgiven. "He shall have judgment without mercy that hath showed no mercy." Only, then, if we do not need, and expect never to beg the mercy of the Lord to ourselves, may we withhold our mercy from our fellow-men.

"ALL THE DAY IDLE"

WHEREFORE idle?—when the harvest beckoning,
Nods its ripe tassels to the brightening sky?
Arise and labour ere the time of reckoning,
Ere the long shadows and the night draw night.

Wherefore idle?—Swing the sickle stoutly!
Bind thy rich sheaves exultingly and fast!
Nothing dismayed, do thy great task devoutly—
Patient and strong, and hopeful to the last!

Wherefore idle?—Labour, not inaction,
Is the soul's birthright, and its truest rest;
Up to thy work!—It is Nature's fit exaction—
He who toils humblest, bravest, toils the best.

Wherefore idle?—God himself is working;
His great thought wearieth not, nor standeth still,
In every throb of his vast heart is lurking
Some mighty purpose of his mightier will.

Wherefore idle?—Not a leaf's slight rustle
But chides thee in thy vain, inglorious rest;
Be a strong actor in the great world,—bustle,—
Not a, weak minion or a pampered guest!

Wherefore idle?—Oh I*my* faint soul, wherefore?
Shake first from thine own powers dull sloth's control;
Then lift thy voice with an exulting "Therefore
Thou, too, shalt conquer, oh, thou striving soul!"

THE BUSHEL OF CORN

FARMER GRAY had a neighbour who was not the best-tempered man in the world though mainly kind and obliging. He was shoemaker. His name was Barton. One day, in harvest-time, when every man on the farm was as busy as a bee, this man came over to Farmer Gray's, and said, in rather a petulant tone of voice,

"Mr. Gray, I wish you would send over, and drive your geese home."

"Why so, Mr. Barton; what have my geese been doing?" said the farmer, in a mild, quiet-tone.

"They pick my pigs' ears when they are eating, and go into my garden, and I will not have it!" the neighbour replied, in a still more petulant voice.

"I am really sorry it, Neighbour Barton, but what can I do?"

"Why, yoke them, and thus keep them on your own premises. It's no kind of a way to let your geese run all over every farm and garden in the neighborhood."

"But I cannot see to it, now. It is harvest-time, Friend Barton, and every man, woman, and child on the farm has as much as he or she can do. Try and bear it for a week or so, and then I will see if I can possibly remedy the evil."

"I can't bear it, and I won't bear it any longer!" said the shoemaker. "So if you do not take care of them, Friend Gray, I shall have to take care of them for you."

"Well, Neighbour Barton, you can do as you please," Farmer Gray replied, in his usual quiet tone. "I am sorry that they trouble you, but I cannot attend to them now."

"I'll attend to them for you, see if I don't," said the shoemaker, still more angrily than when he first called upon Farmer Gray; and then turned upon his heel, and strode off hastily towards his own house, which was quite near to the old farmer's.

"What upon earth can be the matter with them geese?" said Mrs. Gray, about fifteen minutes afterwards.

"I really cannot tell, unless Neighbour Barton is taking care of them. He threatened to do so, if I didn't yoke them right off."

"Taking care of them! How taking care of them?"

"As to that, I am quite in the dark. Killing them, perhaps. He said they picked at his pigs' ears, and drove them away when they were eating, and that he wouldn't have it. He wanted me to yoke them right off, but that I could not do, now, as all the hands are busy. So, I suppose, he is engaged in the neighbourly business of taking care of our geese."

"John! William! run over and see what Mr. Barton is doing with my geese," said Mrs. Gray, in a quick and anxious tone, to two little boys who were playing near.

The urchins scampered off, well pleased to perform any errand.

"Oh, if he has dared to do anything to my geese, I will never forgive him!" the good wife said, angrily.

"H-u-s-h, Sally! make no rash speeches. It is more than probable that he has killed some two or three of them. But never mind, if he has. He will get over this pet, and be sorry for it."

"Yes; but what good will his being sorry do me? Will it bring my geese to life?"

"Ah, well, Sally, never mind. Let us wait until we learn what all this disturbance is about."

In about ten minutes the children came home, bearing the bodies of three geese, each without a head.

"Oh, is not that too much for human endurance?" cried Mrs. Gray. "Where did you find them?"

"We found them lying out in the road," said the oldest of the two children, "and when we picked them up, Mr. Barton said, 'Tell your father that I have yoked his geese for him, to save him the trouble, as his hands are all too busy to do it.'"

"I'd sue him for it!" said Mrs. Gray, in an indignant tone.

"And what good would that do, Sally?"

"Why, it would do a great deal of good. It would teach him better manners. It would punish him; and he deserves punishment."

"And punish us into the bargain. We have lost three geese, now, but we still have their good fat bodies to eat. A lawsuit would cost us many geese, and not leave us even so much as the feathers, besides giving us a world of trouble and vexation. No, no, Sally; just let it rest, and he will be sorry for it, I know."

"Sorry for it, indeed! And what good will his being sorry for it do us, I should like to know? Next he will kill a cow, and then we must be satisfied with his being sorry for it! Now, I can tell you, that I don't believe in that doctrine. Nor do I believe anything about his being sorry—the crabbed, ill-natured wretch!"

"Don't call hard names, Sally," said Farmer Gray, in a mild, soothing tone. "Neighbour Barton was not himself when he killed the geese. Like every other angry person, he was a little insane, and did what he would not have done had he been perfectly in his right mind. When you are a little excited, you know, Sally, that even you do and say unreasonable things."

"Me do and say unreasonable things!" exclaimed Mrs. Gray, with a look and tone of indignant astonishment; "me do and say unreasonable things, when I am angry! I don't understand you, Mr. Gray."

"May-be I can help you a little. Don't you remember how angry you were when Mr. Mellon's old brindle got into our garden, and trampled over your lettuce-bed, and how you struck her with the oven-pole, and knocked off one of her horns?"

"But I didn't mean to do that, though."

"No; but then you were angry, and struck old Brindle with a right good will. And if Mr. Mellon had felt disposed, he might have prosecuted for damages."

"But she had no business there."

"Of course not. Neither had our geese any business in Neighbour Barton's yard. But, perhaps, I can help you to another instance, that will be more conclusive, in regard to your doing and saying unreasonable things, when you are angry. You remember the patent churn?"

"Yes; but never mind about that."

"So you have not forgotten how unreasonable you was about the churn. It wasn't good for anything—you knew it wasn't; and you'd never put a jar of cream into it as long as you lived—that you wouldn't. And yet, on trial, you found that churn the best you had ever used, and you wouldn't part with it on any consideration. So you see, Sally, that even you can say and do unreasonable things, when you are angry, just as well as Mr. Barton can. Let us then consider him a little, and give him time to get over his angry fit. It will be much better to do so."

Mrs. Gray saw that her husband was right, but still she felt indignant at the outrage committed on her geese. She did not, however, say anything about suing the shoemaker—for old Brindle's head, from which the horn had been knocked off, was not yet entirely well, and one prosecution very naturally suggested the idea of another. So she took her three fat geese, and after stripping off their feathers, had them prepared for the table.

On the next morning, as Farmer Gray was going along the road, he met the shoemaker, and as they had to pass very near to each other, the farmer smiled, and bowed, and spoke kindly. Mr. Barton looked and felt very uneasy, but Farmer Gray did not seem to remember the unpleasant incident of the day before.

It was about eleven o'clock of the same day that one of Farmer Gray's little boys came running to him, and crying,

"Oh, father! father! Mr. Barton's hogs are in our cornfield."

"Then I must go and drive them out," said Mr. Gray, in a quiet tone.

"Drive them out!" ejaculated Mrs. Gray; "drive 'em out, indeed! I'd shoot them, that's what I'd do! I'd serve them as he served my geese yesterday."

"But that wouldn't bring the geese to life again, Sally."

"I don't care if it wouldn't. It would be paying him in his own coin, and that's all he deserves."

"You know what the Bible says, Sally, about grievous words, and they apply with stronger force to grievous actions. No, no, I will return Neighbour Barton good for evil. That is the best way. He has done wrong, and I am sure is sorry for it. And as I wish him still to remain sorry for so unkind and unneighbourly an action, I intend making use of the best means for keeping him sorry."

"Then you will be revenged on him, anyhow."

"No, Sally—not revenged. I hope I have no such feeling. For I am not angry with Neighbour Barton, who has done himself a much greater wrong than he has done me. But I wish him to see clearly how wrong he acted, that he may do so no more. And then we shall not have any cause to complain of him, nor he any to be grieved, as I am sure he is, at his own hasty conduct. But while I am talking here, his hogs are destroying my corn."

And so saying, Farmer Gray hurried off, towards his cornfield. When he arrived there, he found four large hogs tearing down the stalks, and pulling off and eating the ripe ears of corn. They had already destroyed a good deal. But he drove them out very calmly, and put up the bars through which they had entered, and then commenced gathering up the half-eaten ears of corn, and throwing them out into the lane for the hogs, that had been so suddenly disturbed in the process of obtaining a liberal meal. As he was thus engaged, Mr. Barton, who had from his own house seen the farmer turn the hogs out of his cornfield, came hurriedly up, and said,

"I am very sorry, Mr. Gray, indeed I am, that my hogs have done this! I will most cheerfully pay you for what they have destroyed."

"Oh, never mind, Friend Barton—never mind. Such things will happen, occasionally. My geese, you know, annoy you very much, sometimes."

"Don't speak of it, Mr. Gray. They didn't annoy me half as much as I imagined they did. But how much corn do you think my hogs have destroyed? One bushel, or two bushels? or how much? Let it be estimated, and I will pay for it most cheerfully."

"Oh, no. Not for the world, Friend Barton. Such things will happen sometimes. And, besides, some of my men must have left the bars down, or your hogs could never have got in. So don't think any more about it. It would be dreadful if one neighbour could not bear a little with another."

All this cut poor Mr. Barton to the heart. His own ill-natured language and conduct, at a much smaller trespass on his rights, presented itself to his mind, and deeply mortified him. After a few moments' silence, he said,

"The fact is, Mr. Gray, I shall feel better if you will let me pay for this corn. My hogs should not be fattened at your expense, and I will not consent to its being done. So I shall insist on paying you for at least one bushel of corn, for I am sure they have destroyed that much, if not more."

But Mr. Gray shook his head and smiled pleasantly, as he replied,

"Don't think anything more about it, Neighbour Barton. It is a matter deserving no consideration. No doubt my cattle have often trespassed on you and will trespass on you again. Let us then bear and forbear."

All this cut the shoemaker still deeper, and he felt still less at ease in mind after he parted from the farmer than he did before. But on one thing he resolved, and that was, to pay Mr. Gray for the corn which his hogs had eaten.

"You told him your mind pretty plainly, I hope," said Mrs. Gray, as her husband came in.

"I certainly did," was the quiet reply.

"And I am glad you had spirit enough to do it! I reckon he will think twice before he kills any more of my geese!"

"I expect you are right, Sally. I don't think we shall be troubled again."

"And what did you say to him? And what did he say for himself?"

"Why he wanted very much to pay me for the corn his pigs had eaten, but I wouldn't hear to it. I told him that it made no difference in the world; that such accidents would happen sometimes."

"You did?"

"Certainly, I did."

"And that's the way you spoke your mind to him?"

"Precisely. And it had the desired effect. It made him feel ten times worse than if I had spoken angrily to him. He is exceedingly pained at what he has done, and says he will never rest until he has paid for that corn. But I am resolved never to take a cent for it. It will be the best possible guarantee I can have for his kind and neighbourly conduct hereafter."

"Well, perhaps you are right," said Mrs. Gray, after a few moments of thoughtful silence. "I like Mrs. Barton very much—and now I come to think of it, I should not wish to have any difference between our families."

"And so do I like Mr. Barton. He has read a good deal, and I find it very pleasant to sit with him, occasionally, during the long winter evenings. His only fault is his quick temper—but I am sure it is much better for us to bear with and soothe that, than to oppose rand excite it and thus keep both his family and our own in hot water."

"You are certainly right," replied Mrs. Gray; "and I only wish that I could always think and feel as you do. But I am little quick, as they say."

"And so is Mr. Barton. Now just the same consideration that you would desire others to have for you, should you exercise towards Mr. Barton, or any one else whose hasty temper leads him into words or actions that, in calmer and more thoughtful moments, are subjects of regret."

On the next day, while Mr. Gray stood in his own door, from which he could see over the two or three acres of ground that the shoemaker cultivated, he observed two of his cows in his neighbour's cornfield, browsing away in quite a contented manner. As he was going to call one of the farm hands to go over and drive them out, he perceived that Mr. Barton had become aware of the mischief that was going on, and had already started for the field of corn.

"Now we will see the effect of yesterday's lesson," said the farmer to himself; and then paused to observe the manner of the shoemaker towards his cattle in driving them out of the field. In a few minutes Mr. Barton came up to the cows, but, instead of throwing stones at them, or striking them with a stick, he merely drove them out in a quiet way, and put up the bars through which they had entered.

"Admirable!" ejaculated Farmer Gray.

"What is admirable?" asked his wife, who came within hearing distance at the moment.

"Why the lesson I gave our friend Barton yesterday. It works admirably."

"How so?"

"Two of our cows were in his cornfield a few minutes ago, destroying the corn at a rapid rate."

"Well! what did he do to them?" in a quick, anxious tone.

"He drove them out."

"Did he stone them, or beat them?"

"Oh no. He was gentle as a child towards them."

"You are certainly jesting."

"Not I. Friend Barton has not forgotten that his pigs were in my cornfield yesterday, and that I turned them out without hurting a hair of one of them. Now, suppose I had got angry and beaten his pigs, what do you think the result would have been? Why, it is much more than probable that one or both of our fine cows would have been at this moment in the condition of Mr. Mellon's old Brindle."

"I wish you wouldn't say anything more about old Brindle," said Mrs. Gray, trying to laugh, while her face grew red in spite of her efforts to keep down her feelings.

"Well, I won't, Sally, if it worries you. But it is such a good illustration that I can't help using it sometimes."

"I am glad he didn't hurt the cows," said Mrs. Gray, after a pause.

"And so am I, Sally. Glad on more than one account. It shows that he has made an effort to keep down his hasty, irritable temper—and if he can do that, it will be a favour conferred on the whole neighbourhood, for almost every one complains, at times, of this fault in his character."

"It is certainly the best policy, to keep fair weather with him," Mrs. Gray remarked, "for a man of his temper could annoy us a good deal."

"That word policy, Sally, is not a good word," replied her husband. "It conveys a thoroughly selfish idea. Now, we ought to look for some higher motives of action than mere policy—motives grounded in correct and unselfish principles."

"But what other motive but policy could we possibly have for putting up with Mr. Barton's outrageous conduct?"

"Other, and far higher motives, it seems to me. We should reflect that Mr. Barton has naturally a hasty temper, and that when excited he does things for which he is sorry afterwards—and that, in nine cases out of ten, he is a greater sufferer from those outbreaks than any one else. In our actions towards him, then, it is a much higher and better motive for us to be governed by a desire to aid him in the correction of this evil, than to look merely to the protection of ourselves from its effects. Do you not think so?"

"Yes. It does seem so."

"When thus moved to action, we are, in a degree, regarding the whole neighbourhood, for the evil of which we speak affects all. And in thus suffering ourselves to be governed by such elevated and unselfish motives, we gain all that we possibly could have gained under the mere instigation of policy—and a great deal more. But to bring the matter into a still narrower compass. In all our actions towards him and every one else, we should be governed by the simple consideration—is it right? If a spirit of retaliation be not right, then it cannot be indulged without a mutual injury. Of course, then, it should never prompt us to action. If cows or hogs get into my field or garden, and destroy my property, who is to blame most? Of course, myself. I should have kept my fences in better repair, or my gate closed. The animals, certainly, are not to blame, for they follow only the promptings of nature; and their owners should not be censured, for they know nothing about it. It would then be very wrong for me to injure both the animals and their owners for my own neglect, would it not?"

"Yes,—I suppose it would."

"So, at least, it seems to me. Then, of course, I ought not to injure Neighbour Barton's cows or hogs, even if they do break into my cornfield or garden, simply because it would be wrong to do so. This is the principle upon which we should act, and not from any selfish policy."

After this there was no trouble about Farmer Gray's geese or cattle. Sometimes the geese would get among Mr. Barton's hogs, and annoy them while eating, but it did not worry him as it did formerly. If they became too troublesome he would drive them away, but not by throwing sticks and stones at them as he once did.

Late in the fall the shoemaker brought in his bill for work. It was a pretty large bill, with sundry credits.

"Pay-day has come at last," said Farmer Gray, good-humouredly, as the shoemaker presented his account.

"Well, let us see!" and he took the bill to examine it item after item.

"What is this?" he asked, reading aloud.

"'Cr. By one bushel of corn, fifty cents.'"

"It's some corn I had from you."

"I reckon you must be mistaken. You never got any corn from me."

"Oh, yes I did. I remember it perfectly. It is all right."

"But when did you get it, Friend Barton? I am sure that I haven't the most distant recollection of it."

"My hogs got it," the shoemaker said, in rather a low and hesitating tone.

"Your hogs!"

"Yes. Don't you remember when my hogs broke into your field, and destroyed your corn?"

"Oh, dear! is that it? Oh, no, no, Friend Barton! Ii cannot allow that item in the bill."

"Yes, but you must. It is perfectly just, and I shall never rest until it is paid."

"I can't, indeed. You couldn't help the hogs getting into my field; and then you know, Friend Barton (lowering his tone), my geese were very troublesome!"

The shoemaker blushed and looked confused; but Farmer Gray slapped him familiarly on the shoulder, and said, in a lively, cheerful way,

"Don't think any more about it, Friend Barton! And hereafter let us endeavour to 'do as we would be done by,' and then everything will go on as smooth as clock-work."

"But you will allow that item in the bill?" the shoemaker urged perseveringly.

"Oh, no, I couldn't do that. I should think it wrong to make you pay for my own or some of my men's negligence in leaving the bars down."

"But then (hesitatingly), those geese—I killed three. Let it go for them."

"If you did kill them, we ate them. So that is even. No, no, let the past be forgotten, and if it makes better neighbours and friends of us, we never need regret what has happened."

Farmer Gray remained firm, and the bill was settled, omitting the item of "corn." From that time forth he never had a better neighbour than the shoemaker. The cows, hogs, and geese of both would occasionally trespass, but the trespassers were always kindly removed. The lesson was not lost on either of them—for even Farmer Gray used to feel, sometimes, a little annoyed when his neighbour's cattle broke into his field. But in teaching the shoemaker a lesson, he had taken a little of it himself.

THE ACCOUNT

THE clock from the city hall struck one;
The merchant's task was not yet done;
He knew the old year was passing away,
And his accounts must all be settled that day;
He must know for a truth how much he should win,
So fast the money was rolling in.

He took the last cash-book, from the pile,
And he summed it up with a happy smile;
For a just and upright man was he,
Dealing with all most righteously,
And now he was sure how much he should win,
How fast the money was rolling in.

He heard not the soft touch on the door—
He heard not the tread on the carpeted floor—
So still was her coming, he thought him alone,
Till she spake in a sweet and silvery tone:
"Thou knowest not yet how much thou shalt win—
How fast the money is rolling in."

Then from 'neath her white, fair arm, she took
A golden-clasped, and, beautiful book—
"'Tis my account thou hast to pay,
In the coming of the New Year's day—
Read—ere thou knowest how much thou shalt win,
How fast the money is rolling in."

He open'd the clasps with a trembling hand—
Therein was Charity's firm demand:

"To the widow, the orphan, the needy, the poor,
Much owest thou of thy yearly store;
Give, ere thou knowest how much thou shalt win—
While fast the money is rolling in."

The merchant took from his box of gold
A goodly sum for the lady bold;
His heart was richer than e'er before,
As she bore the prize from the chamber door.
Ye who would know how much ye can win,
Give, when the money is rolling in.

CONTENTMENT BETTER THAN WEALTH

"IT is vain, to urge, Brother Robert. Out into the world I must go. The impulse is on me. I should die of inaction here."

"You need not be inactive. There is work to do. I shall never be idle."

"And such work! Delving in, and grovelling close to the ground. And for what? Oh no Robert. My ambition soars beyond your 'quiet cottage in a sheltered vale.' My appetite craves something more than simple herbs, and water from the brook. I have set my heart on attaining wealth; and where there is a will there is always a way."

"Contentment is better than wealth."

"A proverb for drones."

"No, William, it is a proverb for the wise."

"Be it for the wise or simple, as commonly, understood, it is no proverb for me. As poor plodder along the way of life, it were impossible for me to know content. So urge no farther, Robert. I am going out into the world a wealth-seeker, and not until wealth is gained do I purpose to return."

"What of Ellen, Robert?"

The young man turned quickly towards his brother, visibly disturbed, and fixed his eyes upon him with an earnest expression.

"I love her as my life," he said, with a strong emphasis on his words.

"Do you love wealth more than life, William?"

"Robert!"

"If you love Ellen as your life, and leave her for the sake of getting riches, then you must love money more than life."

"Don't talk to me after this fashion. I love her tenderly and truly. I am going forth as well for her sake as my own. In all the good fortune that comes as a meed of effort, she will be the sharer."

"You will see her before you leave us?"

"No; I will neither pain her nor myself by a parting interview. Send her this letter and this ring."

A few hours later, and there brothers stood with tightly-grasped hands, gazing into each other's faces.

"Farewell, Robert."

"Farewell, William. Think of the old homestead as still your home. Though it is mine, in the division of our patrimony, let your heart come back to it as yours. Think of it as home; and, should Fortune cheat you with the apples of Sodom, return to it again. Its doors will ever be open, and its hearth-fire bright for you as of old. Farewell!"

And they turned from each other, one going out into the restless world, an eager seeker for its wealth and honours; the other to linger among the pleasant places dear to him by every association of childhood, there to fill up the measure of his days—not idly, for he was no drone in the social hive.

On the evening of that day two maidens sat alone, each in the sanctuary of her own chamber. There was a warm glow on the cheeks of one, and a glad light in her eyes. Pale was the other's face, and wet her drooping lashes. And she that sorrowed held an open letter in her hand. It was full of tender words; but the writer loved wealth more than the maiden, and had gone forth to seek the mistress of his soul. He would "come back," but when? Ah, what a veil of uncertainty was upon the future! Poor, stricken heart! The other maiden—she of the glowing cheeks and dancing eyes—held also a letter in her hand. It was from the brother of the wealth-seeker; and it was also full of loving words; and it said that, on the morrow, he would come to bear her as his bride to his pleasant home. Happy maiden!

Ten years have passed. And what of the wealth-seeker? Has he won the glittering prize? What of the pale-faced maiden he left in tears? Has he returned to her? Does she share now his wealth and honour? Not since the day he went forth from the home of his childhood has a word of intelligence from the wanderer been received; and to those he left behind him he is as one who has passed the final bourne. Yet he still dwells among the living.

In a far-away, sunny clime stands a stately mansion. We will not linger to describe the elegant interior, to hold up before the reader's imagination a picture of rural beauty, exquisitely heightened by art, but enter its spacious hall, and pass up to one of its most luxurious chambers. How hushed and solemn the pervading atmosphere! The inmates, few in number, are grouped around one on whose white forehead Time's trembling finger has written the word "Death!" Over her bends a manly form. There—his face is towards you. Ah! you recognise the wanderer—the wealth-seeker. What does he here? What to him is the dying one? His wife! And has he, then, forgotten the maiden whose dark lashes lay wet on her pale cheeks for many hours after she read his parting words? He has not forgotten, but been false to her. Eagerly sought he the prize, to contend for which he went forth. Years came and departed; yet still hope mocked him with ever-attractive and ever-fading illusions. To-day he stood with his hand just ready to seize the object of his wishes, to-morrow a shadow mocked him. At last, in an evil hour, he bowed down his manhood prostrate even to the dust in woman worship, and took to himself a bride, rich in golden, attractions, but poorer as a woman than ever the beggar at her father's gate. What a thorn in his side she proved! A thorn ever sharp and ever piercing. The closer he attempted to draw her to his bosom, the deeper went the points into his own, until, in the anguish of his soul, again and again he flung her passionately from him.

Five years of such a life! Oh, what is there of earthly good to compensate therefor? But in this last desperate throw did the worldling gain the wealth, station, and honour he coveted? He had wedded the only child of a man whose treasure might be counted by hundreds of thousands; but, in doing so, he had failed to secure the father's approval or confidence. The stern old man regarded him as a mercenary interloper, and ever treated him as such. For five years, therefore, he fretted and chafed in the narrow prison whose gilded bars his own hands had forged. How often, during that time, had his heart wandered back to the dear old home, and the beloved ones with whom he had passed his early years! And, ah! how many, many times came between him and the almost hated countenance of his wife the gentle, the loving face of that one to whom he had been false! How often her soft blue eyes rested on his own How often he started and looked up suddenly, as if her sweet voice came floating on the air!

And so the years moved on, the chain galling more deeply, and a bitter sense of humiliation as well as bondage robbing him of all pleasure in his life.

Thus it is with him when, after ten years, we find him waiting, in the chamber of death, for the stroke that is to break the fetters that so long have bound him. It has fallen. He is free again. In dying, the sufferer made no sign. Suddenly she plunged into the dark profound, so impenetrable to mortal eyes, and as the turbid waves closed, sighing over her, he who had called her wife turned from the couch on which her frail body remained, with an inward "Thank God! I am a man again!"

One more bitter dreg yet remained for his cup. Not a week had gone by ere the father of his dead wife spoke to him these cutting words:—

"You were nothing to me while my daughter lived—you are less than nothing to me now. It was my wealth, not my child you loved. She has passed away. What affection would have given to her, dislike will never bestow on you. Henceforth we are strangers."

When the next sun went down on that stately mansion, which the wealth-seeker had coveted, he was a wanderer again—poor, humiliated, broken in spirit.

How bitter had been the mockery of all his early hopes! How terrible the punishment he had suffered!

One more eager, almost fierce struggle with alluring fortune, with which the worldling came near steeping his soul in crime, and then fruitless ambition died in his bosom.

"My brother said well," he murmured, as a ray of light fell suddenly on the darkness of his spirit; "'contentment is better than wealth.' Dear brother! Dear old home! Sweet Ellen! Ah, why did I leave you? Too late! too late! A cup, full of the wine of life, was at my lips; but, I turned my head away, asking for a more fiery and exciting draught. How vividly comes before me now that parting scene! I am looking into my brother's face. I feel the tight grasp of his hand. His voice is in my ears. Dear brother! And his parting words, I hear them now, even more earnestly than when they were first spoken. 'Should fortune cheat you with the apples of Sodom, return to your home again. Its doors will ever be open, and its hearth-fires bright for you as of old.' Ah, do the fires still burn? How many years have passed since I went forth! And Ellen? Even if she be living and unchanged in her affections, I can never lay this false heart at her feet. Her look of love would smite me as with a whip of scorpions."

The step of time has fallen so lightly on the flowery path of those to whom contentment was a higher boon than wealth, but few footmarks were visible. Yet there had been changes in the old homestead. As the smiling years went by, each, as it looked in at the cottage window, saw the home circle widening, or new beauty crowning the angel brows of happy children. No thorn to his side had Robert's gentle wife proved. As time passed on, closer and closer was she drawn to his bosom; yet never a point had pierced him. Their home was a type of Paradise.

It is near the close of a summer day. The evening meal is spread, and they are about gathering round the table, when a stranger enters. His words are vague and brief, his manner singular, his air slightly mysterious. Furtive, yet eager glances go from face to face.

"Are these all your children?" he asks, surprise and admiration mingling in his tones.

"All ours, and, thank God, the little flock is yet unbroken."

The stranger averts his face. He is disturbed by emotions that it is impossible to conceal.

"Contentment is better than wealth," he murmurs. "Oh that I had comprehended the truth."

The words were not meant for others; but the utterance had been too distinct. They have reached the ears of Robert, who instantly recognises in the stranger his long-wandering, long-mourned brother.

"William!"

The stranger is on his feet. A moment or two the brothers stand gazing at each other, then tenderly embrace.

"William!"

How the stranger starts and trembles! He had not seen, in the quiet maiden, moving among and ministering to the children so unobtrusively, the one he had parted from years before—the one to whom he had been so false. But her voice has startled his ears with the familiar tones of yesterday.

"Ellen!" Here is an instant oblivion of all the intervening years. He has leaped back over the gulf, and stands now as he stood ere ambition and lust for gold lured him away from the side of his first and only love. It is well both for him and the faithful maiden that he cannot so forget the past as to take her in his arms and clasp her almost wildly to his heart. But for this, conscious shame would have betrayed his deeply-repented perfidy.

And here we leave them, reader. "Contentment is better than wealth." So the worldling proved, after a bitter experience, which may you be spared! It is far better to realize a truth perceptibly, and thence make it a rule of action, than to prove its verity in a life of sharp agony. But how few are able to rise into such a realization!

RAINBOWS EVERYWHERE

BENDING over a steamer's side, a face looked down into the clear, green depths of Lake Erie, where the early moonbeams were showering rainbows through the dancing spray, and chasing the white-crusted waves with serpents of gold. The face was clouded with thought, a shade too sombre, yet there glowed over it something like a reflection from the iris-hues beneath. A voice of using was borne away into the purple and vermilion haze that twilight began to fold over the bosom of the lake.

"Rainbows! Ye follow me everywhere! Gloriously your arches arose from the horizon of the prairies, when the storm-king and the god of day met within them to proclaim a treaty and an alliance. You spanned the Father of Waters with a bridge that put to the laugh man's clumsy structures of chain, and timber, and wire. You floated in a softening veil before the awful grandeur of Niagara; and here you gleam out from the light foam in the steamboat's wake.

"Grateful am I for you, oh rainbows! for the clouds, the drops, and the sunshine of which you are wrought, and for the gift of vision through which my spirit quaffs the wine of your beauty.

"Grateful also for faith, which hangs an ethereal halo over the fountains of earthly joy, and wraps grief in robes so resplendent that, like Iris of the olden time, she is at once recognised as a messenger from Heaven.

"Blessings on sorrow, whether past or to come! for in the clear shining of heavenly love, every tear-drop becomes a pearl. The storm of affliction crushes weak human nature to the dust; the glory of the eternal light overpowers it; but, in the softened union of both, the stricken spirit beholds the bow of promise, and knows that it shall not utterly be destroyed. When we say that for us there is nothing but darkness and tears, it is because we are weakly brooding over the shadows within us. If we dared look up, and face our sorrow, we should see upon it the seal of God's love, and be calm.

"Grant me, Father of Light, whenever my eyes droop heavily with the rain of grief, at least to see the reflection of thy signet-bow upon the waves over which I am sailing unto thee. And through the steady toiling of the voyage, through the smiles and tears of every day's progress, let the iris-flash appear, even as now it brightens the spray that rebounds from the labouring wheels."

The voice died away into darkness which returned no answer to its murmurings. The face vanished from the boat's side, but a flood of light was pouring into the serene depths of a trusting soul.